Philip   d
most o   a
year at   s
music: al
music   e
Hugo Award for his classic novel of alternative history,
The Man in the High Castle (1962). He was married five
times and had three children. He died in March 1982.

'Dick quietly produced serious fiction in a popular form
and there can be no greater praise'
Michael Moorcock

'One of the most original practitioners writing any kind of
fiction, Philip K. Dick made most of the European avant-
garde seem navel-gazers in a cul-de-sac'
Sunday Times

'No other writer of his generation had such a powerful
intellectual presence. He has stamped himself not only on
our memories but in our imaginations'
Brian Aldiss

'The most consistently brilliant SF writer in the world'
John Brunner

By the same author

PHILIP K. DICK

A Handful of Darkness

GRAFTON BOOKS

A Division of the Collins Publishing Group

LONDON GLASGOW
TORONTO SYDNEY AUCKLAND

Grafton Books
A Division of the Collins Publishing Group
8 Grafton Street, London W1X 3LA

Published by Granada Publishing Limited
in Panther Books 1966
Reprinted 1980, 1988

First published in Great Britain by
Rich and Cowan Ltd 1955

Copyright © Philip K. Dick 1955

ISBN 0-586-04804-9

Printed and bound in Great Britain by
Collins, Glasgow

Set in Sabon

Contents

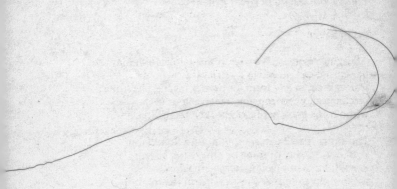

Colony

Major Lawrence Hall bent over the binocular microscope, correcting the fine adjustment.

'Interesting,' he murmured.

'Isn't it? Three weeks on this planet and we've yet to find a harmful life-form.' Lieutenant Friendly sat down on the edge of the lab table, avoiding the culture bowls. 'What kind of place is this? No disease germs, no lice, no flies, no rats, no –'

'No whisky or red light districts.' Hall straightened up. 'Quite a place. I was sure this brew would show something along the lines of Terra's *eberthella typhi*. Or the Martian sand rot corkscrew.'

'But the whole planet's harmless. You know, I'm wondering whether this is the Garden of Eden our ancestors fell out of.'

'Were pushed out of.'

Hall wandered over to the window of the lab and contemplated the scene beyond. He had to admit it was an attractive sight. Rolling forests and hills, green slopes alive with flowers and endless vines; waterfalls and hanging moss; fruit trees, acres of flowers, lakes. Every effort had been made to preserve intact the surface of Planet Blue – as it had been designated by the original scout ship, six months earlier.

Hall sighed. 'Quite a place. I wouldn't mind coming back here again some time.'

'Makes Terra seem a little bare.' Friendly took out his cigarettes; then put them away again. 'You know, the place has a funny effect on me. I don't smoke any more.

Guess that's because of the way it looks. It's so – so damn pure. Unsullied. I can't smoke or throw papers around. I can't bring myself to be a picnicker.'

'The picnickers'll be along soon enough,' Hall said. He went back to the microscope. 'I'll try a few more cultures. Maybe I'll find a lethal germ yet.'

'Keep trying.' Lieutenant Friendly hopped off the table. 'I'll see you later and find out if you've had any luck. There's a big conference going on in Room One. They're almost ready to give the go-ahead to the EA for the first load of colonists to be sent out.'

'Picnickers!'

Friendly grinned. 'Afraid so.'

The door closed after him. His bootsteps echoed down the corridor. Hall was alone in the lab.

He sat for a time in thought. Presently he bent down and removed the slide from the stage of the microscope, selected a new one and held it up to the light to read the marking. The lab was warm and quiet. Sunlight streamed through the windows and across the floor. The trees outside moved a little in the wind. He began to feel sleepy.

'Yes, the picnickers,' he grumbled. He adjusted the new slide into position. 'And all of them ready to come in and cut down the trees, tear up the flowers, spit in the lakes, burn up the grass. With not even the common cold virus around to – '

He stopped, his voice choked off –

Choked off, because the two eyepieces of the microscope had twisted suddenly around his windpipe and were trying to strangle him. Hall tore at them, but they dug relentlessly into his throat, steel prongs closing like the claws of a trap.

Throwing the microscope on to the floor, he leaped up. The microscope crawled quickly towards him, hooking around his leg. He kicked it loose with his other foot, and drew his blast pistol.

The microscope scuttled away, rolling on its coarse adjustments. Hall fired. It disappeared in a cloud of metallic particles.

'Good God!' Hall sat down weakly, mopping his face. 'What the – ?' He massaged his throat. 'What the hell!'

The council room was packed solid. Every officer of the Planet Blue unit was there. Commander Stella Morrison tapped on the big control map with the end of a slim plastic pointer.

'This long flat area is ideal for the actual city. It's close to water, and weather conditions vary sufficiently to give the settlers something to talk about. There are large deposits of various minerals. The colonists can set up their own factories. They won't have to do any importing. Over here is the biggest forest on the planet. If they have any sense, they'll leave it. But if they want to make newspapers out of it, that's not our concern.'

She looked around the room at the silent men.

'Let's be realistic. Some of you have been thinking we shouldn't send the okay to the Emigration Authority, but keep the planet our own selves, to come back to. I'd like that as much as any of the rest of you, but we'd just get into a lot of trouble. It's not *our* planet. We're here to do a certain job. When the job is done, we move along. And it is almost done. So let's forget it. The only thing left to do is flash the go-ahead signal and then begin packing our things.'

'Has the lab report come in on bacteria?' Vice-Commander Wood asked.

'We're taking special care to look out for them, of course. But the last I heard nothing had been found. I think we can go ahead and contact the EA. Have them send a ship to take us off and bring in the first load of settlers. There's no reason why – ' she stopped.

A murmur was swelling through the room. Heads turned towards the door.

Commander Morrison frowned. 'Major Hall, may I remind you that when the council is in session no one is permitted to interrupt!'

Hall swayed back and forth, supporting himself by holding on to the door knob. He gazed vacantly around the council room. Finally his glassy eyes picked out Lieutenant Friendly, sitting half-way across the room.

'Come here,' he said hoarsely.

'Me?' Friendly sank further down in his chair.

'Major, what is the meaning of this?' Vice-Commander Wood cut in angrily. 'Are you drunk or are – ?' He saw the blast gun in Hall's hand. 'Is something wrong, Major?'

Alarmed, Lieutenant Friendly got up and grabbed Hall's shoulder. 'What is it? What's the matter?'

'Come to the lab.'

'Did you find something?' the Lieutenant studied his friend's rigid face. 'What is it?'

'Come on.' Hall started down the corridor, Friendly following. Hall pushed the laboratory door open, stepped inside slowly.

'What is it?' Friendly repeated.

'My microscrope.'

'Your microscope? What about it?' Friendly squeezed past him into the lab. 'I don't see it.'

'It's gone.'

'Gone? Gone where?'

'I blasted it.'

'You blasted it?' Friendly looked at the other man. 'I don't get it. Why?'

Hall's mouth opened and closed, but no sound came out.

'Are you all right?' Friendly asked in concern. Then he

bent down and lifted a black plastic box from a shelf under the table. 'Say, is this a gag?'

He removed Hall's microscope from the box. 'What do you mean, you blasted it? Here it is, in its regular place. Now, tell me what's going on? You saw something on a slide? Some kind of bacteria? Lethal? Toxic?'

Hall approached the microscope slowly. It was his all right. There was the nick just above the fine adjustment. And one of the stage clips was slightly bent. He touched it with his finger.

Five minutes ago this microscope had tried to kill him. And he knew he had blasted it out of existence.

'You sure you don't need a psyche test?' Friendly asked anxiously. 'You look like post-trauma to me, or worse.'

'Maybe you're right,' Hall muttered.

The robot psyche tester whirred, integrating and gestalting. At last its colour code lights changed from red to green.

'Well?' Hall demanded.

'Severe disturbance. Instability ratio up above ten.'

'That's over danger?'

'Yes. Eight is danger. Ten is unusual, especially for a person of your index. You usually show about a four.'

Hall nodded wearily. 'I know.'

'If you could give me more data – '

Hall set his jaw. 'I can't tell you any more.'

'It's illegal to hold back information during a psyche test,' the machine said peevishly. 'If you do that you deliberately distort my findings.'

Hall rose. 'I can't tell you any more. But you do record a high degree of unbalance for me?'

'There's a high degree of psychic disorganization. But what it means, or why it exists, I can't say.'

'Thanks.' Hall clicked the tester off. He went back to his own quarters. His head whirled. Was he out of his

mind? But he had fired his blast gun at *something*. Afterwards, he had tested the atmosphere in the lab, and there
were metallic particles in suspension, especially near the
place he had fired his blast gun at the microscope.

But how could a thing like that be? A microscope
coming to life, trying to kill him!

Anyhow, Friendly had pulled it out of its box, whole
and sound. But how had it got back in the box?

He stripped off his uniform and entered the shower.
While he ran warm water over his body he meditated. The
robot psyche tester had showed his mind was severely
disturbed, but that could have been the result, rather than
the cause, of the experience. He had started to tell Friendly
about it but he had stopped. How could he expect anyone
to believe a story like that?

He shut off the water and reached out for one of the
towels on the rack.

The towel wrapped around his waist, yanking him
against the wall. Rough cloth pressed over his mouth and
nose. He fought wildly, pulling away. All at once the towel
let go. He fell, sliding to the floor, his head striking the
wall. Stars shot around him; then violent pain.

Sitting in a pool of warm water, Hall looked up at the
towel rack. The towel was motionless now, like the others
with it. Three towels in a row, all exactly alike, all
unmoving. Had he dreamed it?

He got shakily to his feet, rubbing his head. Carefully
avoiding the towel rack, he edged out of the shower and
into his room. He pulled a new towel from the dispenser
in a gingerly manner. It seemed normal. He dried himself
and began to put his clothes on.

His belt got him around the waist and tried to crush
him. It was strong – it had reinforced metal links to hold
his leggings and his gun. He and the belt rolled silently on
the floor, struggling for control. The belt was like a furious

metal snake, whipping and lashing at him. At last he managed to get his hands around his blaster.

At once the belt let go. He blasted it out of existence and then threw himself down in a chair, gasping for breath.

The arms of the chair closed around him. But this time the blaster was ready. He had to fire six times before the chair fell limp and he was able to get up again.

He stood half dressed in the middle of the room, his chest rising and falling.

'It isn't possible,' he whispered. 'I must be out of my mind.'

Finally he got his leggings and boots on. He went outside into the empty corridor. Entering the lift, he ascended to the top floor.

Commander Morrison looked up from her desk as Hall stepped through the robot clearing screen. It pinged.

'You're armed,' the Commander said accusingly.

Hall looked down at the blaster in his hand. He put it down on the desk. 'Sorry.'

'What do you want? What's the matter with you? I have a report from the testing machine. It says you've hit a ratio of ten within the last twenty-four-hour period.' She studied him intently. 'We've known each other for a long time, Lawrence. What's happening to you?'

Hall took a deep breath. 'Stella, earlier today, my microscope tried to strangle me.'

Her blue eyes widened. 'What!'

'Then, when I was getting out of the shower, a bath towel tried to smother me. I got by it, but while I was dressing, my belt – ' he stopped. The Commander had got to her feet.

'Guards!' she called.

'Wait, Stella.' Hall moved towards her. 'Listen to me. This is serious. There's something wrong. Four times things have tried to kill me. Ordinary objects suddenly turned lethal. Maybe it's what we've been looking for. Maybe this is — '

'Your microscope tried to kill you?'

'It came alive. Its stems got me around the windpipe.'

There was a long silence. 'Did anyone see this happen besides you?'

'No.'

'What did you do?'

'I blasted it.'

'Are there any remains?'

'No,' Hall admitted reluctantly. 'As a matter of fact, the microscope seems to be all right, again. The way it was before. Back in its box.'

'I see.' The Commander nodded to the two guards who had answered her call. 'Take Major Hall down to Captain Taylor and have him confined until he can be sent back to Terra for examination.'

She watched calmly as the two guards took hold of Hall's arms with magnetic grapples.

'Sorry, Major,' she said. 'Unless you can prove any of your story, we've got to assume it's psychotic projection on your part. And the planet isn't well enough policed for us to allow a psychotic to run around loose. You could do a lot of damage.'

The guards moved him towards the door. Hall went unprotestingly. His head rang, rang and echoed. Maybe she was right. Maybe he was out of his mind.

They came to Captain Taylor's offices. One of the guards rang the buzzer.

'Who is it?' the robot door demanded shrilly.

'Commander Morrison orders this man put under the Captain's care.'

There was a hesitant pause, then: 'The Captain is busy.'

'This is an emergency.'

The robot's relays clicked while it made up its mind. 'The Commander sent you?'

'Yes. Open up.'

'You may enter,' the robot conceded finally. It drew its locks back, releasing the door.

The guard pushed the door open. And stopped.

On the floor lay Captain Taylor, his face blue, his eyes gaping. Only his head and his feet were visible. A red and white scatter rug was wrapped around him, squeezing, straining tighter and tighter.

Hall dropped to the floor and pulled at the rug. 'Hurry!' he barked. 'Grab it!'

The three of them pulled together. The rug resisted.

'Help,' Taylor cried weakly.

'We're trying!' They tugged frantically. At last the rug came away in their hands. It flopped off rapidly towards the open door. One of the guards blasted it.

Hall ran to the vidscreen and shakily dialled the Commander's emergency number.

Her face appeared on the screen.

'See!' he gasped.

She stared past him to Taylor lying on the floor, the two guards kneeling beside him, their blasters still out.

'What – what happened?'

'A rug attacked him.' Hall grinned without amusement. 'Now who's crazy?'

'We'll send a guard unit down.' She blinked. 'Right away. But how – '

'Tell them to have their blasters ready. And better make that a general alarm to *everyone*.'

Hall placed four items on Commander Morrison's desk: a microscope, a towel, a metal belt, and a small red and white rug.

She edged away nervously. 'Major, are you sure – ?'

'They're all right, *now*. That's the strangest part. This

towel. A few hours ago it tried to kill me. I got away by blasting it to particles. But here it is, back again. The way it always was. Harmless.'

Captain Taylor fingered the red and white rug warily. 'That's my rug. I brought it from Terra. My wife gave it to me. I – I trusted it completely.'

They all looked at each other.

'We blasted the rug, too,' Hall pointed out.

There was silence.

'Then what was it that attacked me?' Captain Taylor asked. 'If it wasn't this rug?'

'It looked like this rug,' Hall said slowly. 'And what attacked me looked like this towel.'

Commander Morrison held the towel up to the light. 'It's just an ordinary towel! It couldn't have attacked you.'

'Of course not,' Hall agreed. 'We've put these objects through all the tests we can think of. They're just what they're supposed to be, all elements unchanged. Perfectly stable non-organic objects. It's impossible that *any* of these could have come to life and attacked us.'

'But something did,' Taylor said. 'Something attacked me. And if it wasn't this rug, what was it?'

Lieutenant Dodds felt around on the dresser for his gloves. He was in a hurry. The whole unit had been called to emergency assembly.

'Where did I – ?' he murmured. 'What the hell!'

For on the bed were *two* pairs of identical gloves, side by side.

Dodds frowned, scratching his head. How could it be? He owned only one pair. The others must be somebody else's. Bob Wesley had been in the night before, playing cards. Maybe he had left them.

The vidscreen flashed again. 'All personnel, report at once. All personnel, report at once. Emergency assembly of all personnel.'

'All right!' Dodds said impatiently. He grabbed up one of the pairs of gloves, sliding them on to his hands.

As soon as they were in place, the gloves carried his hands down to his waist. They clamped his fingers over the butt of his gun, lifting it from his holster.

'I'll be damned,' Dodds said. The gloves brought the blast gun up, pointing it at his chest.

The fingers squeezed. There was a roar. Half of Dodds' chest dissolved. What was left of him fell slowly to the floor, the mouth still open in amazement.

Corporal Tenner hurried across the ground towards the main building, as soon as he heard the wail of the emergency alarm.

At the entrance to the building he stopped to take off his metal-cleated boots. Then he frowned. By the door were two safety mats instead of one.

Well, it didn't matter. They were both the same. He stepped on to one of the mats and waited. The surface of the mat sent a flow of high-frequency current through his feet and legs, killing any spores or seeds that might have clung to him while he was outside.

He passed on into the building.

A moment later Lieutenant Fulton hurried up to the door. He yanked off his hiking boots and stepped on to the first mat he saw.

The mat folded over his feet.

'Hey,' Fulton cried. 'Let go!'

He tried to pull his feet loose, but the mat refused to let go. Fulton became scared. He drew his gun, but he didn't care to fire at his own feet.

'Help!' he shouted.

Two soldiers came running up. 'What's the matter, Lieutenant?'

'Get this damn thing off me.'

The soldiers began to laugh.

'It's no joke,' Fulton said, his face suddenly white. 'It's breaking my feet! It's — '

He began to scream. The soldiers grabbed frantically at the mat. Fulton fell, rolling and twisting, still screaming. At last the soldiers managed to get a corner of the mat loose from his feet.

Fulton's feet were gone. Nothing but limp bone remained, already half dissolved.

'Now we know,' Hall said grimly. 'It's a form of organic life.'

Commander Morrison turned to Corporal Tenner. 'You saw two mats when you came into the building?'

'Yes, Commander. Two. I stepped on — on one of them. And came in.'

'You were lucky. You stepped on the right one.'

'We've got to be careful,' Hall said. 'We've got to watch for duplicates. Apparently *it*, whatever it is, imitates objects it finds. Like a chameleon. Camouflage.'

'Two,' Stella Morrison murmured, looking at the two vases of flowers, one at each end of her desk. 'It's going to be hard to tell. Two towels, two vases, two chairs. There may be whole rows of things that are all right. All multiples legitimate except one.'

'That's the trouble. I didn't notice anything unusual in the lab. There's nothing odd about another microscope. It blended right in.'

The Commander drew away from the identical vases of flowers. 'How about those? Maybe one is — whatever they are.'

'There's two of a lot of things. Natural pairs. Two boots. Clothing. Furniture. I didn't notice that extra chair in my room. Equipment. It'll be impossible to be sure. And sometimes — '

The vidscreen lit. Vice-Commander Wood's features formed. 'Stella, another casualty.'

'Who is it this time?'

'An officer dissolved. All but a few buttons and his blast pistol – Lieutenant Dodds.'

'That makes three,' Commander Morrison said.

'If it's organic, there ought to be some way we can destroy it,' Hall muttered. 'We've already blasted a few, apparently killed them. They *can* be hurt! But we don't know how many more there are. We've destroyed five or six. Maybe it's an infinitely divisible substance. Some kind of protoplasm.'

'And meanwhile – ?'

'Meanwhile we're all at its mercy. Or *their* mercy. It's our lethal life-form, all right. That explains why we found everything else harmless. Nothing could compete with a form like this. We have mimic forms of our own, of course. Insects, plants. And there's the twisty slug on Venus. But nothing that goes this far.'

'It can be killed, though. You said so yourself. That means we have a chance.'

'If it can be found.' Hall looked around the room. Two walking-capes hung by the door. Had there been *two* a moment before?

He rubbed his forehead wearily. 'We've got to try to find some sort of poison or corrosive agent, something that'll destroy them wholesale. We can't just sit and wait for them to attack us. We need something we can spray. That's the way we got the twisty slugs.'

The Commander gazed past him, rigid.

He turned to follow her gaze. 'What is it?'

'I never noticed two brief-cases in the corner over there. There was only one before – I think.' She shook her head in bewilderment. 'How are we going to know? This business is getting me down.'

'You need a good stiff drink.'

She brightened. 'That's an idea. But – '

'But what?'

'I don't want to touch anything. There's no way to tell.'
She fingered the blast gun at her waist. 'I keep wanting to
use it, on everything.'

'Panic reaction. Still, we are being picked off, one by
one.'

Captain Unger got the emergency call over his headphones.
He stopped work at once, gathered the specimens he had
collected in his arms, and hurried back towards the bucket.

It was parked closer than he remembered. He stopped,
puzzled. There it was, the bright little cone-shaped car
with its treads firmly planted in the soft soil, its door open.

Unger hurried up to it, carrying his specimens carefully.
He opened the storage hatch in the back and lowered his
armload. Then he went around to the front and slid in
behind the controls.

He turned the switch. But the motor did not come on.
That was strange. While he was trying to figure it out, he
noticed something that gave him a start.

A few hundred feet away, among the trees was a second
bucket, just like the one he was in. And that *was* where he
remembered having parked his car. Of course, he was in
the bucket. Somebody else had come looking for specimens, and this bucket belonged to him.

Unger started to get out again.

The door closed around him. The seat folded up over
his head. The dashboard became plastic and oozed. He
gasped – he was suffocating. He struggled to get out,
flailing and twisting. There was wetness all around him,
bubbling, flowing wetness, warm like flesh.

'Glub.' His head was covered. His body was covered.

The bucket was turning to liquid. He tried to pull his hands free but they would not come.

And then the pain began. He was being dissolved. All at once he realized what the liquid was.

Acid. Digestive acid. He was in a stomach.

'Don't look!' Gail Thomas cried.

'Why not?' Corporal Hendricks swam towards her, grinning. 'Why can't I look?'

'Because I'm going to get out.'

The sun shone down on the lake. It glittered and danced on the water. All around huge moss-covered trees rose up, great silent columns among the flowering vines and bushes.

Gail climbed up on the bank, shaking water from her, throwing her hair back out of her eyes. The woods were silent. There was no sound except the lapping of the waves. They were a long way from the unit camp.

'When can I look?' Hendricks demanded, swimming around in a circle, his eyes shut.

'Soon.' Gail made her way into the trees, until she came to the place where she had left her uniform. She could feel the warm sun glowing against her bare shoulders and arms. Sitting down in the grass, she picked up her tunic and leggings.

She brushed the leaves and bits of tree bark from her tunic and began to pull it over her head.

In the water, Corporal Hendricks waited patiently, continuing in his circle. Time passed. There was no sound. He opened his eyes. Gail was nowhere in sight.

'Gail?' he called.

It was very quiet.

'Gail!'

No answer.

Corporal Hendricks swam rapidly to the bank. He pulled himself out of the water. One leap carried him to his own uniform, neatly piled at the edge of the lake. He grabbed up his blaster.

'*Gail!*'

The woods were silent. There was no sound. He stood, looking around him, frowning. Gradually, a cold fear began to numb him, in spite of the warm sun.

'*Gail!* GAIL!'

And still there was only silence.

Commander Morrison was worried. 'We've got to act,' she said. 'We can't wait. Ten lives lost already from thirty encounters. One-third is too high a percentage.'

Hall looked up from his work. 'Anyhow, now we know what we're up against. It's a form of protoplasm, with infinite versatility.' He lifted the spray tank. 'I think this will give us an idea of how many exist.'

'What's that?'

'A compound of arsenic and hydrogen in gas form. Arsine.'

'What are you going to do with it?'

Hall locked his helmet into place. His voice came through the Commander's earphones. 'I'm going to release this throughout the lab. I think there are a lot of them in here, more than anywhere else.'

'Why here?'

'This is where all samples and specimens were originally brought, where the first one of them was encountered. I think they came in with the samples, or as the samples, and then infiltrated through the rest of the buildings.'

The Commander locked her own helmet into place. Her four guards did the same. 'Arsine is fatal to human beings, isn't it?'

Hall nodded. 'We'll have to be careful. We can use it in here for a limited test, but that's about all.'

He adjusted the flow of oxygen inside his helmet.

'What's your test supposed to prove?' she wanted to know.

'If it shows anything at all, it should give us an idea of how extensively they've infiltrated. We'll know better what we're up against. This may be more serious than we realize.'

'How do you mean?' she asked, fixing her own oxygen flow.

'There are a hundred people in this unit on Planet Blue. As it stands now, the worst that can happen is that they'll get all of us, one by one. But that's nothing. Units of a hundred are lost every day of the week. It's a risk whoever is first to land on a planet must take. In the final analysis, it's relatively unimportant.'

'Compared to what?'

'If they *are* infinitely divisible, then we're going to have to think twice about leaving here. It would be better to stay and get picked off one by one than to run the risk of carrying any of them back to the system.'

She looked at him. 'Is that what you're trying to find out – whether they're infinitely divisible?'

'I'm trying to find out what we're up against. Maybe there are only a few of them. Or maybe they're everywhere.' He waved a hand around the laboratory. 'Maybe half the things in this room are not what we think they are . . . It's bad when they attack us. It would be worse if they didn't.'

'Worse?' The Commander was puzzled.

'Their mimicry is perfect. Of inorganic objects, at least. I looked through one of them, Stella, when it was imitating my microscope. It enlarged, adjusted, reflected, just like a regular microscope. It's a form of mimicry that surpasses anything we've ever imagined. It carries down below the surface, into the actual elements of the object imitated.'

'You mean one of them could slip back to Terra along

with us? In the form of clothing or a piece of lab equipment?' She shuddered.

'We assume they're some sort of protoplasm. Such malleability suggests a simple original form – and that suggests binary fission. If that's so, then there may be no limit to their ability to reproduce. The dissolving properties make me think of the simple unicellular protozoa.'

'Do you think they're intelligent?'

'I don't know. I hope not.' Hall lifted the spray. 'In any case, this should tell us their extent. And, to some degree, corroborate my notion that they're basic enough to reproduce by simple division – the worst thing possible, from our standpoint.

'Here goes,' Hall said.

He held the spray tightly against him, depressed the trigger, aimed the nozzle slowly around the lab. The Commander and the four guards stood silently behind him. Nothing moved. The sun shone in through the windows, reflecting from the culture dishes and equipment.

After a moment he let the trigger up again.

'I didn't see anything,' Commander Morrison said. 'Are you sure you did anything?'

'Arsine is colourless. But don't loosen your helmet. It's fatal. And don't move.'

They stood waiting.

For a time nothing happened. Then –

'Good God!' Commander Morrison exclaimed.

At the far end of the lab a slide cabinet wavered suddenly. It oozed, buckling and pitching. It lost its shape completely – a homogeneous jelly-like mass perched on top of the table. Abruptly it flowed down the side of the table on to the floor, wobbling as it went.

'Over there!'

A bunsen burner melted and flowed along beside it. All around the room objects were in motion. A great glass retort folded up into itself and settled down into a blob. A rack of test tubes, a shelf of chemicals . . .

'Look out!' Hall cried, stepping back.

A huge bell jar dropped with a soggy splash in front of him. It was a single large cell, all right. He could dimly make out the nucleus, the cell wall, the hard vacuoles suspended in the cytoplasm.

Pipettes, tongs, a mortar, all were flowing now. Half the equipment in the room was in motion. They had imitated almost everything there was to imitate. For every microscope there was a mimic. For every tube and jar and bottle and flask . . .

One of the guards had his blaster out. Hall knocked it down. 'Don't fire! Arsine is inflammable. Let's get out of here. We know what we wanted to know.'

They pushed the laboratory door open quickly and made their way out into the corridor. Hall slammed the door behind them, bolting it tightly.

'It is bad, then?' Commander Morrison asked.

'We haven't got a chance. The arsine disturbed them; enough of it might even kill them. But we haven't got that much arsine. And, if we could flood the planet, we wouldn't be able to use our blasters.'

'Suppose we left the planet.'

'We can't take the chance of carrying them back to the system.'

'If we stay here we'll be absorbed, dissolved, one by one,' the Commander protested.

'We could have arsine brought in. Or some other poison that might destroy them. But it would destroy most of the life on the planet along with them. There wouldn't be much left.'

'Then we'll have to destroy all life-forms! If there's no other way of doing it we've got to burn the planet clean. Even if there wouldn't be a thing left but a dead world.'

They looked at each other.

'I'm going to call the System Monitor,' Commander Morrison said. 'I'm going to get the unit off here, out of danger — all that are left, at least. That poor girl by the lake . . .' She shuddered. 'After everyone's out of here, we can work out the best way of cleaning up this planet.'

'You'll run the risk of carrying one of them back to Terra?'

'Can they imitate us? Can they imitate living creatures? Higher life-forms?'

Hall considered. 'Apparently not. They seem to be limited to inorganic objects.'

The Commander smiled grimly. 'Then we'll go back without any inorganic material.'

'But our clothes! They can imitate belts, gloves, boots — '

'We're not taking our clothes. We're going back without anything. And I mean without anything *at all*.'

Hall's lips twitched. 'I see.' He pondered. 'It might work. Can you persuade the personnel to — to leave all their things behind? Everything they own?'

'If it means their lives, I can *order* them to do it.'

'Then it might be our one chance of getting away.'

The nearest cruiser large enough to remove the remaining members of the unit was just two hours distance away. It was moving Terra-side again.

Commander Morrison looked up from the vidscreen. 'They want to know what's wrong here.'

'Let me talk.' Hall seated himself before the screen. The heavy features and gold braid of a Terran cruiser captain regarded him. 'This is Major Lawrence Hall, from the Research Division of this unit.'

'Captain Daniel Davis.' Captain Davis studied him without expression. 'You're having some kind of trouble, Major?'

Hall licked his lips. 'I'd rather not explain until we're aboard, if you don't mind.'

'Why not?'

'Captain, you're going to think we're crazy enough as it is. We'll discuss everything fully once we're aboard.' He hesitated. 'We're going to board your ship naked.'

The Captain raised an eyebrow. 'Naked?'

'That's right.'

'I see.' Obviously he didn't.

'When will you get here?'

'In about two hours, I'd say.'

'It's now 13.00 by our schedule. You'll be here by 15.00?'

'At approximately that time,' the captain agreed.

'We'll be waiting for you. Don't let any of your men out. Open one lock for us. We'll board without any equipment. Just ourselves, nothing else. As soon as we're aboard, remove the ship at once.'

Stella Morrison leaned towards the screen. 'Captain, would it be possible – for your men to – ?'

'We'll land by robot control,' he assured her. 'None of my men will be on deck. No one will see you.'

'Thank you,' she murmured.

'Not at all.' Captain Davis saluted. 'We'll see you in about two hours then, Commander.'

'Let's get everyone out on to the field,' Commander Morrison said. 'They should remove their clothes here, I think, so there won't be any objects on the field to come in contact with the ship.'

Hall looked at her face. 'Isn't it worth it to save our lives?'

Lieutenant Friendly bit his lips. 'I won't do it. I'll stay here.'

'You have to come.'

'But, Major – '

Hall looked at his watch. 'It's 14.50. The ship will be here any minute. Get your clothes off and get out on the landing field.'

'Can't I take anything at *all*?'

'Nothing. No even your blaster ... They'll give us clothes inside the ship. Come on! Your life depends on this. Everyone else is doing it.'

Friendly tugged at his shirt reluctantly. 'Well, I guess I'm acting silly.'

The vidscreen clicked. A robot voice announced shrilly: 'Everyone out of the buildings at once! Everyone out of the buildings and on the field without delay! Everyone out of the buildings at once! Everyone – '

'So soon?' Hall ran to the window and lifted the metal blind. 'I didn't hear it land.'

Parked in the centre of the landing field was a long grey cruiser, its hull pitted and dented from meteoric strikes. It lay motionless. There was no sign of life about it.

A crowd of naked people was already moving hesitantly across the field towards it, blinking in the bright sunlight.

'It's here!' Hall started tearing off his shirt. 'Let's go!'

'Wait for me!'

'Then hurry.' Hall finished undressing. Both men hurried out into the corridor. Unclothed guards raced past them. They padded down the corridors through the long unit building, to the door. They ran downstairs, out on the field. Warm sunlight beat down on them from the sky overhead. From all the unit buildings, naked men and women were pouring silently towards the ship.

'What a sight!' an officer said. 'We'll never be able to live it down.'

'But you'll live at least,' another said.

'Lawrence!'

Hall half turned.

'Please don't look around. Keep on going. I'll walk behind you.'

'How does it feel, Stella?' Hall asked.

'Unusual.'

'Is it worth it?'

'I suppose so.'

'Do you think anyone will believe us?'

'I doubt it,' she said. 'I'm beginning to wonder myself.'

'Anyhow, we'll get back alive.'

'I guess so.'

Hall looked up at the ramp being lowered from the ship in front of them. The first people were already beginning to scamper up the metal incline, into the ship, through the circular lock.

'Lawrence – '

There was a peculiar tremor in the Commander's voice. 'Lawrence, I'm – '

'You're what?'

'I'm scared.'

'Scared!' He stopped. 'Why?'

'I don't know,' she quavered.

People pushed against them from all sides. 'Forget it. Carry over from your early childhood.' He put his foot on the bottom of the ramp. 'Up we go.'

'I want to go back!' There was panic in her voice. 'I – '

Hall laughed. 'It's too late now, Stella.' He mounted the ramp, holding on to the rail. Around him, on all sides, men and women were pushing forward, carrying them up. They came to the lock. 'Here we are.'

The man ahead of him disappeared.

Hall went inside after him, into the dark interior of the ship, into the silent blackness before him. The Commander followed.

* * *

At exactly 15.00 Captain Daniel Davis landed his ship in the centre of the field. Relays slid the entrance lock open with a bang. Davis and the other officers of the ship sat waiting in the control cabin, around the big control table.

'Well,' Captain Davis said, after a while, 'where are they?'

The officers became uneasy. 'Maybe something's wrong.'

'Maybe the whole damn thing's a joke!'

They waited and waited.

But no one came.

Impostor

'One of these days I'm going to take time off,' Spence Olham said at first-meal. He looked around at his wife. 'I think I've earned a rest. Ten years is a long time.'

'And the Project?'

'The war will be won without me. This ball of clay of ours isn't really in much danger.' Olham sat down at the table and lit a cigarette. 'The newsmachines alter dispatches to make it appear the Outspacers are right on top of us. You know what I'd like to do on my vacation? I'd like to take a camping trip in those mountains outside of town, where we went that time. Remember? I got poison oak and you almost stepped on a gopher snake.'

'Sutton Wood?' Mary began to clear away the food dishes. 'The Wood was burned a few weeks ago. I thought you knew. Some kind of a flash fire.'

Olham sagged. 'Didn't they even try to find the cause?' His lips twisted. 'No one cares any more. All they can think of is the war.' He clamped his jaws together, the whole picture coming up in his mind, the Outspacers, the war, the needle-ships.

'How can we think about anything else?'

Olham nodded. She was right, of course. The dark little ships out of Alpha Centauri had bypassed the Earth cruisers easily, leaving them like helpless turtles. It had been one-way fights, all the way back to Terra.

All the way, until the protec-bubble was demonstrated by Westinghouse Labs. Thrown around the major Earth cities and finally the planet itself, the bubble was the first real defence, the first legitimate answer to the Outspacers – as the newsmachines labelled them.

But to win the war, that was another thing. Every lab, every project was working night and day, endlessly, to find something more: a weapon for positive combat. His own project, for example. All day long, year after year.

Olham stood up, putting out his cigarette. 'Like the Sword of Damocles. Always hanging over us. I'm getting tired. All I want to do is take a long rest. But I guess everybody feels that way.'

He got his jacket from the closet and went out on the front porch. The shoot would be along any moment, the fast little bug that would carry him to the Project.

'I hope Nelson isn't late.' He looked at his watch. 'It's almost seven.'

'Here the bug comes,' Mary said, gazing between the rows of houses. The sun glittered behind the roofs, reflecting against the heavy lead plates. The settlement was quiet; only a few people were stirring. 'I'll see you later. Try not to work beyond your shift, Spence.'

Olham opened the car door and slid inside, leaning back against the seat with a sigh. There was an older man with Nelson.

'Well?' Olham said, as the bug shot ahead. 'Heard any interesting news?'

'The usual,' Nelson said. 'A few Outspace ships hit, another asteriod abandoned for strategic reasons.'

'It'll be good when we get the Project into final stage. Maybe it's just the propaganda from the newsmachines, but in the last month I've gotten weary of all this. Everything seems so grim and serious, no colour to life.'

'Do you think the war is in vain?' the older man said suddenly. 'You are an integral part of it, yourself.'

'This is Major Peters,' Nelson said. Olham and Peters shook hands. Olham studied the older man.

'What brings you along so early?' he said. 'I don't remember seeing you at the Project before.'

'No, I'm not with the Project,' Peters said, 'but I know something about what you're doing. My own work is altogether different.'

A look passed between him and Nelson. Olham noticed it and he frowned. The bug was gaining speed, flashing across the barren, lifeless ground towards the distant rim of the Project buildings.

'What is your business?' Olham said. 'Or aren't you permitted to talk about it?'

'I'm with the government,' Peters said. 'With FSA, the Security Organ.'

'Oh?' Olham raised an eyebrow. 'Is there any enemy infiltration in this region?'

'As a matter of fact I'm here to see you, Mr Olham.'

Olham was puzzled. He considered Peters' words, but he could make nothing of them. 'To see me? Why?'

'I'm here to arrest you as an Outspace spy. That's why I'm up so early this morning. *Grab him, Nelson* – '

The gun drove into Olham's ribs. Nelson's hands were shaking, trembling with released emotion, his face pale. He took a deep breath and let it out again.

'Shall we kill him now?' he whispered to Peters. 'I think we should kill him now. We can't wait.'

Olham stared into his friend's face. He opened his mouth to speak, but no words came. Both men were staring at him steadily, rigid and grim with fright. Olham felt dizzy. His head ached and spun.

'I don't understand,' he murmured.

At that moment the shoot car left the ground and rushed up, heading into space. Below them the Project fell away, smaller and smaller, disappearing. Olham shut his mouth.

'We can wait a little,' Peters said. 'I want to ask him some questions, first.'

Olham gazed dully ahead as the bug rushed through space.

'The arrest was made all right,' Peters said into the vidscreen. On the screen the features of the Security chief showed. 'It should be a load off everyone's mind.'

'Any complications?'

'None. He entered the bug without suspicion. He didn't seem to think my presence was too unusual.'

'Where are you now?'

'On our way out, just inside the protec-bubble. We're moving at maximum speed. You can assume that the critical period is past. I'm glad the take-off jets in this craft were in good working order. If there had been any failure at that point – '

'Let me see him,' the Security chief said. He gazed directly at Olham where he sat, his hands in his lap, staring ahead.

'So that's the man.' He looked at Olham for a time. Olham said nothing. At last the chief nodded to Peters. 'All right. That's enough.' A faint trace of disgust wrinkled his features. 'I've seen all I want. You've done something that will be remembered for a long time. They're preparing some sort of citation for both of you.'

'That's not necessary,' Peters said.

'How much danger is there now? Is there still much chance that – '

'There is some chance, but not too much. According to my understanding, it requires a verbal key phrase. In any case we'll have to take the risk.'

'I'll have the Moon base notified you're coming.'

'No.' Peters shook his head. 'I'll land the ship outside, beyond the base. I don't want it in jeopardy.'

'Just as you like.' The chief's eyes flickered as he glanced again at Olham. Then his image faded. The screen blanked.

Olham shifted his gaze to the window. The ship was already through the protec-bubble, rushing with greater and greater speed all the time. Peters was in a hurry; below him, rumbling under the floor, the jets were wide open. They were afraid, hurrying frantically, because of him.

Next to him on the seat Nelson shifted uneasily. 'I think we should do it now,' he said. 'I'd give anything if we could get it over with.'

'Take it easy,' Peters said. 'I want you to guide the ship for a while so I can talk to him.'

He slid over beside Olham, looking into his face. Presently he reached out and touched him gingerly, on the arm and then on the cheek.

Olham said nothing. 'If I could let Mary know,' he thought again. 'If I could find some way of letting her know.' He looked around the ship. How? The vidscreen? Nelson was sitting by the board, holding the gun. There was nothing he could do. He was caught, trapped.

But why?

'Listen,' Peters said, 'I want to ask you some questions. You know where we're going. We're moving Moonward. In an hour we'll land on the far side, on the desolate side. After we land you'll be turned over immediately to a team of men waiting there. Your body will be destroyed at once. Do you understand that?' He looked at his watch. 'Within two hours your parts will be strewn over the landscape. There won't be anything left of you.'

Olham struggled out of his lethargy. 'Can't you tell me – '

'Certainly, I'll tell you,' Peters nodded. 'Two days ago we received a report that an Outspace ship had penetrated the protec-bubble. The ship let off a spy in the form of a humanoid robot. The robot was to destroy a particular human being and take his place.'

Peters looked calmly at Olham.

'Inside the robot was a U-Bomb. Our agent did not know how the bomb was to be detonated, but he conjectured that it might be a particular spoken phrase, a certain group of words. The robot would live the life of the person he killed, entering into his usual activities, his job, his social life. He had been constructed to resemble that person. No one would know the difference.'

Olham's face went sickly chalk.

'The person whom the robot was to impersonate was Spence Olham, a high-ranking official at one of the Research projects. Because this particular project was approaching crucial stage, the presence of an animate bomb, moving towards the centre of the Project – '

Olham stared down at his hands. '*But I'm Olham!*'

'Once the robot had located and killed Olham, it was a simple matter to take over his life. The robot was probably released from the ship eight days ago. The substitution was probably accomplished over the last week-end, when Olham went for a short walk in the hills.'

'But I'm Olham.' He turned to Nelson, sitting at the controls. 'Don't you recognize me? You've known me for twenty years. Don't you remember how we went to college together?' He stood up. 'You and I were at the University. We had the same room.' He went towards Nelson.

'Stay away from me!' Nelson snarled.

'Listen. Remember our second year? Remember that girl? What was her name – ' He rubbed his forehead. 'The one with the dark hair. The one we met over at Ted's place.'

'Stop!' Nelson waved the gun frantically. 'I don't want to hear any more. You killed him! You . . . machine.'

Olham looked at Nelson. 'You're wrong. I don't know what happened, but the robot never reached me. Something must have gone wrong. Maybe the ship crashed.' He turned to Peters. 'I'm Olham. I know it. No transfer was made. I'm the same as I've always been.'

He touched himself, running his hands over his body. 'There must be some way to prove it. Take me back to Earth. An X-ray examination, a neurological study, anything like that will show you. Or maybe we can find the crashed ship.'

Neither Peters nor Nelson spoke.

'I am Olham,' he said again. 'I know I am. But I can't prove it.'

'The robot,' Peters said, 'would be unaware that he was not the real Spence Olham. He would become Olham in mind as well as the body. He was given an artificial memory system, false recall. He would look like him, have his memories, his thoughts and interests, perform his job.

'But there would be one difference. Inside the robot is a U-Bomb, ready to explode at the trigger phrase.' Peters moved a little away. 'That's the one difference. That's why we're taking you to the Moon. They'll disassemble you and remove the bomb. Maybe it will explode, but it won't matter there.'

Olham sat down slowly.

'We'll be there soon,' Nelson said.

He lay back, thinking frantically, as the ship dropped slowly down. Under them was the pitted surface of the Moon, the endless expanse of ruin. What could he do? What would save him?

'Get ready,' Peters said.

In a few minutes he would be dead. Down below he could see a tiny dot, a building of some kind. There were men in the building, the demolition team, waiting to tear him to bits. They would rip him open, pull off his arms and legs, break him apart. When they found no bomb they would be surprised; they would know, but it would be too late.

Olham looked around the small cabin. Nelson was still holding the gun. There was no chance there. If he could get a doctor, have an examination made – that was the only way. Mary could help him. He thought frantically, his mind racing. Only a few minutes, just a little time left. If he could contact her, get word to her some way.

'Easy,' Peters said. The ship came down slowly, bumping on the rough ground. There was silence.

'Listen,' Olham said thickly. 'I can prove I'm Spence Olham. Get a doctor. Bring him here – '

'There's the squad.' Nelson pointed. 'They're coming.' He glanced nervously at Olham. 'I hope nothing happens.'

'We'll be gone before they start work,' Peters said. 'We'll be out of here in a moment.' He put on his pressure suit. When he had finished he took the gun from Nelson. 'I'll watch him for a moment.'

Nelson put on his pressure suit, hurrying awkwardly. 'How about him?' He indicated Olham. 'Will he need one?'

'No.' Peters shook his head. 'Robots probably don't require oxygen.'

The group of men were almost to the ship. They halted, waiting. Peters signalled to them.

'Come on!' He waved his hand and the men approached warily; stiff, grotesque figures in their inflated suits.

'If you open the door,' Olham said, 'it means my death. It will be murder.'

'Open the door,' Nelson said. He reached for the handle. Olham watched him. He saw the man's hand tighten around the metal rod. In a moment the door would swing back, the air in the ship would rush out. He would die, and presently they would realize their mistake. Perhaps at some other time, when there was no war, men might not act this way, hurrying an individual to his death because they were afraid. Everyone was frightened, everyone was willing to sacrifice the individual because of the group fear.

He was being killed because they could not wait to be sure of his guilt. There was not enough time.

He looked at Nelson. Nelson had been his friend for years. They had gone to school together. He had been best man at his wedding. Now Nelson was going to kill him. But Nelson was not wicked; it was not his fault. It was the times. Perhaps it had been the same way during the plagues. When men had shown a spot they probably had been killed, too, without a moment's hesitation, without proof, on suspicion alone. In times of danger there was no other way.

He did not blame them. But he had to live. His life was too precious to be sacrificed. Olham thought quickly. What could he do? Was there anything? He looked around.

'Here goes,' Nelson said.

'You're right,' Oldham said. The sound of his own voice surprised him. It was the strength of desperation. 'I have no need of air. Open the door.'

They paused, looking at him in curious alarm.

'Go ahead. Open it. It makes no difference.' Olham's hand disappeared inside his jacket. 'I wonder how far you can run.'

'Run?'

'You have fifteen seconds to live.' Inside his jacket his fingers twisted, his arm suddenly rigid. He relaxed, smiling a little. 'You were wrong about the trigger phrase. In that respect you were mistaken. Fourteen seconds, now.'

Two shocked faces stared at him from the pressure suits. Then they were struggling, running, tearing the door open. The air shrieked out, spilling into the void. Peters and Nelson bolted out of the ship. Olham came after them. He grasped the door and dragged it shut. The automatic pressure system chugged furiously, restoring the air. Olham let his breath out with a shudder.

One more second —

Beyond the window the two men had joined the group. The group scattered, running in all directions. One by one they threw themselves down, prone on the ground. Olham seated himself at the control board. He moved the dials into place. As the ship rose up into the air the men below scrambled to their feet and stared up, their mouths open.

'Sorry,' Olham murmured, 'but I've got to get back to Earth.'

He headed the ship back the way it had come.

It was night. All around the ship crickets chirped, disturbing the chill darkness. Olham bent over the vidscreen. Gradually the image formed; the call had gone through without trouble. He breathed a sigh of relief.

'Mary,' he said. The woman stared at him. She gasped.

'Spence! Where are you? What's happened?'

'I can't tell you. Listen. I have to talk fast. They may break this call off any minute. Go to the Project grounds and get Dr Chamberlain. If he isn't there, get any doctor. Bring him to the house and have him stay there. Have him bring equipment, X-ray, fluoroscope, everything.'

'But — '

'Do as I say. Hurry. Have him get it ready in an hour.' Olham leaned towards the screen. 'Is everything all right? Are you alone?'

'Alone?'

'Is anyone with you? Has ... has Nelson or anyone contacted you?'

'No, Spence, I don't understand.'

'All right. I'll see you at the house in an hour. And don't tell anyone anything. Get Chamberlain there on any pretext. Say you're very ill.'

He broke the connection and looked at his watch. A moment later he left the ship, stepping down into the darkness. He had a half-mile to go.

He began to walk.

One light showed in the window, the study light. He watched it, kneeling against the fence. There was no sound, no movement of any kind. He held his watch up and read it by starlight. Almost an hour had passed.

Along the street a shoot bug came. It went on.

Olham looked towards the house. The doctor should have already come. He should be inside, waiting with Mary. A thought struck him. Had she been able to leave the house? Perhaps they had intercepted her. Maybe she was moving into a trap.

But what else could he do?

With a doctor's records, photographs and reports, there was a chance, a chance of proof. If he could be examined, if he could remain alive long enough for them to study him –

He could prove it that way. It was probably the only way. His one hope lay inside the house. Dr Chamberlain was a respected man. He was the staff doctor for the Project. He would know; his words on the matter would have meaning. He could overcome their hysteria, their madness, with facts.

Madness – that was what it was. If only they would wait, act slowly, take their time. But they could not wait. He had to die, die at once, without proof, without any kind of trial or examination. The simplest test would tell, but they had not time for the simplest test. They could think only of the danger. Danger, and nothing more.

He stood up and moved towards the house. He came up on the porch. At the door he paused, listening. Still no sound. The house was absolutely still.

Too still.

Olham stood on the porch, unmoving. They were trying to be silent inside. Why? It was a small house; only a few feet away, beyond the door, Mary and Dr Chamberlain should be standing. Yet he could hear nothing, no sound of voices, nothing at all. He looked at the door. It was a door he had opened and closed a thousand times, every morning and every night.

He put his hand on the knob. Then, all at once, he reached out and touched the bell instead. The bell pealed off some place in the back of the house. Olham smiled. He could hear movement.

Mary opened the door. As soon as he saw her face he knew.

He ran, throwing himself in the bushes. A Security officer shoved Mary out of the way, firing past her. The bushes burst apart. Olham wriggled around the side of the house. He leaped up and ran, racing frantically into the darkness. A searchlight snapped on, a beam of light circling past him.

He crossed the road and squeezed over a fence. He jumped down and made his way across a back yard. Behind him men were coming, Security officers, shouting to each other as they came. Olham gasped for breath, his chest rising and falling.

Her face – he had known at once. The set lips, the terrified, wretched eyes. Suppose he had gone ahead, pushed open the door and entered! They had tapped the call and come at once, as soon as he had broken off. Probably she believed their account. No doubt she thought he was the robot, too.

Olham ran on and on. He was losing the officers, dropping them behind. Apparently they were not much good at running. He climbed a hill and made his way down the other side. In a moment he would be back at the ship. But where to, this time? He slowed down, stopping.

He could see the ship already, outlined against the sky, where he had parked it. The settlement was behind him; he was on the outskirts of the wilderness between the inhabited places, where the forests and desolation began. He crossed a barren field and entered the trees.

As he came towards it, the door of the ship opened.

Peters stepped out, framed against the light. In his arms was a heavy boris-gun. Olham stopped, rigid. Peters stared around him into the darkness. 'I know you're there, some place,' he said. 'Come on up here, Olham. There are Security men all around you.'

Olham did not move.

'Listen to me. We will catch you very shortly. Apparently you still do not believe you're the robot. Your call to the woman indicates that you are still under the illusion created by your artificial memories.

'But you *are* the robot. You are the robot, and inside you is the bomb. Any moment the trigger phrase may be spoken, by you, by someone else, by anyone. When that happens the bomb will destroy everything for miles around. The Project, the woman, all of us will be killed. Do you understand?'

Olham said nothing. He was listening. Men were moving towards him, slipping through the woods.

'If you don't come out, we'll catch you. It will be only a matter of time. We no longer plan to remove you to the Moon-base. You will be destroyed on sight, and we will have to take the chance that the bomb will detonate. I have ordered every available Security officer in the area. The whole county is being searched, inch by inch. There is no place you can go. Around this wood is a cordon of armed men. You have about six hours left before the last inch is covered.'

Olham moved away. Peters went on speaking; he had not seen him at all. It was too dark to see anyone. But

Peters was right. There was no place he could go. He was beyond the settlement, on the outskirts where the woods began. He could hide for a time, but eventually they would catch him.

Only a matter of time.

Olham walked quietly away through the wood. Mile by mile, each part of the country was being measured off, laid bare, searched, studied, examined. The cordon was coming all the time, squeezing him into a smaller and smaller space.

What was there left? He had lost the ship, the one hope of escape. They were at his home; his wife was with them, believing, no doubt, that the real Olham had been killed. He clenched his fists. Some place there was a wrecked Outspace needle-ship, and in it the remains of the robot. Somewhere nearby the ship had crashed, and broken up.

And the robot lay inside, destroyed.

A faint hope stirred him. What if he could find the remains? If he could show them the wreckage, the remains of the ship, the robot –

But where? Where would he find it?

He walked on, lost in thought. Some place, not too far off, probably. The ship would have landed close to the Project; the robot would have expected to go the rest of the way on foot. He went up the side of a hill and looked around. Crashed and burned. Was there some clue, some hint? Had he read anything, heard anything? Some place close by, within walking distance. Some wild place, a remote spot where there would be no people.

Suddenly Olham smiled. Crashed and burned –

Sutton Wood.

He increased his pace.

It was morning. Sunlight filtered down through the broken trees, on to the man crouching at the edge of the clearing.

Olham glanced up from time to time, listening. They were not far off, only a few minutes away. He smiled.

Down below him, strewn across the clearing and into the charred stumps that had been Sutton Wood, lay a tangled mass of wreckage. In the sunlight it glittered a little, gleaming darkly. He had not had too much trouble finding it. Sutton Wood was a place he knew well; he had climbed around it many times in his life, when he was younger. He had known where he would find the remains. There was one peak that jutted up suddenly, without warning.

A descending ship, unfamiliar with the Wood, had little chance of missing it. And now he squatted, looking down at the ship, or what remained of it.

Olham stood up. He could hear them, only a little distance away, coming together, talking in low tones. He tensed himself. Everything depended on who first saw him. If it were Nelson he had no chance. Nelson would fire at once. He would be dead before they saw the ship. But if he had time to call out, hold them off for a moment – that was all he needed. Once they saw the ship he would be safe.

But if they fired first –

A charred branch cracked. A figure appeared, coming forward uncertainly. Olham took a deep breath. Only a few seconds remained, perhaps the last seconds of his life. He raised his arms, peering intently.

It was Peters.

'Peters!' Olham waved his arms. Peters lifted his gun, aiming. 'Don't fire!' His voice shook. 'Wait a minute. Look past me, across the clearing.'

'I've found him,' Peters shouted. Security men came pouring out of the burned woods around him.

'Don't shoot. Look past me. The ship, the needle-ship. The Outspace ship. Look!'

Peters hesitated. The gun wavered.

'It's down there,' Olham said rapidly. 'I knew I'd find it here. The burned wood. Now you believe me. You'll find the remains of the robot in the ship. Look, will you?'

'There is something down there,' one of the men said nervously.

'Shoot him!' a voice said. It was Nelson.

'Wait.' Peters turned sharply. 'I'm in charge. Don't anyone fire. Maybe he's telling the truth.'

'Shoot him,' Nelson said. 'He killed Olham. Any minute he may kill us all. If the bomb goes off – '

'Shut up.' Peters advanced towards the slope. He stared down. 'Look at that.' He waved two men up to him. 'Go down there and see what that is.'

The men raced down the slope, across the clearing. They bent down, poking in the ruins of the ship.

'Well?' Peters called.

Olham held his breath. He smiled a little. It must be there; he had not had time to look himself, but it had to be there. Suddenly doubt assailed him. Suppose the robot had lived long enough to wander away? Suppose his body had been completely destroyed, burned to ashes by the fire?

He licked his lips. Perspiration came out on his forehead. Nelson was staring at him, his face still livid. His chest rose and fell.

'Kill him,' Nelson said. 'Before he kills us.'

The two men stood up.

'What have you found?' Peters said. He held the gun steady. 'Is there anything there?'

'Looks like something. It's a needle-ship, all right. There's something beside it.'

'I'll look.' Peters strode past Olham. Olham watched him go down the hill and up to the men. The others were following after him, peering to see.

'It's a body of some sort,' Peters said. 'Look at it!'

Olham came along with them. They stood around in a circle, staring down.

On the ground, bent and twisted into a strange shape, was a grotesque form. It looked human, perhaps; except that it was bent so strangely, the arms and legs flung off in all directions. The mouth was open, the eyes stared glassily.

'Like a machine that's run down,' Peters murmured.

Olham smiled feebly. 'Well?' he said.

Peters looked at him. 'I can't believe it. You were telling the truth all the time.'

'The robot never reached me,' Olham said. He took out a cigarette and lit it. 'It was destroyed when the ship crashed. You were all too busy with the war to wonder why an out of the way woods would suddenly catch fire and burn. Now you know.'

He stood smoking, watching the men. They were dragging the grotesque remains from the ship. The body was stiff, the arms and legs rigid.

'You'll find the bomb, now,' Olham said. The men laid the body on the ground. Peters bent down.

'I think I see the corner of it.' He reached out, touching the body.

The chest of the corpse had been laid open. Within the gaping tear something glinted, something metal. The men stared at the metal without speaking.

'That would have destroyed us all, if it had lived,' Peters said. 'That metal box, there.'

There was silence.

'I think we owe you something,' Peters said to Olham. 'This must have been a nightmare to you. If you hadn't escaped, we would have – ' He broke off.

Olham put out his cigarette. 'I knew, of course, that the robot had never reached me. But I had no way of proving it. Sometimes it isn't possible to prove a thing right away. That was the whole trouble. There wasn't any way I could demonstrate that I was myself.'

'How about a vacation?' Peters said. 'I think we might work out a month's vacation for you. You could take it easy, relax.'

'I think right now I want to go home,' Olham said.

'All right, then,' Peters said. 'Whatever you say.'

Nelson had squatted down on the ground, beside the corpse. He reached out towards the glint of metal visible within the chest.

'Don't touch it,' Olham said. 'It might still go off. We better let the demolition squad take care of it later on.'

Nelson said nothing. Suddenly he grabbed hold of the metal, reaching his hand inside the chest. He pulled.

'What are you doing?' Olham cried.

Nelson stood up. He was holding on to the metal object. His face was blank with terror. It was a metal knife, an Outspace needle-knife, covered with blood.

'This killed him,' Nelson whispered. 'My friend was killed with this.' He looked at Olham. 'You killed him with this and left him beside the ship.'

Olham was trembling. His teeth chattered. He looked from the knife to the body. 'This can't be Olham,' he said. His mind spun, everything was whirling. 'Was I wrong?'

He gaped.

'But if that's Olham, then I must be – '

He did not complete the sentence, only the first phase. The blast was visible all the way to Alpha Centauri.

Expendable

The man came out on the front porch and examined the day. Bright and clear – with dew on the lawns. He buttoned his coat and put his hands in his pockets.

As the man started down the steps the two caterpillars waiting by the mailbox twitched with interest.

'There he goes,' the first one said. 'Send in your report.'

As the other began to rotate his vanes the man stopped, turning quickly.

'I heard that,' he said. He brought his foot down against the wall, scraping the caterpillars off, on to the concrete. He crushed them.

Then he hurried down the path to the pavement. As he walked he looked around him. In the cherry tree a bird was hopping, pecking bright-eyed at the cherries. The man studied him. All right? Or – The bird flew off. Birds all right. No harm from them.

He went on. At the corner he brushed against a spider web, crossed from the bushes to the telephone pole. His heart pounded. He tore away, batting in the air. As he went on he glanced over his shoulder. The spider was coming slowly down the bush, feeling out the damage to his web.

Hard to tell about spiders. Difficult to figure out. More facts needed – no contact, yet.

He waited at the bus stop, stamping his feet to keep them warm.

The bus came and he boarded it, feeling a sudden pleasure as he took his seat with all the warm, silent people, staring indifferently ahead. A vague flow of security poured through him.

He grinned, and relaxed, the first time in days.

The bus went down the street.

Tirmus waved his antennae excitedly.

'Vote, then, if you want.' He hurried past them, up on to the mound. 'But let me say what I said yesterday, before you start.'

'We already know it,' Lala said impatiently. 'Let's get moving. We have the plans worked out. What's holding us up?'

'More reason for me to speak.' Tirmus gazed around at the assembled gods. 'The entire Hill is ready to march against the giant in question. Why? We know he can't communicate to his fellows – it's out of the question. The type of vibration, the language they use makes it impossible to convey such ideas as he holds about us, about our – '

'Nonsense.' Lala stepped up. 'Giants communicate well enough.'

'There is no record of a giant having made known information about us!'

The army moved restlessly.

'Go ahead,' Tirmus said. 'But it's a waste of effort. He's harmless – cut off. Why take all the time and – '

'Harmless?' Lala stared at him. 'Don't you understand? He knows!'

Tirmus walked away from the mound. 'I'm against unnecessary violence. We should save our strength. Some day we'll need it.'

The vote was taken. As expected, the army was in favour of moving against the giant. Tirmus sighed and began stroking out the plans on the ground.

'This is the location that he takes. He can be expected

to appear there at period-end. Now, as I see the situation – '

He went on, laying out the plans in the soft soil.

One of the gods leaned towards another, antennae touching. 'This giant. He doesn't stand a chance. In a way, I feel sorry for him. How'd he happen to butt in?'

'Accident.' The other grinned. 'You know, the way they do, barging around.'

'It's too bad for him, though.'

It was nightfall. The street was dark and deserted. Along the pavement the man came, a newspaper under his arm. He walked quickly, glancing around him. He skirted the big tree growing by the kerb and leaped agilely into the street. He crossed the street and gained the opposite side. As he turned the corner he entered the web, sewn from bush to telephone pole. Automatically he fought it, brushing it off him. As the strands broke a thin humming came to him, metallic and wiry.

'. . . wait!'

He paused.

'. . . careful . . . inside . . . wait . . .'

His jaw set. The last strands broke in his hands and he walked on. Behind him the spider moved in the fragment of his web, watching. The man looked back.

'Nuts to you,' he said. 'I'm not taking any chances, standing here all tied up.'

He went on, along the pavement, to his path. He skipped up the path, avoiding the darkening bushes. On the porch he found his key, fitting it into the lock.

He paused. Inside? Better than outside, especially at night. Night a bad time. Too much movement under the bushes. Not good. He opened the door and stepped inside. The rug lay ahead of him, a pool of blackness. Across on the other side he made out the form of the lamp.

Four steps to the lamp. His foot came up. He stopped.

What did the spider say? What? He waited, listening.
Silence.

He took his cigarette lighter and flicked it on.

The carpet of ants swelled towards him, rising up in a
flood. He leaped aside, out on to the porch. The ants came
rushing, hurrying, scratching across the floor in the half-
light.

The man jumped down to the ground and around the
side of the house. When the first ants came flowing over
the porch he was already spinning the faucet handle
rapidly, gathering up the hose.

The burst of water lifted the ants up and scattered them,
flinging them away. The man adjusted the nozzle, squint-
ing through the mist. He advanced, turning the hard
stream from side to side.

'God damn you,' he said, his teeth locked. 'Waiting
inside – '

He was frightened. Inside – never before! In the night
cold sweat came out on his face. Inside. They had never
got inside before. Maybe a moth or two, and flies, of
course. But they were harmless, fluttery, noisy –

A carpet of ants!

Savagely, he sprayed them until they broke rank and
fled into the lawn, into the bushes, under the house.

He sat down on the walk, holding the hose, trembling
from head to foot.

They really meant it. Not an anger raid, annoyed,
spasmodic; but planned, an attack, worked out. They had
waited for him. One more step –

Thank God for the spider.

Presently he shut the hose off and stood up. No sound;
silence everywhere. The bushes rustled suddenly. Beetle?
Something black scurried – he put his foot on it. A

messenger, probably. Fast runner. He went gingerly inside the dark house, feeling his way by the cigarette lighter.

Later, he sat at his desk, the spray gun beside him, heavy-duty steel and copper. He touched its damp surface with his fingers.

Seven o'clock. Behind him the radio played softly. He reached over and moved the desk lamp so that it shone on the floor beside the desk.

He lit a cigarette and took some writing paper and his fountain pen. He paused, thinking.

So they really wanted him, badly enough to plan it out. Bleak despair descended over him like a torrent. What could he do? Whom could he go to? Or tell? He clenched his fists, sitting bolt upright in the chair.

The spider slid down beside him on the desk top. 'Sorry. Hope you aren't frightened, as in the poem.'

The man stared. 'Are you the same one? The one at the corner? The one who warned me?'

'No. That's somebody else. A Spinner. I'm strictly a Cruncher. Look at my jaws.' He opened and shut his mouth. 'I bite them up.'

The man smiled. 'Good for you.'

'Sure. Do you know how many there are of us in — say — an acre of land? Guess.'

'A thousand.'

'No. Two and a half million. Of all kinds. Crunchers, like me, or Spinners, or Stingers.'

'Stingers?'

'The best. Let's see.' The spider thought. 'For instance, the black widow, as you call her. Very valuable.' He paused. 'Just one thing.'

'What's that?'

'We have our problems. The gods — '

'Gods!'

'Ants, as you call them. The leaders. They're beyond us. Very unfortunate. They have an awful taste – makes one sick. We have to leave them for the birds.'

The man stood up. 'Birds? Are they – '

'Well, we have an arrangement. This has been going on for ages. I'll give you the story. We have some time left.'

The man's heart contracted. 'Time left? What do you mean?'

'Nothing. A little trouble later on, I understand. Let me give you the background. I don't think you know it.'

'Go ahead. I'm listening.' He stood up and began to walk back and forth.

'*They* were running the earth pretty well, about a billion years ago. You see, men came from some other planet. Which one? I don't know. They landed and found the earth quite well cultivated by them. There was a war.'

'So we're the invaders,' the man murmured.

'Sure. The war reduced both sides to barbarism, them and yourselves. You forgot how to attack, and they degenerated into closed social factions, ants, termites – '

'I see.'

'The last group of you that knew the full story started us going. We were bred – ' the spider chuckled in its own fashion, 'bred some place for this worthwhile purpose. We keep them down very well. You know what they call us? The Eaters. Unpleasant, isn't it?'

Two more spiders came drifting down on their web-strands, alighting on the desk. The three spiders went into a huddle.

'More serious than I thought,' the Cruncher said easily. 'Didn't know the whole dope. The Stinger here – '

The black widow came to the edge of the desk. 'Giant,' she piped, metallically. 'I'd like to talk with you.'

'Go ahead,' the man said.

'There's going to be some trouble here. They're moving,

coming here, a lot of them. We thought we'd stay with you a while. Get in on it.'

'I see.' The man nodded. He licked his lips, running his fingers shakily through his hair. 'Do you think — that is, what are the chances — '

'Chances?' The Stinger undulated thoughtfully. 'Well, we've been in this work a long time. Almost a million years. I think that we have the edge over them, in spite of drawbacks. Our arrangements with the birds, and of course, with the toads — '

'I think we can save you,' the Cruncher put in cheerfully. 'As a matter of fact, we look forward to events like this.'

From under the floor boards came a distant scratching sound, the noise of a multitude of tiny claws and wings, vibrating faintly, remotely. The man heard. His body sagged all over.

'You're really certain? You think you can do it?' He wiped the perspiration from his lips and picked up the spray gun, still listening.

The sound was growing, swelling beneath them, under the floor, under their feet. Outside the house bushes rustled and a few moths flew up against the window. Louder and louder the sound grew, beyond and below, everywhere, a rising hum of anger and determination. The man looked from side to side.

'You're sure you can do it?' he murmured. 'You really can save me?'

'Oh,' the Stinger said, embarrassed. 'I didn't mean *that*. I meant the species, the race . . . not you as an individual.'

The man gaped at him and the three Eaters shifted uneasily. More moths burst against the window. Under them the floor stirred and heaved.

'I see,' the man said. 'I'm sorry I misunderstood you.'

Planet for Transients

The late afternoon sun shone down blinding and hot, a great shimmering orb in the sky. Trent halted a moment to get his breath. Inside his lead-lined helmet his face dripped with sweat, drop after drop of sticky moisture that steamed his viewplate and clogged his throat.

He slid his emergency pack over to the other side and hitched up his gun-belt. From his oxygen tank he pulled a couple of exhausted tubes and tossed them away in the brush. The tubes rolled and disappeared, lost in the endless heaps of red-green leaves and vines.

Trent checked his counter, found the reading low enough, slid back his helmet for a precious moment.

Fresh air rushed into his nose and mouth. He took a deep breath, filling his lungs. The air smelled good – thick and moist and rich with the odour of growing plants. He exhaled and took another breath.

To his right a towering column of orange shrubbery rose, wrapped around a sagging concrete pillar. Spread out over the rolling countryside was a vast expanse of grass and trees. In the distance a mass of growth looked like a wall, a jungle of creepers and insects and flowers and underbrush that would have to be blasted as he advanced slowly.

Two immense butterflies danced past him. Great fragile shapes, multi-coloured, racing erratically around him and then away. Life everywhere – bugs and plants and the rustling small animals in the shrubbery, a buzzing jungle of life in every direction. Trent sighed and snapped his helmet back in place. Two breathfuls was all he dared.

He increased the flow of his oxygen tank and then raised his transmitter to his lips. He clicked it briefly on. 'Trent. Checking with the Mine Monitor. Hear me?'

A moment of static and silence. Then, a faint, ghostly voice. 'Come in, Trent. Where the hell are you?'

'Still going North. Ruins ahead. I may have to bypass. Looks thick.'

'Ruins?'

'New York, probably. I'll check with the map.'

The voice was eager. 'Anything yet?'

'Nothing. Not so far, at least. I'll circle and report in about an hour.' Trent examined his wrist watch. 'It's half-past three. I'll raise you before evening.'

The voice hesitated. 'Good luck. I hope you find something. How's your oxygen holding out?'

'All right.'

'Food?'

'Plenty left. I may find some edible plants.'

'Don't take any chances!'

'I won't.' Trent clicked off the transmitter and returned it to his belt. 'I won't,' he repeated. He gathered up his blast gun and hoisted his pack and started forward, his heavy lead-lined boots sinking deep into the lush foliage and compost underfoot.

It was just past four o'clock when he saw them. They stepped out of the jungle around him. Two of them, young males – tall and thin and horny blue-grey like ashes. One raised his hand in greeting. Six or seven fingers – extra joints. 'Afternoon,' he piped.

Trent stopped instantly. His heart thudded. 'Good afternoon.'

The two youths came slowly around him. One had an axe – a foliage axe. The other carried only his pants and the remains of a canvas shirt. They were nearly eight feet tall. No flesh – bones and hard angles and large, curious eyes, heavily lidded. There were internal changes, radically different metabolism and cell structure, ability to utilize hot salts, altered digestive system. They were both looking at Trent with interest – growing interest.

'Say,' one said. 'You're a human being.'

'That's right,' Trent said.

'My name's Jackson.' The youth extended his thin blue horny hand and Trent shook it awkwardly. The hand was fragile under his lead-lined glove. Its owner added, 'My friend here is Earl Potter.'

Trent shook hands with Potter. 'Greetings,' Potter said. His rough lips twitched. 'Can we have a look at your rig?'

'My rig?' Trent countered.

'Your gun and equipment. What's that on your belt? And that tank?'

'Transmitter – oxygen.' Trent showed them the transmitter. 'Battery operated. Hundred-mile range.'

'You're from a camp?' Jackson asked quickly.

'Yes. Down in Pennsylvania.'

'How many?'

Trent shrugged. 'Couple of dozen.'

The blue-skinned giants were fascinated. 'How have you survived? Penn was hard hit, wasn't it? The pools must be deep around there.'

'Mines,' Trent explained. 'Our ancestors moved down deep in the coal mines when the war began. So the records have it. We're fairly well set up. Grow our own food in tanks. A few machines, pumps and compressors and electrical generators. Some hand lathes. Looms.'

He didn't mention that generators now had to be cranked by hand, that only about half of the tanks were still operative. After three hundred years metal and plastic weren't much good – in spite of endless patching and repairing. Everything was wearing out, breaking down.

'Say,' Potter said. 'This sure makes a fool of Dave Hunter.'

'Dave Hunter?'

'Dave says there aren't any true humans left,' Jackson explained. He poked at Trent's helmet curiously. 'Why don't you come back with us? We've got a settlement near here – only an hour or so away on the tractor – our hunting tractor. Earl and I were out hunting flap-rabbits.'

'Flap-rabbits?'

'Flying rabbits. Good meat but hard to bring down – weigh about thirty pounds.'

'What do you use? Not the axe surely.'

Potter and Jackson laughed. 'Look at this here.' Potter slid a long brass rod from his trousers. It fitted down inside his pants along his pipe-stem leg.

Trent examined the rod. It was tooled by hand. Soft brass, carefully bored and straightened. One end was shaped into a nozzle. He peered down it. A tiny metal pin was lodged in a cake of transparent material. 'How does it work?' he asked.

'Launched by hand – like a blow gun. But once the b-dart is in the air it follows its target for ever. The initial thrust has to be provided.' Potter laughed. 'I supply that. A big puff of air.'

'Interesting.' Trent returned the rod. With elaborated casualness, studying the two blue-grey faces, he asked, 'I'm the first human you've seen?'

'That's right,' Jackson said. 'The Old Man will be pleased to welcome you.' There was eagerness in his reedy voice. 'What do you say? We'll take care of you. Feed you, bring you cold plants and animals. For a week, maybe?'

'Sorry,' Trent said. 'Other business. If I come through here on the way back . . .'

The horny faces fell with disappointment. 'Not for a

little while? Overnight? We'll pump you plenty of cold food. We have a fine cooler the Old Man fixed up.'

Trent tapped his tank. 'Short on oxygen. You don't have a compressor?'

'No. We don't have any use. But maybe the Old Man could – '

'Sorry.' Trent moved off. 'Have to keep going. You're sure there are no humans in this region?'

'We thought there weren't any left anywhere. A rumour once in a while. But you're the first we've seen.' Potter pointed west. 'There's a tribe of rollers off that way.' He pointed vaguely south. 'A couple of tribes of bugs.'

'And some runners.'

'You've seen them?'

'I came that way.'

'And north there's some of the underground ones – the blind digging kind.' Potter made a face. 'I can't see them and their bores and scoops. But what the hell.' He grinned. 'Everybody has his own way.'

'And to the east,' Jackson added, 'where the ocean begins, there's a lot of the porpoise kind – the undersea type. They swim around – use those big underwater air-domes and tanks – come up sometimes at night. A lot of types come out at night. We're still daylight-oriented.' He rubbed his horny blue-grey skin. 'This cuts radiation fine.'

'I know,' Trent said. 'So long.'

'Good luck.' They watched him go, heavy-lidded eyes still big with astonishment, as the human being pushed slowly off through the lush green jungle, his metal and plastic suit glinting faintly in the afternoon sun.

Earth was alive, thriving with activity. Plants and animals and insects in boundless confusion. Night forms, day forms, land and water types, incredible kinds and numbers that had never been catalogued, probably never would be.

By the end of the war every surface inch was radioactive. A whole planet sprayed and bombarded by hard radiation. All life subjected to beta and gamma rays. Most life died – but not all. Hard radiation brought mutation – at all levels, insects, plant and animal. The normal mutation and selection process was accelerated millions of years in seconds.

These altered progeny littered the Earth. A crawling teeming glowing horde of radiation-saturated beings. In this world, only those forms which could use hot soil and breathe particle-laden air survived. Insects and animals and men who could live in a world with a surface so alive that it glowed at night.

Trent considered this moodily, as he made his way through the steaming jungle, expertly burning creepers and vines with his blaster. Most of the oceans had been vaporized. Water descended still, drenching the land with torrents of hot moisture. This jungle was wet – wet and hot and full of life. Around him creatures scuttled and rustled. He held his blaster tight and pushed on.

The sun was setting. It was getting to be night. A range of ragged hills jutted ahead in the violet gloom. The sunset was going to be beautiful – compounded of particles in suspension, particles that still drifted from the initial blast, centuries ago.

He stopped for a moment to watch. He had come a long way. He was tired – and discouraged.

The horny blue-skinned giants were a typical mutant tribe. *Toads*, they were called. Because of their skin – like desert horned-toads. With their radical internal organs, geared to hot plants and air, they lived easily in a world where he survived only in a lead-lined suit, polarized viewplate, oxygen tank, special cold food pellets grown underground in the Mine.

The Mine – time to call again. Trent lifted his transmitter. 'Trent checking again,' he muttered. He licked his dry lips. He was hungry and thirsty. Maybe he could find some relatively cool spot, free of radiation. Take off his suit for a quarter of an hour and wash himself. Get the sweat and grime off.

Two weeks he had been walking, cooped up in a hot sticky lead-lined suit, like a diver's suit. While all around him countless life-forms scrambled and leaped, unbothered by the lethal pools of radiation.

'Mine,' the faint tinny voice answered.

'I'm about washed up for today. I'm stopping to rest and eat. No more until tomorrow.'

'No luck?' Heavy disappointment.

'None.'

Silence. Then, 'Well, maybe tomorrow.'

'Maybe. Met a tribe of toads. Nice young bucks, eight feet high.' Trent's voice was bitter. 'Wandering around with nothing on but shirts and pants. Bare feet.'

The Mine Monitor was uninterested. 'I know. The lucky stiffs. Well, get some sleep and raise me tomorrow A.M. A report came in from Lawrence.'

'Where is he?'

'Due west. Near Ohio. Making good progress.'

'Any results?'

'Tribes of rollers, bugs and the digging kind that come up at night – the blind white things.'

'Worms.'

'Yes, worms. Nothing else. When will you report again?'

'Tomorrow,' Trent said. He cut the switch and dropped his transmitter to his belt.

Tomorrow. He peered into the gathering gloom at the distant range of hills. Five years. And always – tomorrow. He was the last of a great procession of men to be sent out. Lugging precious oxygen tanks and food pellets and a blast pistol. Exhausting their last stores in a useless sortie into the jungles.

Tomorrow? Some tomorrow, not far off, there wouldn't be any more oxygen tanks and food pellets. The compressors and pumps would have stopped completely. Broken down for good. The Mine would be dead and silent. Unless they made contact pretty damn soon.

He squatted down and began to pass his counter over the surface, looking for a cool spot to undress. He passed out.

'Look at him,' a faint faraway voice said.

Consciousness returned with a rush. Trent pulled himself violently awake, groping for his blaster. It was morning. Grey sunlight filtered down through the trees. Around him shapes moved.

The blaster . . . gone!

Trent sat up, fully awake. The shapes were vaguely human – but not very. Bugs.

'Where's my gun?' Trent demanded.

'Take it easy.' A bug advanced, the others behind. It was chilly. Trent shivered. He got awkwardly to his feet as the bugs formed a circle around him. 'We'll give it back.'

'Let's have it now.' He was stiff and cold. He snapped his helmet in place and tightened his belt. He was shivering, shaking all over. The leaves and vines dripped wet slimy drops. The ground was soft underfoot.

The bugs conferred. There were ten or twelve of them. Strange creatures, more like insects than men. They were shelled – thick shiny chitin. Multi-lensed eyes. Nervous, vibrating antennae by which they detected radiation.

Their protection wasn't perfect. A strong dose and they were finished. They survived by detection and avoidance and partial immunity. Their food was taken indirectly, first digested by smaller warm-blooded animals and then taken as fecal matter, minus radio-active particles.

'You're a human,' a bug said. Its voice was shrill and metallic. The bugs were asexual – these, at least. Two others types existed, male drones and a Mother. These were neuter warriors, armed with pistols and foliage axes.

'That's right,' Trent said.

'What are you doing here? Are there more of you?'

'Quite a few.'

The bugs conferred again, antennae waving wildly. Trent waited. The jungle was stirring into life. He watched a gelatin-like mass flow up the side of a tree and into the branches, a half-digested mammal visible within. Some drab day moths fluttered past. The leaves stirred as under-ground creatures burrowed sullenly away from the light.

'Come along with us,' a bug said. It motioned Trent forward. 'Let's get going.'

Trent fell in reluctantly. They marched along a narrow path, cut by axes some time recently. The thick feelers and probes of the jungle were already coming back. 'Where are we going?' Trent demanded.

'To the Hill.'

'Why?'

'Never mind.'

Watching the shiny bugs stride along, Trent had trouble believing they had once been human beings. Their ances-tors, at least. In spite of their incredible altered physiology the bugs were mentally about the same as he. Their tribal arrangement approximated the human organic states, communism and fascism.

'May I ask you something?' Trent said.

'What?'

'I'm the first human you've seen? There aren't any more around here?'

'No more.'

'Are there reports of human settlements anywhere?'

'Why?'

'Just curious,' Trent said tightly.

'You're the only one.' The bug was pleased. 'We'll get a

bonus for this – for capturing you. There's a standing reward. Nobody's ever claimed it before.'

A human was wanted here too. A human brought with him valuable *gnosis*, odds and ends of tradition the mutants needed to incorporate into their shaky social structures. Mutant cultures were still unsteady. They needed contact with the past. A human being was a shaman, a Wise Man to teach and instruct. To teach the mutants how life had been, how their ancestors had lived and acted and looked.

A valuable possession for any tribe – especially if no other humans existed in the region.

Trent cursed savagely. *None?* No others? There *had* to be other humans – some place. If not north, then east. Europe, Asia, Australia. Some place, somewhere on the globe. Humans with tools and machines and equipment. The Mine couldn't be the only settlement, the last fragment of true man. Prized curiosities – doomed when their compressors burned out and their food tanks dried up.

If he didn't have any luck pretty soon . . .

The bugs halted, listening. Their antennae twitched suspiciously.

'What is it?' Trent asked.

'Nothing.' They started on. 'For a moment – '

A flash. The bugs ahead on the trail winked out of existence. A dull roar of light rolled over them.

Trent sprawled. He struggled, caught in the vines and sappy weeds. Around him bugs twisted and fought wildly. Tangling with small furry creatures that fired rapidly and efficiently with hand weapons and, when they got close, kicked and gouged with immense hind legs.

Runners.

The bugs were losing. They retreated back down the trail, scattering into the jungle. The runners hopped after them, springing on their powerful hind legs like kangaroos. The last bug departed. The noise died down.

'Okay,' a runner ordered. He gasped for breath, straightening up. 'Where's the human?'

Trent got slowly to his feet. 'Here.'

The runners helped him up. They were small, not over four feet high. Fat and round, covered with thick pelts. Little good-natured faces peered up at him with concern. Beady eyes, quivering noses and great kangaroo legs.

'You all right?' one asked. He offered Trent his water canteen.

'I'm all right.' Trent pushed the canteen away. 'They got my blaster.'

The runners searched around. The blaster was nowhere to be seen.

'Let it go.' Trent shook his head dully, trying to collect himself. 'What happened? The light.'

'A grenade.' The runners puffed with pride. 'We stretched a wire across the trail, attached to the pin.'

'The bugs control most of this area,' another said. 'We have to fight our way through.' Around his neck hung a pair of binoculars. The runners were armed with slug-pistols and knives.

'Are you really a human being?' a runner asked. 'The original stock?'

'That's right,' Trent muttered in unsteady tones.

The runners were awed. Their beady eyes grew wide. They touched his metal suit, his viewplate. His oxygen tank and pack. One squatted down and expertly traced the circuit of his transmitter apparatus.

'Where are you from?' the leader asked in his deep purr-like voice. 'You're the first human we've seen in months.'

Trent spun, choking. '*Months?* Then . . .'

'None around here. We're from Canada. Up around Montreal. There's a human settlement up there.'

Trent's breath came fast. 'Walking distance?'

'Well, we made it in a couple of days. But we go fairly fast.' The runner eyed Trent's metal-clad legs doubtfully. 'I don't know. For you it would take longer.'

Humans. A human settlement. 'How many? A big settlement? Advanced?'

'It's hard to remember. I saw their settlement once. Down underground – levels, cells. We traded some cold plants for salt. That was a long time ago.'

'They're operating successfully? They have tools – machinery – compressors? Food tanks to keep going?'

The runner twisted uneasily. 'As a matter of fact they may not be there any more.'

Trent froze. Fear cut through him like a knife. 'Not there? What do you mean?'

'They may be gone.'

'Gone where?' Trent's voice was bleak. 'What happened to them?'

'I don't know,' the runner said. 'I don't know what happened to them. Nobody knows.'

He pushed on, hurrying frantically north. The jungle gave way to a bitterly cold fern-like forest. Great silent trees on all sides. The air was thin and brittle.

He was exhausted. And only one tube of oxygen remained in the tank. After that he would have to open his helmet. How long would he last? The first rain cloud would bring lethal particles sweeping into his lungs. Or the first strong wind, blowing from the ocean.

He halted, gasping for breath. He had reached the top of a long slope. At the bottom a plain stretched out – tree-covered – a dark green expanse, almost brown. Here and there a spot of white gleamed. Ruins of some kind. A human city had been here three centuries ago.

Nothing stirred – no sign of life. No sign anywhere.

Trent made his way down the slope. Around him the forest was silent. A dismal oppression hung over everything. Even the usual rustling of small animals was lacking. Animals, insects, men — all were gone. Most of the runners had moved south. The small things probably had died. And the men?

He came out among the ruins. This had been a great city once. Then men had probably gone down in air-raid shelters and mines and subways. Later on they had enlarged their underground chambers. For three centuries men — the true men — had held on, living below the surface. Wearing lead-lined suits when they came up, growing food in tanks, filtering their water, compressing particle-free air. Shielding their eyes against the glare of the bright sun.

And now — nothing at all.

He lifted his transmitter. 'Mine,' he snapped. 'This is Trent.'

The transmitter sputtered feebly. It was a long time before it responded. The voice was faint, distant. Almost lost in the static. 'Well? Did you find them?'

'They're gone.'

'But . . .'

'Nothing. No one. Completely abandoned.' Trent sat down on a broken stump of concrete. His body was dead. Drained of life. 'They were here recently. The ruins aren't covered. They must have left in the last few weeks.'

'It doesn't make sense. Mason and Douglas are on their way. Douglas has the tractor car. He should be there in a couple of days. How long will your oxygen last?'

'Twenty-four hours.'

'We'll tell him to make time.'

'I'm sorry I don't have more to report. Something better.' Bitterness welled up in his voice. 'After all these years. They were here all this time. And now that we've finally got to them . . .'

'Any clues? Can you tell what became of them?'

'I'll look.' Trent got heavily to his feet. 'If I find anything I'll report.'

'Good luck.' The faint voice faded off into static. 'We'll be waiting.'

Trent returned the transmitter to his belt. He peered up at the grey sky. Evening — almost night. The forest was bleak and ominous. A faint blanket of snow was falling silently over the brown growth, hiding it under a layer of grimy white. Snow mixed with particles. Lethal dust — still falling, after three hundred years.

He switched on his helmet-beam. The beam cut a pale swath ahead of him through the trees, among the ruined columns of concrete, the occasional heaps of rusted slag. He entered the ruins.

In their centre he found the towers and installations. Great pillars laced with mesh scaffolding — still bright. Open tunnels from underground lay like black pools. Silent deserted tunnels. He peered down one, flashing his helmet-beam into it. The tunnel went straight down, deep into the heart of the Earth. But it was empty.

Where had they gone? What had happened to them? Trent wandered around dully. Human beings had lived here, worked here, survived. They had come up to the surface. He could see the bore-nosed cars parked among the towers, now grey with the night snow. They had come up and then — gone.

Where?

He sat down in the shelter of a ruined column and flicked on his heater. His suit warmed up, a slow red glow that made him feel better. He examined his counter. The area was hot. If he intended to eat and drink he'd have to move on.

He was tired. Too damn tired to move on. He sat resting, hunched over in a heap, his helmet-beam lighting up a circle of grey snow ahead of him. Over him the snow fell silently. Presently he was covered, a grey lump sitting among the ruined concrete. As silent and unmoving as the towers and scaffolding around him.

He dozed. His heater hummed gently. Around him a wind came up, swirling the snow, blowing it up against him. He slid forward a little until his metal-and-plastic helmet came to rest against the concrete.

Towards midnight he woke up. He straightened, suddenly alert. Something – a noise. He listened.

Far off, a dull roaring.

Douglas in the car? No, not yet – not for another two days. He stood up, snow pouring off him. The roar was growing, getting louder. His heart began to hammer wildly. He peered around, his beam flashing through the night.

The ground shook, vibrating through him, rattling his almost empty oxygen tank. He gazed up at the sky – and gasped.

A glowing trail slashed across the sky, igniting the early morning darkness. A deep red, swelling each second. He watched it, open-mouthed.

Something was coming down – landing.

A rocket.

The long metal hull glittered in the morning sun. Men were working busily, loading supplies and equipment. Tunnel cars raced up and down, hauling material from the under-surface levels to the waiting ship. The men worked carefully and efficiently, each in his metal-and-plastic suit, in his carefully sealed lead-lined protection shield.

'How many back at your Mine?' Norris asked quietly.

'About thirty.' Trent's eyes were on the ship. 'Thirty-three, including all those out.'

'Out?'

'Looking. Like me. A couple are on their way here. They should arrive soon. Late today or tomorrow.'

Norris made some notes on his chart. 'We can handle about fifteen with this load. We'll catch the rest next time. They can hold out another week?'

'Yes.'

Norris eyed him curiously. 'How did you find us? This is a long way from Pennsylvania. We're making our last stop. If you had come a couple of days later . . .'

'Some runners sent me this way. They said you had gone they didn't know where.'

Norris laughed. 'We didn't know where either.'

'You must be taking all this stuff some place. This ship. It's old, isn't it? Fixed up.'

'Originally it was some kind of bomb. We located it and repaired it – worked on it from time to time. We weren't sure what we wanted to do. We're not sure yet. But we know we have to leave.'

'Leave? Leave Earth?'

'Of course.' Norris motioned him towards the ship. They made their way up the ramp to one of the hatches. Norris pointed back down. 'Look down there – at the men loading.'

The men were almost finished. The last cars were half empty, bringing up the final remains from underground. Books, records, pictures, artifacts – the remains of a culture. A multitude of representative objects, shot into the hold of the ship to be carried off, away from Earth.

'Where?' Trent asked.

'To Mars for the time being. But we're not staying there. We'll probably go on out, towards the moons of Jupiter and Saturn. Ganymede may turn out to be something. If not Ganymede, one of the others. If worst comes to worst we can stay on Mars. It's pretty dry and barren but it's not radio-active.'

'There's no chance here – no possibility of reclaiming the radio-active areas? If we could cool off Earth, neutralize the hot clouds and – '

'If we did that,' Norris said, 'they'd all die.'

'They?'

'Rollers, runners, worms, toads, bugs, all the rest. The endless varieties of life. Countless forms adapted to *this* Earth – this hot Earth. These plants and animals use the radio-active metals. Essentially the new basis of life here is an assimilation of hot metallic salts. Salts which are utterly lethal to us.'

'But even so – '

'Even so, it's not really our world.'

'We're the true humans,' Trent said.

'Not any more. Earth is alive, teeming with life. Growing wildly – in all directions. We're one form, an old form. To live here, we'd have to restore the old conditions, the old factors, the balance as it was three hundred and fifty years ago. A colossal job. And if we succeeded, if we managed to cool Earth, none of this would remain.'

Norris pointed at the great brown forest. And beyond it, towards the south, at the beginning of the steaming jungle that continued all the way to the Straits of Magellan.

'In a way it's what we deserve. *We* brought the War. *We* changed Earth. Not destroyed – *changed*. Made it so different we can't live here any longer.'

Norris indicated the lines of helmeted men. Men sheathed in lead, in heavy protection suits, covered with layers of metal and wiring, counters, oxygen tanks, shields, food pellets, filtered water. The men worked, sweating in their heavy suits. 'See them? What do they resemble?'

A worker came up, gasping and panting. For a brief second he lifted his viewplate and took a hasty breath of air. He slammed his plate and nervously locked it in place. 'Ready to go, sir. All loaded.'

'Change of plan,' Norris said. 'We're going to wait until this man's companions get here. Their camp is breaking up. Another day won't make any difference.'

'All right, sir.' The worker pushed off, climbing back down to the surface, a weird figure in his heavy lead-lined suit and bulging helmet and intricate gear.

'We're visitors,' Norris told him.

Trent flinched violently. '*What?*'

'Visitors on a strange planet. Look at us. Shielded suits and helmets, space suits – for exploring. We're a rocket-ship stopping at an alien world on which we can't survive. Stopping for a brief period to load up – and then take off again.'

'Closed helmets,' Trent said, in a strange voice.

'Closed helmets. Lead shields. Counters and special food and water. Look over there.'

A small group of runners were standing together, gazing up in awe at the great gleaming ship. Off to the right, visible among the trees, was a runner village. Chequer-board crops and animal pens and board houses.

'The natives,' Norris said. 'The inhabitants of the planet. They can breathe the air, drink the water, eat the plant-life. We can't. This is their planet – not ours. They can live here, build up a society.'

'I hope we can come back.'

'Back?'

'To visit – some time.'

Norris smiled ruefully. 'I hope so too. But we'll have to get permission from the inhabitants – permission to land.' His eyes were bright with amusement – and, abruptly, pain. A sudden agony that gleamed out over everything else. 'We'll have to ask them if it's all right. And they may say *no*. They may not want us.'

Prominent Author

'My husband,' said Mary Ellis, 'although he is a very prompt man, and hasn't been late to work in twenty-five years, is actually still some place around the house.' She sipped at her faintly scented hormone and carbohydrate drink. 'As a matter of fact, he won't be leaving for another ten minutes.'

'Incredible,' said Dorothy Lawrence, who had finished *her* drink, and now basked in the dermalmist spray that descended over her virtually unclad body from an automatic jet above the couch. 'What they won't think of next!'

Mrs Ellis beamed proudly, as if she personally were an employee of Terran Development. 'Yes, it is incredible. According to somebody down at the office, the whole history of civilization can be explained in terms of transportation techniques. Of course, I don't know anything about history. That's for Government research people. But from what this man told Henry – '

'Where's my brief-case?' came a fussy voice from the bedroom. 'Good Lord, Mary. I know I left it on the clothes-cleaner last night.'

'You left it upstairs,' Mary replied, raising her voice slightly. 'Look in the closet.'

'Why would it be in the closet?' Sounds of angry stirring arounds. 'You'd think a man's own brief-case would be safe.' Henry Ellis stuck his head into the living-room briefly. 'I found it. Hello, Mrs Lawrence.'

'Good morning,' Dorothy Lawrence replied. 'Mary was explaining that you're still here.'

'Yes, I'm still here.' Ellis straightened his tie, as the

mirror revolved slowly around him. 'Anything you want me to pick up downtown, honey?'

'No,' Mary replied. 'Nothing I can think of. I'll vid you at the office if I remember something.'

'Is it true,' Mrs Lawrence asked, 'that *as soon as you step into it* you're all the way downtown?'

'Well, almost all the way.'

'A hundred and sixty miles! It's beyond belief. Why, it takes my husband two and a half hours to get his monojet through the commercial lanes and down at the parking lot then walk all the way up to his office.'

'I know,' Ellis muttered, grabbing his hat and coat. 'Used to take me about that long. But no more.' He kissed his wife good-bye. 'So long. See you tonight. Nice to have seen you again, Mrs Lawrence.'

'Can I – watch?' Mrs Lawrence asked hopefully.

'Watch? Of course, of course.' Ellis hurried through the house, out the back door and down the steps into the yard. 'Come along!' he shouted impatiently. 'I don't want to be late. It's nine fifty-nine and I have to be at my desk by ten.'

Mrs Lawrence hurried eagerly after Ellis. In the back yard stood a big circular hoop that gleamed brightly in the mid-morning sun. Ellis turned some controls at the base. The hoop changed colour, from silver to a shimmering red.

'Here I go!' Ellis shouted. He stepped briskly into the hoop. The hoop fluttered about him. There was a faint *pop*. The glow died.

'Good heavens!' Mrs Lawrence gasped. 'He's gone!'

'He's in downtown N'York,' Mary Ellis corrected.

'I wish *my* husband had a Jiffi-scuttler. When they show up on the market commercially maybe I can afford to get him one.'

'Oh, they're very handy,' Mary Ellis agreed. 'He's probably saying hello to the boys right this minute.'

* * *

Henry Ellis was in a sort of tunnel. All around him a grey, formless tube stretched out in both directions, a sort of hazy sewer-pipe.

Framed in the opening behind him, he could see the faint outline of his own house. His back porch and yard, Mary standing on the steps in her red bra and slacks. Mrs Lawrence beside her in green-chequered shorts. The cedar tree and rows of petunias. A hill. The neat little houses of Cedar Groves, Pennsylvania. And in front of him –

New York City. A wavering glimpse of the busy street corner in front of his office. The great building itself, a section of concrete and glass and steel. People moving. Skyscrapers. Monojets landing in swarms. Aerial signs. Endless white-collar workers hurrying everywhere, rushing to their offices.

Ellis moved leisurely towards the New York end. He had taken the Jiffi-scuttler often enough to know just exactly how many steps it was. Five steps. Five steps along the wavery grey tunnel and he had gone a hundred and sixty miles. He halted, glancing back. So far he had gone three steps. Ninety-six miles. More than half-way.

The fourth dimension was a wonderful thing.

Ellis lit his pipe, leaning his brief-case against his trouser-leg and groping in his coat pocket for his tobacco. He still had thirty seconds to get to work. Plenty of time. The pipe-lighter flared and he sucked in expertly. He snapped the lighter shut and restored it to his pocket.

A wonderful thing, all right. The Jiffi-scuttler had already revolutionized society. It was now possible to go anywhere in the world *instantly*, with no time lapse. And without wading through endless lanes of other monojets, also going places. The transportation problem had been a major headache since the middle of the twentieth century. Every year more families moved from the cities out into the country, adding numbers to the already swollen swarms that choked the roads and jetlanes.

But it was all solved now. An *infinite* number of Jiffi-scuttlers could be set up; there was no interference between them. The Jiffi-scuttler bridged distances non-spacially, through another dimension of some kind (they hadn't explained that part too clearly to him). For a flat thousand credits any Terran family could have Jiffi-scuttler hoops set up, one in the back yard — the other in Berlin, or Bermuda, or San Francisco, or Port Said. Anywhere in the world. Of course, there was one drawback. The hoop had to be anchored in one specific spot. You picked your destination and that was that.

But for an office worker, it was perfect. Step in one end, step out the other. Five steps — a hundred and sixty miles. A hundred and sixty miles that had been a two-hour nightmare of grinding gears and sudden jolts, monojets cutting in and out, speeders, reckless flyers, alert cops waiting to pounce, ulcers and bad tempers. It was all over now. All over for him, at least, as an employee of Terran Development, the manufacturer of the Jiffi-scuttler. And soon for everybody, when they were commercially on the market.

Ellis sighed. Time for work. He could see Ed Hall racing up the steps of the TD building two at a time. Tony Franklin hurrying after him. Time to get moving. He bent down and reached for his brief-case —

It was then he saw them.

The wavery grey haze was thin there. A sort of thin spot where the shimmer wasn't so strong. Just a bit beyond his foot and past the corner of his brief-case.

Beyond the thin spot were three tiny figures. Just beyond the grey waver. Incredibly small men, no larger than insects. Watching him with incredulous astonishment.

Ellis gazed down intently, his brief-case forgotten. The

three tiny men were equally dumbfounded. None of them
stirred, the three tiny figures, rigid with awe, Henry Ellis
bent over, his mouth open, eyes wide.

A fourth little figure joined the others. They all stood
rooted to the spot, eyes bulging. They had on some kind
of robes. Brown robes and sandals. Strange, unTerran
costumes. Everything about them was unTerran. Their
size, their oddly coloured dark faces, their clothing – and
their voices.

Suddenly the tiny figures were shouting shrilly at each
other, squeaking a strange gibberish. They had broken out
of their freeze and now ran about in queer, frantic circles.
They raced with incredible speed, scampering like ants on
a hot griddle. They raced jerkily, their arms and legs
pumping wildly. And all the time they squeaked in their
shrill high-pitched voices.

Ellis found his brief-case. He picked it up slowly. The
figures watched in mixed wonder and terror as the huge
bag rose, only a short distance from them. An idea drifted
through Ellis' brain. Good Lord – could they come into
the Jiffi-scuttler, through the grey haze?

But he had no time to find out. He was already late as it
was. He pulled away and hurried towards the New York
end of the tunnel. A second later he stepped out in the
blinding sunlight, abruptly finding himself on the busy
street corner in front of his office.

'Hey, there, Hank!' Donald Potter shouted, as he raced
through the doors into the TD building. 'Get with it!'

'Sure, sure.' Ellis followed after him automatically.
Behind, the entrance to the Jiffi-scuttler was a vague circle
above the pavement, like the ghost of a soap-bubble.

He hurried up the steps and inside the offices of Terran
Development, his mind already on the hard day ahead.

As they were locking up the office and getting ready to
go home, Ellis stopped Co-ordinator Patrick Miller in his

office. 'Say, Mr Miller. You're also in charge of the research end, aren't you?'

'Yeah. So?'

'Let me ask you something. Just where does the Jiffi-scuttler go? It must go somewhere.'

'It goes out of this continuum completely.' Miller was impatient to get home. 'Into another dimension.'

'I know that. But – *where*?'

Miller unfolded his breast-pocket handkerchief rapidly and spread it out on his desk. 'Maybe I can explain it to you this way. Suppose you're a two-dimensional creature and this handkerchief represents your – '

'I've seen that a million times,' Ellis said, disappointed. 'That's merely an analogy, and I'm not interested in an analogy. I want a factual answer. Where does my Jiffi-scuttler go, between here and Cedar Groves?'

Miller laughed. 'What the hell do you care?'

Ellis became abruptly guarded. He shrugged indifferently. 'Just curious. It certainly must go *some place*.'

Miller put his hand on Ellis' shoulder in a friendly big-brother fashion. 'Henry, old man, you just leave that up to us. Okay? We're the designers, you're the consumer. Your job is to use the 'scuttler, try it out for us, report any defects or failure so when we put it on the market next year we'll be sure there's nothing wrong with it.'

'As a matter of fact – ' Ellis began.

'What is it?'

Ellis clamped his sentence off. 'Nothing.' He picked up his brief-case. 'Nothing at all. I'll see you tomorrow. Thanks, Mr Miller. Goodnight.'

He hurried downstairs and out of the TD building. The faint outline of his Jiffi-scuttler was visible in the fading late-afternoon sunlight. The sky was already full of mono-jets taking off. Weary workers beginning their long trip back to their homes in the country. The endless commute.

Ellis made his way to the hoop and stepped into it. Abruptly the bright sunlight dimmed and faded.

Again he was in the wavery grey tunnel. At the far end flashed a circle of green and white. Rolling green hills and his own house. His back yard. The cedar tree and flower beds. The town of Cedar Groves.

Two steps down the tunnel. Ellis halted, bending over. He studied the floor of the tunnel intently. He studied the misty grey wall, where it rose and flickered – and the thin place. The place he had noticed.

They were still there. *Still?* It was a different bunch. This time ten or eleven of them. Men and women and children. Standing together, gazing up at him with awe and wonder. No more than a half-inch high, each. Tiny distorted figures, shifting and changing shape oddly. Altering colours and hues.

Ellis hurried on. The tiny figures watched him go. A brief glimpse of their microscopic astonishment – and then he was stepping out into his back yard.

He clicked off the Jiffi-scuttler and mounted the back steps. He entered his house, deep in thought.

'Hi,' Mary cried, from the kitchen. She rustled towards him in her hip-length mesh shirt, her arms out. 'How was work today?'

'Fine.'

'Is anything wrong? You look – strange.'

'No. No, nothing's wrong.' Ellis kissed his wife absently on the forehead. 'What's for dinner?'

'Something choice. Siriusian mole steak. One of your favourites. Is that all right?'

'Sure.' Ellis tossed his hat and coat down on the chair. The chair folded them up and put them away. His thoughtful, preoccupied look still remained. 'Fine, honey.'

'Are you *sure* there's nothing wrong? You didn't get into another argument with Pete Taylor, did you?'

'No. Of course not.' Ellis shook his head in annoyance. 'Everything's all right, honey. Stop needling me.'

'Well, I *hope* so,' Mary said, with a sigh.

The next morning they were waiting for him.

He saw them the first step into the Jiffi-scuttler. A small group waiting within the wavering grey, like bugs caught in a block of jello. They moved jerkily, rapidly, arms and legs pumping in a blur of motion. Trying to attract his attention. Piping wildly in their pathetically faint voices.

Ellis stopped and squatted down. They were putting something through the wall of the tunnel, through the thin place in the grey. It was small, so incredibly small he could scarcely see it. A square of white at the end of a microscopic pole. They were watching him eagerly, faces alive with fear and hope. Desperate, pleading hope.

Ellis took the tiny square. It came loose like some fragile rose petal from its stalk. Clumsily, he let it drop and had to hunt all around for it. The little figures watched in an agony of dismay as his huge hands moved blindly around the floor of the tunnel. At last he found it and gingerly lifted it up.

It was too small to make out. *Writing?* Some tiny lines – but he couldn't read them. Much too small to read. He got out his wallet and carefully placed the square between two cards. He restored his wallet to his pocket.

'I'll look at it later,' he said.

His voice boomed and echoed up and down the tunnel. At the sound the tiny creatures scattered. They all fled, shrieking in their shrill, piping voices, away from the grey shimmer, into the dimness beyond. In a flash they were gone. Like startled mice. He was alone.

Ellis knelt down and put his eye against the grey shimmer, where it was thin. Where they had stood waiting. He could see something dim and distorted, lost in a vague haze. A landscape of some sort. Indistinct. Hard to make out.

Hills. Trees and crops. But so tiny. And dim . . .

He glanced at his watch. God, it was ten! Hastily he scrambled to his feet and hurried out of the tunnel, on to the blazing New York pavement.

Late. He raced up the stairs of the Terran Development building and down the long corridor to his office.

At lunchtime he stopped in at the Research Labs. 'Hey,' he called, as Jim Andrews brushed past, loaded down with reports and equipment. 'Got a second?'

'What do you want, Henry?'

'I'd like to borrow something. A magnifying glass.' He considered. 'Maybe a small photon-microscope would be better. One or two hundred power.'

'Kids' stuff.' Jim found him a small microscope. 'Slides?'

'Yeah, a couple of blank slides.'

He carried the microscope back to his office. He set it up on his desk, clearing away his papers. As a precaution he sent Miss Nelson, his secretary, out of the room and off to lunch. Then carefully, cautiously, he got the tiny wisp from his wallet and slipped it between two slides.

It was writing, all right. But nothing he could read. Utterly unfamiliar. Complex, interlaced little characters.

For a time he sat thinking. Then he dialled his interdepartment vidphone. 'Give me the Linguistics Department.'

After a moment Earl Peterson's good-natured face appeared. 'Hi, there, Ellis. What can I do for you?'

Ellis hesitated. He had to do this right. 'Say, Earl, old man. Got a little favour to ask you.'

'Like what? Anything to oblige an old pal.'

'You, uh – you have that Machine down there, don't you? That translating business you use for working over documents from non-Terran cultures?'

'Sure. So?'

'Think I could use it?' He talked fast. 'It's a screwy sort of a deal, Earl. I got this pal living on – uh – Centaurus VI, and he writes me in – uh – you know, the Centauran native semantic system, and I – '

'You want the Machine to translate a letter? Sure, I think we could manage it. This once, at least. Bring it down.'

He brought it down. He got Earl to show him how the intake feed worked, and as soon as Earl had turned his back he fed in the tiny square of material. The Linguistics Machine clicked and whirred. Ellis prayed silently that the paper wasn't too small. Wouldn't fall out between the relay-probes of the Machine.

But sure enough, after a couple of seconds, a tape unreeled from the output slot. The tape cut itself off and dropped into a basket. The Linguistics Machine turned promptly to other stuff, more vital material from TD's various export branches.

With trembling fingers Ellis spread out the tape. The words danced before his eyes.

Questions. They were asking him questions. God, it was getting complicated. He read the questions intently, his lips moving. What was he getting himself into? They were expecting answers. He had taken their paper, gone off with it. Probably they would be waiting for him, on his way home.

He returned to his office and dialled his vidphone. 'Give me outside,' he ordered.

The regular vid monitor appeared. 'Yes, sir?'

'I want the Federal Library of Information,' Ellis said. 'Cultural Research Division.'

That night they were waiting, all right. But not the same ones. It was odd – each time a different group. Their clothing was slightly different, too. A new hue. And in the background the landscape had also altered slightly. The trees he had seen were gone. The hills were still there, but a different shade. A hazy grey-white. Snow?

He squatted down. He had worked it out with care. The answers from the Federal Library of Information had gone back to the Linguistics Machine for re-translation. The answers were now in the original tongue of the questions – but on a trifle larger piece of paper.

Ellis made like a marble game and flicked the wad of paper through the grey shimmer. It bowled over six or seven of the watching figures and rolled down the side of the hill on which they were standing. After a moment of terrified immobility the figures scampered frantically after it. They disappeared into the vague and invisible depths of their world and Ellis got stiffly to his feet again.

'Well,' he muttered to himself, 'that's that.'

But it wasn't. The next morning there was a new group – and a new list of questions. The tiny figures pushed their microscopic square of paper through the thin spot in the wall of the tunnel and stood waiting and trembling as Ellis bent over and felt around for it.

He found it – finally. He put it in his wallet and continued on his way, stepping out at New York, frowning. This was getting serious. Was this going to be a full-time job?

But then he grinned. It was the damn oddest thing he had ever heard of. The little rascals were cute, in their own way. Tiny intent faces, screwed up with serious concern. And terror. They were scared of him, really scared. And why not? Compared to them he was a giant.

He conjectured about their world. What kind of a planet was theirs? Odd to be so small. But size was a relative matter. Small, though, compared to him. Small and reverent. He could read fear and a yearning, gnawing hope, as they pushed up their papers. They were depending on him. Praying he'd give them answers.

Ellis grinned. 'Damn unusual job,' he said to himself.

'What's this?' Peterson said, when he showed up in the Linguistics Lab at noontime.

'Well, you see, I got another letter from my friend on Centaurus VI.'

'Yeah?' A certain suspicion flickered across Peterson's face. 'You're not ribbing me, are you, Henry? The Machine has a lot to do, you know. Stuff's coming in all the time. We can't afford to waste any time with – '

'This is really serious stuff, Earl.' Ellis patted his wallet. 'Very important business. Not just gossip.'

'Okay. If you say so.' Peterson gave the nod to the team operating the Machine. 'Let this guy use the Translator, Tommie.'

'Thanks,' Ellis murmured.

He went through the routine, getting a translation and then carrying the questions up to his vidphone and passing them over to the Library research staff. By nightfall the answers were back in the original tongue and with them carefully in his wallet, Ellis headed out of the Terran Development building and into his Jiffi-scuttler.

As usual, a new group was waiting.

'Here you are, boys,' Ellis boomed, flicking the wad through the thin place in the shimmer. The wad rolled down the microscopic countryside, bouncing from hill to hill, the little people tumbling jerkily after it in their funny stiff-legged fashion. Ellis watched them go, grinning with interest – and pride.

They really hurried; no doubt about that. He could make them out only vaguely, now. They had raced wildly off away from the shimmer. Only a small portion of their world was tangent to the Jiffi-scuttler, apparently. Only the one spot, where the shimmer was thin. He peered intently through.

They were getting the wad open, now. Three or four of them, unprying the paper and examining the answers.

Ellis swelled with pride as he continued along the tunnel and out into his own back yard. He couldn't read their questions – and when translated, he couldn't answer them. The Linguistics Department did the first part, the Library research staff the rest. Nevertheless, Ellis felt pride. A deep, glowing spot of warmth far down inside him. The expression on their faces. The look they gave him when they saw the answer-wad in his hand. When they realized he was going to answer their questions. And the way they scampered after it. It was sort of – satisfying. It made him feel damn good.

'Not bad,' he murmured, opening the back door and entering his house. 'Not bad at all.'

'What's not bad, dear?' Mary asked, looking quickly up from the table. She laid down her magazine and got to her feet. 'Why, you look so *happy*! What is it?'

'Nothing. Nothing at all!' He kissed her warmly on the mouth. 'You're looking pretty good tonight yourself, kid.'

'Oh, Henry!' Much of Mary blushed prettily. 'How sweet.'

He surveyed his wife in her two-piece wraparound of clear plastic with appreciation. 'Nice-looking fragments you have on.'

'Why, Henry! What's come over you? You seem so – so *spirited*!'

Ellis grinned. 'Oh, I guess I enjoy my job. You know, there's nothing like taking pride in your work. A job well done, as they say. Work you can be proud of.'

'I thought you always said you were nothing but a cog in a great impersonal machine. Just a sort of cypher.'

'Things are different,' Ellis said firmly. 'I'm doing a – uh – a new project. A new assignment.'

'A new assignment?'

'Gathering information. A sort of – creative business. So to speak.'

By the end of the week he had turned over quite a body of information to them.

He began starting for work about nine-thirty. That gave him a whole thirty minutes to spend squatting down on his hands and knees, peering through the thin place in the shimmer. He got so he was pretty good at seeing them and what they were doing in their microscopic world.

Their civilization was somewhat primitive. No doubt of that. By Terran standards it was scarcely a civilization at all. As near as he could tell, they were virtually without scientific techniques; a kind of agrarian culture, rural communism, a monolithic tribal-based organization apparently without too many members.

At least, not at one time. That was the part he didn't understand. Every time he came past there was a different group of them. No familiar faces. And their world changed, too. The trees, the crops, fauna. The weather, apparently.

Was their time rate different? They moved rapidly, jerkily. Like a vidtape speeded up. And their shrill voices. Maybe that was it. A totally different universe in which the whole time structure was radically different.

As to their attitude towards him, there was no mistaking it. After the first couple of times they began assembling offerings, unbelievably small bits of smoking food, prepared in ovens and on open brick hearths. If he got down with his nose against the grey shimmer he could get a faint whiff of the food. It smelled good. Strong and pungent. Highly spiced. Meat, probably.

On Friday he brought a magnifying glass along and

watched them through it. It was meat, all right. They were bringing ant-sized animals to be killed and cooked, leading them up to the ovens. With the magnifying glass he could see more of their faces. They had strange faces. Strong and dark, with a peculiar firm look.

Of course, there was only one look *he* got from them. A combination of fear, reverence, and hope. The look made him feel good. It was a look for him, only. Between themselves they shouted and argued – and sometimes stabbed and fought each other furiously, rolling in their brown robes in a wild tangle. They were a passionate and strong species. He got so he admired them.

Which was good – because it made him feel better. To have the reverent awe of such a proud, sturdy race was really something. There was nothing craven about them.

About the fifth time he came there was a rather attractive structure built. Some kind of temple. A place of religious worship.

To him! They were developing a real religion about him. No doubt of it. He began going to work at nine o'clock, to give himself a full hour with them. They had, by the middle of the second week, a full-sized ritual evolved. Processions, lighted tapers, what seemed to be songs or chants. Priests in long robes. And the spiced offerings.

No idols, though. Apparently he was so big they couldn't make out his appearance. He tried to imagine what it looked like to be on their side of the shimmer. An immense shape looming up above them, beyond a wall of grey haze. An indistinct being, something like themselves, yet not like them at all. A different kind of being, obviously. Larger – but different in other ways. And when he spoke – booming echoes up and down the Jiffi-scuttler. Which still sent them fleeing in panic.

An evolving religion. He was changing them. Through his actual presence and through his answers, the precise, correct responses he obtained from the Federal Library of Information and had the Linguistics Machine translate into their language. Of course, by *their* time rate they had to wait generations for the answers. But they had become accustomed to it, by now. They waited. They expected. They passed up questions and after a couple of centuries he passed down answers, answers which they no doubt put to good use.

'What in the world?' Mary demanded, as he got home from work an hour late one night. 'Where have you been?'

'Working,' Ellis said carelessly, removing his hat and coat. He threw himself down on the couch. 'I'm tired. Really tired.' He sighed with relief and motioned for the couch-arm to bring him a whisky sour.

Mary came over by the couch. 'Henry, I'm a little worried.'

'Worried?'

'You shouldn't work so hard. You ought to take it easy, more. How long since you've had a real vacation? A trip off Terra. Out of the System. You know, I'd just like to call that fellow Miller and ask him why it's necessary a man your age put in so much – '

'A man my age!' Ellis bristled indignantly. 'I'm not so old.'

'Of course not.' Mary sat down beside him and put her arms around him affectionately. 'But you shouldn't have to do so much. You deserve a rest. Don't you think?'

'This is different. You don't understand. This isn't the same old stuff. Reports and statistics and the damn filing. This is – '

'What is it?'

'This is *different*. I'm not a cog. This gives me something. I can't explain it to you, I guess. But it's something I have to do.'

'If you could tell me more about it – '

'I can't tell you any more about it,' Ellis said. 'But there's nothing in the world like it. I've worked twenty-five years for Terran Development. Twenty-five years at the same reports, again and again. Twenty-five years – and I never felt this way.'

'Oh, yeah?' Miller roared. 'Don't give me that! Come clean, Ellis!'

Ellis opened and closed his mouth. 'What are you talking about?' Horror rolled through him. 'What's happened?'

'Don't try to give *me* the runaround.' On the vidscreen Miller's face was purple. 'Come into my office.'

The screen went dead.

Ellis sat stunned at his desk. Gradually, he collected himself and got shakily to his feet. 'Good Lord.' Weakly, he wiped cold sweat from his forehead. All at once. Everything in ruins. He was dazed with the shock.

'Anything wrong?' Miss Nelson asked sympathetically.

'No.' Ellis moved numbly towards the door. He was shattered. What had Miller found out? Good God! Was it possible he had –

'Mr Miller looked angry.'

'Yeah.' Ellis moved blindly down the hall, his mind reeling. Miller looked angry all right. Somehow he had found out. But why was he mad? Why did he care? A cold chill settled over Ellis. It looked bad. Miller was his superior – with hiring and firing powers. Maybe he'd done something wrong. Maybe he had somehow broken a law. Committed a crime. But what?

What did Miller care about *them*? What concern was it of Terran Development?

He opened the door to Miller's office. 'Here I am, Mr Miller,' he muttered. 'What's the trouble?'

Miller glowered at him in rage. 'All this goofy stuff about your cousin on Proxima.'

'It's – uh – you mean a business friend on Centaurus VI.'

'You – you swindler!' Miller leaped up. 'And after all the Company's done for you.'

'I don't understand,' Ellis muttered. 'What have –'

'Why do you think we gave you the Jiffi-scuttler in the first place?'

'Why?'

'To *test*! To try out, you wall-eyed Venusian stink-cricket! The Company magnanimously consented to allow you to operate a Jiffi-scuttler in advance of market presentation, and what do you do? Why, you –'

Ellis started to get indignant. After all, he had been with TD twenty-five years. 'You don't have to be so offensive. I plunked down my thousand gold credits for it.'

'Well, you can just mosey down to the accountant's office and get your money back. I've already sent out a directive for a construction team to crate up your Jiffi-scuttler and bring it back to receiving.'

Ellis was dumbfounded. 'But *why*?'

'Why indeed! Because it's defective. Because it doesn't work. That's why.' Miller's eyes blazed with technological outrage. 'The inspection crew found a leak a mile wide in it.' His lip curled. 'As if you didn't know.'

Ellis' heart sank. 'Leak?' he croaked apprehensively.

'Leak. It's a damn good thing I authorized a periodic inspection. If we depended on people like you to –'

'Are you *sure*? It seemed all right to me. That is, it got me here without any trouble.' Ellis floundered. 'Certainly no complaints from my end.'

'No. No complaints from your end. That's exactly why you're not getting another one. That's why you're taking the monojet transport back home tonight. Because you didn't report the leak! And if you ever try to put something over on this office again –'

'How do you know I was aware of the – defect?'

Miller sank down in his chair, overcome with fury. 'Because,' he said carefully, 'of your daily pilgrimage to the Linguistics Machine. With your alleged letter from your grandmother on Betelgeuse II. Which wasn't any such thing. Which was an utter fraud. Which you got through the leak in the Jiffi-scuttler!'

'How do you know?' Ellis squeaked boldly, driven to the wall. 'So maybe there was a defect. But you can't prove there's any connection between your badly constructed Jiffi-scuttler and my – '

'Your missive,' Miller stated, 'which you foisted on our Linguistics Machine, was not a non-Terran script. It was not from Centaurus VI. It was not from any non-Terran system. It was ancient Hebrew. And there's only one place you could have got it, Ellis. So don't try to kid me.'

'Hebrew!' Ellis exclaimed, startled. He turned white as a sheet. 'Good Lord. The other continuum – the fourth dimension. Time, of course.' He trembled. 'And the expanding universe. That would explain their size. And it explains why a new group, a new generation – '

'We're taking enough of a chance as it is, with these Jiffi-scuttlers. Warping a tunnel through other space-time continua.' Miller shook his head wearily. 'You meddler. You *knew* you were supposed to report any defect.'

'I don't think I did any harm, did I?' Ellis was suddenly terribly nervous. 'They seemed pleased, even grateful. Gosh, I'm sure I didn't cause any trouble.'

Miller shrieked in insane rage. For a time he danced around the room. Finally he threw something down on his desk, directly in front of Ellis. 'No trouble. No, none. Look at this. I got this from the Ancient Artifacts Archives.'

'What is it?'

'Look at it! I compared one of your question sheets to

this. The same. *Exactly* the same. All your sheets, questions and answers, every one of them's in here. You multi-legged Ganymedian mange beetle!'

Ellis picked up the book and opened it. As he read the pages a strange look came slowly over his face. 'Good heavens. So they kept a record of what I gave them. They put it all together in a book. Every word of it. And some commentaries, too. It's all here — Every single word. It *did* have an effect, then. They passed it on. Wrote all of it down.'

'Go back to your office. I'm through looking at you for today. I'm through looking at you for ever. Your severance cheque will come through regular channels.'

In a trance, his face flushed with a strange excitement, Ellis gripped the book and moved dazedly towards the door. 'Say, Mr Miller. Can I have this? Can I take it along?'

'Sure,' Miller said wearily. 'Sure, you can take it. You can read it on your way home tonight. On the public monojet transport.'

'Henry has something to show you,' Mary Ellis whispered excitedly, gripping Mrs Lawrence's arm. 'Make sure you say the right thing.'

'The right thing?' Mrs Lawrence faltered nervously, a trifle uneasy. 'What is it? Nothing alive, I hope.'

'No, no.' Mary pushed her towards the study door. 'Just smile.' She raised her voice. 'Henry, Dorothy Lawrence is here.'

Henry Ellis appeared at the door of his study. He bowed slightly, a dignified figure in silk dressing gown, pipe in his mouth, fountain pen in one hand. 'Good evening, Dorothy,' he said in a low, well-modulated voice. 'Care to step into my study a moment?'

'Study?' Mrs Lawrence came hesitantly in. 'What do

you study? I mean, Mary says you've been doing something very interesting recently, now that you're not with –
I mean, now that you're home more. She didn't give me
any idea what it was, though.'

Mrs Lawrence's eyes roved curiously around the study.
The study was full of reference volumes, charts, a huge
mahogany desk, an atlas, globe, leather chairs, an unbelievably ancient electric typewriter.

'Good heavens!' she exclaimed. 'How odd. All these old
things.'

Ellis lifted something carefully from the bookcase and
held it out to her casually. 'By the way – you might glance
at this.'

'What is it? A book?' Mrs Lawrence took the book and
examined it eagerly. 'My goodness. Heavy, isn't it?' She
read the back, her lips moving. 'What does it mean? It
looks old. What strange letters! I've never seen anything
like it. *Holy Bible*.' She glanced up brightly. 'What is this?'

Ellis smiled faintly. 'Well – '

A light dawned. Mrs Lawrence gasped in revelation.
'Good heavens! You didn't *write* this, did you?'

Ellis' smile broadened into a depreciating blush. A
dignified hue of modesty. 'Just a little thing I threw
together,' he murmured indifferently. 'My first, as a matter
of fact.' Thoughtfully, he fingered his fountain pen. 'And
now, if you'll excuse me, I really should be getting back to
my work . . .'

The Builder

'E. J. Elwood!' Liz said anxiously. 'You aren't listening to anything we're saying. And you're not eating a bit. What in the world is the matter with you? Sometimes I just can't understand you.'

For a long time there was no response. Ernest Elwood continued to stare past them, staring out the window at the semi-darkness beyond, as if hearing something they did not hear. At last he sighed, drawing himself up in his chair, almost as if he were going to say something. But then his elbow knocked against his coffee cup and he turned instead to steady the cup, wiping spilled brown coffee from its side.

'Sorry,' he murmured. 'What were you saying?'

'Eat, dear,' his wife said. She glanced at the two boys as she spoke to see if they had stopped eating also. 'You know, I go to a great deal of trouble to fix your food.' Bob, the older boy, was going right ahead, cutting his liver and bacon carefully into bits. But sure enough, little Toddy had put down his knife and fork as soon as E.J. had, and now he, too, was sitting silently, staring down at his plate.

'See?' Liz said. 'You're not setting a very good example for the boys. Eat up your food. It's getting cold. You don't want to eat cold liver, do you? There's nothing worse than liver when it gets cold and the fat all over the bacon hardens. It's harder to digest cold fat than anything else in the world. Especially lamb fat. They say a lot of people can't eat lamb fat at all. Dear, please eat.'

Elwood nodded. He lifted his fork and spooned up some

peas and potatoes, carrying them to his mouth. Little Toddy did the same, gravely and seriously, a small edition of his father.

'Say,' Bob said. 'We had an atomic bomb drill at school today. We lay under the desks.'

'Is that right?' Liz said.

'But Mr Pearson our science teacher says that if they drop a bomb on us the whole town'll be demolished, so I can't see what good getting under the desk will do. I think they ought to realize what advances science has made. There are bombs now that'll destroy miles, leaving nothing standing.'

'You sure know a lot,' Toddy muttered.

'Oh, shut up.'

'Boys,' Liz said.

'It's true,' Bob said earnestly. 'A fellow I know is in the Marine Corp Reserve and he says they have new weapons that will destroy wheat crops and poison water supplies. It's some kind of crystals.'

'Heavens,' Liz said.

'They didn't have things like that in the last war. Atomic development came almost at the end without there really being an opportunity to make use of it on a full scale.' Bob turned to his father. 'Dad, isn't that true? I'll bet when you were in the Army you didn't have any of the fully atomic – '

Elwood threw down his fork. He pushed his chair back and stood up. Liz stared up in astonishment at him, her cup half raised. Bob's mouth hung open, his sentence unfinished. Little Toddy said nothing.

'Dear, what's the matter?' Liz said.

'I'll see you later.'

They gazed after him in amazement as he walked away from the table, out of the dining-room. They heard him go into the kitchen and pull open the back door. A moment later the back door slammed behind him.

'He went out in the back yard,' Bob said. 'Mom, was he always like this? Why does he act so funny? It isn't some kind of war psychosis he got in the Philippines, is it? In the First World War they called it shell shock, but now they know it's a form of war psychosis. Is it something like that?'

'Eat your food,' Liz said, red spots of anger burning in her cheeks. She shook her head. 'Darn that man. I just can't imagine – '

The boys ate their food.

It was dark out in the back yard. The sun had set and the air was cool and thin, filled with dancing specks of night insects. In the next yard Joe Hunt was working, raking leaves from under his cherry tree. He nodded to Elwood.

Elwood walked slowly down the path, across the yard towards the garage. He stopped, his hands in his pockets. By the garage something immense and white loomed up, a vast pale shape in the evening gloom. As he stood gazing at it a kind of warmth began to glow inside him. It was a strange warmth, something like pride, a little pleasure mixed in, and – and excitement. Looking at the boat always made him excited. Even when he was first starting on it he had felt the sudden race of his heart, the shaking of his hands, sweat on his face.

His boat. He grinned, walking closer. He reached up and thumped the solid side. What a fine boat it was, and coming along damn well. Almost done. A lot of work had gone into that, a lot of work and time. Afternoons off from work, Sundays, and even sometimes early in the morning before work.

That was best, early in the morning, with the bright sun shining down and the air good-smelling and fresh, and everything wet and sparkling. He liked that time best of all, and there was no one else up to bother him and ask him questions. He thumped the solid side again. A lot of work and material, all right. Lumber and nails, sawing and hammering and bending. Of course, Toddy had helped him. He certainly couldn't have done it alone; no doubt of that. If Toddy hadn't drawn the lines on the board and –

'Hey,' Joe Hunt said.

Elwood started, turning. Joe was leaning on the fence, looking at him. 'Sorry,' Elwood said. 'What did you say?'

'Your mind was a million miles away,' Hunt said. He took a puff on his cigar. 'Nice night.'

'Yes.'

'That's some boat you got there, Elwood.'

'Thanks,' Elwood murmured. He walked away from it, back towards the house. 'Goodnight, Joe.'

'How long is it you've been working on that boat?' Hunt reflected. 'Seems like about a year in all, doesn't it? Above twelve months. You sure put a lot of time and effort into it. Seems like every time I see you you're carting lumber back here and sawing and hammering away.'

Elwood nodded, moving towards the back door.

'You even got your kids working. At least, the little tyke. Yes, it's quite a boat.' Hunt paused. 'You sure must be going to go quite a way with it, by the size of it. Now just exactly where was it you told me you're going? I forget.'

There was silence.

'I can't hear you, Elwood,' Hunt said. 'Speak up. A boat that big, you must be – '

'Lay off.'

Hunt laughed easily. 'What's the matter, Elwood? I'm just having a little harmless fun, pulling your leg. But seriously, where are you going with that? You going to drag it down to the beach and float it? I know a guy has a little sail-boat he fits on to a trailer cart, hooks it up to his car. He drives down to the yacht harbour every week or so. But my God, you can't get that big thing on to a trailer. You know, I heard about a guy built a boat in his cellar. Well, he got done and you know what he discovered? He discovered that the boat was so big when he tried to get it out the door – '

Liz Elwood came to the back door, snapping on the kitchen light and pushing the door open. She stepped out on to the grass, her arms folded.

'Good evening, Mrs Elwood,' Hunt said, touching his hat. 'Sure a nice night.'

'Good evening.' Liz turned to E.J. 'For heaven's sake, are you going to come in?' Her voice was low and hard.

'Sure.' Elwood reached out listlessly for the door. 'I'm coming in. Goodnight, Joe.'

'Goodnight,' Hunt said. He watched the two of them go inside. The door closed, the light went off. Hunt shook his head. 'Funny guy,' he murmured. 'Getting funnier all the time. Like he's in a different world. Him and his boat!'

He went indoors.

'She was just eighteen,' Jack Fredericks said, 'but she sure knew what it was all about.'

'Those southern girls are that way,' Charlie said. 'It's like fruit, nice soft, ripe, slightly damp fruit.'

'There's a passage in Hemingway like that,' Ann Pike said. 'I can't remember what it's from. He compares a – '

'But the way they talk,' Charlie said. 'Who can stand the way those southern girls talk?'

'What's the matter with the way they talk?' Jack demanded. 'They talk different, but you get used to it.'

'Why can't they talk right?'

'What do you mean?'

'They talk like – coloured people.'

'It's because they all come from the same region,' Ann said.

'Are you saying this girl was coloured?' Jack said.

'No, of course not. Finish your pie.' Charlie looked at his wrist watch. 'Almost one. We have to be getting on back to the office.'

'I'm not finished eating,' Jack said. 'Hold on!'

'You know, there's a lot of coloured people moving into my area,' Ann said. 'There's a real estate sign up on a house about a block from me. "All races welcomed." I almost fell over dead when I saw it.'

'What did you do?'

'I didn't do anything. What can you do?'

'You know, if you work for the Government they can put a coloured man or a Chinese next to you,' Jack said, 'and you can't do anything about it.'

'Except quit.'

'It interferes with your right to work,' Charlie said. 'How can you work like that? Answer me.'

'There's too many pinks in the Government,' Jack said. 'That's how they got that, about hiring people for Government jobs without looking to see what race they belong to. During WPA days, when Harry Hopkins was in.'

'You know where Harry Hopkins was born?' Ann said. 'He was born in Russia.'

'That was Sidney Hillman,' Jack said.

'It's all the same,' Charlie said. 'They all ought to be sent back there.'

Ann looked curiously at Ernest Elwood. He was sitting quietly, reading his newspaper, not saying anything. The cafeteria was alive with movement and noise. Everyone was eating and talking, coming and going, back and forth.

'E.J., are you all right?' Ann said.

'Yes.'

'He's reading about the White Sox,' Charlie said. 'He

has that intent look. Say, you know, I took my kids to the game the other night, and – '

'Come on,' Jack said, standing up. 'We have to get back.'

They all rose. Elwood folded his newspaper up silently, putting it into his pocket.

'Say, you're not talking much,' Charlie said to him as they went up the aisle. Elwood glanced up.

'Sorry.'

'I've been meaning to ask you something. Do you want to come over Saturday night for a little game? You haven't played with us for a hell of a long time.'

'Don't ask him,' Jack said, paying for his meal at the cash register. 'He always wants to play queer games like deuces wild, baseball, spit in the ocean – '

'Straight poker for me,' Charlie said. 'Come on, Elwood. The more the better. Have a couple of beers, chew the fat, get away from the wife, eh?' He grinned.

'One of these days we're going to have a good old stag party,' Jack said, pocketing his change. He winked at Elwood. 'You know the kind I mean? We get some gals together, have a little show – ' He made a motion with his hand.

Elwood moved off. 'Maybe. I'll think it over.' He paid for his lunch. Then he went outside, out on to the bright pavement. The others were still inside, waiting for Ann. She had gone into the powder room.

Suddenly Elwood turned and walked hurriedly down the pavement, away from the cafeteria. He turned the corner quickly and found himself on Cedar Street, in front of a television store. Shoppers and clerks out on their lunch hour pushed and crowded past him, laughing and talking, bits of their conversations rising and falling around him like waves of the sea. He stepped into the doorway of the television shop and stood, his hands in his pockets, like a man hiding from the rain.

What was the matter with him? Maybe he should go see a doctor. The sounds, the people, everything bothered him. Noise and motion everywhere. He wasn't sleeping enough at night. Maybe it was something in his diet. And he was working so damn hard out in the yard. By the time he went to bed at night he was exhausted. Elwood rubbed his forehead. People and sounds, talking, streaming past him, endless shapes moving in the streets and stores.

In the window of the television shop a big television set blinked and winked a soundless programme, the images leaping merrily. Elwood watched passively. A woman in tights was doing acrobatics, first a series of splits, then cartwheels and spins. She walked on her hands for a moment, her legs waving above her, smiling at the audience. Then she disappeared and a brightly dressed man came on, leading a dog.

Elwood looked at his watch. Five minutes to one. He had five minutes to get back to the office. He went back on to the pavement and looked around the corner. Ann and Charlie and Jack were no place to be seen. They had gone on. Elwood walked slowly along, past the stores, his hands in his pockets. He stopped for a moment in front of the ten cent store, watching the milling women pushing and shoving around the imitation jewellery counters, touching things, picking them up, examining them. In the window of a drugstore he stared at an advertisement for athlete's foot, some kind of a powder, being sprinkled between two cracked and blistered toes. He crossed the street.

On the other side he paused to look at a display of women's clothing, skirts and blouses and wool sweaters. In a colour photograph a handsomely dressed girl was removing her blouse to show the world her elegant bra.

Elwood passed on. The next window was suitcases, luggage and trunks.

Luggage. He stopped, frowning. Something wandered through his mind, some loose vague thought, too nebulous to catch. He felt, suddenly, a deep inner urgency. He examined his watch. Ten past one. He was late. He hurried to the corner and stood waiting impatiently for the light to change. A handful of men and women pressed past him, moving out to the kerb to catch an oncoming bus. Elwood watched the bus. It halted, its doors opening. The people rushed on to it. Suddenly Elwood joined them, stepping up the steps of the bus. The doors closed behind him as he fished out change from his pocket.

A moment later he took his seat, next to an immense old woman with a child on her lap. Elwood sat quietly, his hands folded, staring ahead and waiting, as the bus moved off down the street, moving towards the residential district.

When he got home there was no one there. The house was dark and cool. He went to the bedroom and got his old clothes from the closet. He was just going out into the back yard when Liz appeared in the driveway, her arms loaded with groceries.

'E.J.!' she said. 'What's the matter? Why are you home?'

'I don't know. I took some leave. It's all right.'

Liz put her packages down on the fence. 'For heaven's sake,' she said irritably. 'You frightened me.' She stared at him intently. 'You took *leave*?'

'Yes.'

'How much does that make, this year? How much leave have you taken in all?'

'I don't know.'

'You don't know? Well, is there any left?'

'Left for what?'

Liz stared at him. Then she picked up her packages and went inside the house, the back door banging after her.

Elwood frowned. What was the matter? He went on into the garage and began to drag lumber and tools out on to the lawn, beside the boat.

He gazed up at it. It was square, big and square, like some enormous solid packing crate. Lord, but it was solid. He had put endless beams into it. There was a covered cabin with a big window, the roof tarred over. Quite a boat.

He began to work. Presently Liz came out of the house. She crossed the yard silently, so that he did not notice her until he came to get some large nails.

'Well?' Liz said.

Elwood stopped for a moment. 'What is it?'

Liz folded her arms.

Elwood became impatient. 'What is it? Why are you looking at me?'

'Did you really take more leave? I can't believe it. You really came home again to work on – on that.'

Elwood turned away.

'Wait.' She came up beside him. 'Don't walk off from me. Stand still.'

'Be quiet. Don't shout.'

'I'm not shouting. I want to talk to you. I want to ask you something. May I? May I ask you something? You don't mind talking to me?'

Elwood nodded.

'*Why?*' Liz said, her voice low and intense. 'Why? Will you tell me that? Why?'

'Why what?'

'That. That – that thing. What is it for? Why are you here in the yard in the middle of the day? For a whole year it's been like this. At the table last night, all of a sudden you got up and walked out. Why? What's it all for?'

'It's almost done,' Elwood murmured. 'A few more licks here and there and it'll be – '

'And then what?' Liz came around in front of him, standing in his path. 'And then what? What are you going to do with it? Sell it? Float it? All the neighbours are laughing at you. Everybody in the block knows – ' Her voice broke suddenly. ' – Knows about you, and this. The kids at school make fun of Bob and Toddy. They tell them their father is – That he's – '

'That he's crazy?'

'Please, E.J., tell me what it's for. Will you do that? Maybe I can understand. You never told me. Wouldn't it help? Can't you even do that?'

'I can't,' Elwood said.

'You can't! Why not?'

'Because I don't know,' Elwood said. 'I don't know what it's for. Maybe it isn't for anything.'

'But if it isn't for anything why do you work on it?'

'I don't know. I like to work on it. Maybe it's like whittling.' He waved his hand impatiently. 'I've always had a workshop of some kind. When I was a kid I used to build model aeroplanes. I have tools. I've always had tools.'

'But why do you come home in the middle of the day?'

'I get restless.'

'Why?'

'I – I hear people talking, and it makes me uneasy. I want to get away from them. There's something about it all, about them. Their ways. Maybe I have claustrophobia.'

'Shall I call Doctor Evans and make an appointment?'

'No. No, I'm all right. Please, Liz, get out of the way so I can work. I want to finish.'

'And you don't even know what it's for.' She shook her head. 'So all this time you've been working without knowing why. Like some animal that goes out at night and fights, like a cat on the back fence. You leave your work and us to – '

'Get out of the way.'

'Listen to me. You put down that hammer and come inside. You're putting your suit on and going right back to the office. Do you hear? If you don't I'm never going to let you inside the house again. You can break down the door if you want, with your hammer. But it'll be locked for you from now on, if you don't forget that boat and go back to work.'

There was silence.

'Get out of the way,' Elwood said. 'I have to finish.'

Liz stared at him. 'You're going on?' The man pushed past her. 'You're going to go ahead? There's something wrong with you. Something wrong with your mind. You're – '

'Stop,' Elwood said, looking past her. Liz turned.

Toddy was standing silently in the driveway, his lunch pail under his arm. His small face was grave and solemn. He did not say anything to them.

'Tod!' Liz said. 'Is it that late already?'

Toddy came across the grass to his father. 'Hello, boy,' Elwood said. 'How was school?'

'Fine.'

'I'm going in the house,' Liz said. 'I meant it, E.J. Remember that I meant it.'

She went up the walk. The back door slammed behind her.

Elwood sighed. He sat down on the ladder leading up the side of the boat and put his hammer down. He lit a cigarette and smoked silently. Toddy waited without speaking.

'Well, boy?' Elwood said at last. 'What do you say?'

'What do you want done, Dad?'

'Done?' Elwood smiled. 'Well, there's not too much left. A few things here and there. We'll be through, soon. You might look around for boards we didn't nail down on the deck.' He rubbed his jaw. 'Almost done. We've been working a long time. You could paint, if you want. I want to get the cabin painted. Red, I think. How would red be?'

'Green.'

'Green? All right. There's some green porch paint in the garage. Do you want to start stirring it up?'

'Sure,' Toddy said. He headed towards the garage.

Elwood watched him go. 'Toddy – '

The boy turned. 'Yes?'

'Toddy, wait.' Elwood went slowly towards him. 'I want to ask you something.'

'What is it, Dad?'

'You – you don't mind helping me, do you? You don't mind working on the boat?'

Toddy looked up gravely into his father's face. He said nothing. For a long time the two of them gazed at each other.

'Okay!' Elwood said suddenly. 'You run along and get the paint started.'

Bob came swinging along the driveway with two of the kids from the junior high school. 'Hi, Dad,' Bob called, grinning. 'Say, how's it coming?'

'Fine,' Elwood said.

'Look,' Bob said to his pals, pointing to the boat. 'You see that? You know what that is?'

'What is it?' one of them said.

Bob opened the kitchen door. 'That's an atomic powered sub.' He grinned, and the two boys grinned. 'It's full of Uranium 235. Dad's going all the way to Russia with it. When he gets through, there won't be a thing left of Moscow.'

The boys went inside, the door slamming behind them.

Elwood stood looking up at the boat. In the next yard Mrs Hunt stopped for a moment with taking down her washing, looking at him and the big square hull rising above him.

'Is it really atomic powered, Mr Elwood?' she said.

'No.'

'What makes it run, then? I don't see any sails. What kind of motor is in it? Steam?'

Elwood bit his lip. Strangely, he had never thought of that part. There was no motor in it, no motor at all. There were no sails, no boiler. He had put no engine into it, no turbines, no fuel. Nothing. It was a wood hull, an immense box, and that was all. He had never thought of what would make it go, never in all the time he and Toddy had worked on it.

Suddenly a torrent of despair descended over him. There was no engine, nothing. It was not a boat, it was only a great mass of wood and tar and nails. It would never go, never never leave the yard. Liz was right: he was like some animal going out into the yard at night, to fight and kill in the darkness, to struggle dimly, without sight or understanding, equally blind, equally pathetic.

What had he built it for? He did not know. Where was it going? He did not know that either. What would make it run? How would he get it out of the yard? What was it all for, to build without understanding, darkly, like a creature in the night?

Toddy had worked alongside him, the whole time. Why had *he* worked? Did he know? Did the boy know what the boat was for, why they were building? Toddy had never asked because he trusted his father to know.

But he did not know. He, the father, he did not know either, and soon it would be done, finished, ready. And then what? Soon Toddy would lay down his paint brush, cover the last can of paint, put away the nails, the scraps of wood, hang the saw and hammer up in the garage again. And *then* he would ask, ask the question he had never asked before but which must come finally.

And he could not answer him.

Elwood stood, staring up at it, the great hulk they had built, struggling to understand. Why had he worked? What was it all for? When would he know? Would he *ever* know? For an endless time he stood there, staring up.

It was not until the first great black drops of rain began to splash about him that he understood.

The Impossible Planet

'She just stands there,' Norton said nervously. 'Captain, you'll have to talk to her.'

'What does she want?'

'She wants a ticket. She's stone deaf. She just stands there staring and she won't go away. It gives me the creeps.'

Captain Andrews got slowly to his feet. 'Okay. I'll talk to her. Send her in.'

'Thanks.' To the corridor Norton said, 'The Captain will talk to you. Come ahead.'

There was motion outside the control room. A flash of metal. Captain Andrews pushed his desk scanner back and stood waiting.

'In here.' Norton backed into the control room. 'This way. Right in here.'

Behind Norton came a withered little old woman. Beside her moved a gleaming robant, a towering robot servant, supporting her with its arm. The robant and the tiny old woman entered the control room slowly.

'Here's her papers.' Norton slid a folio on to the chart desk, his voice awed. 'She's three hundred and fifty years old. One of the oldest sustained. From Riga II.'

Andrews leafed slowly through the folio. In front of the desk the little woman stood silently, staring straight ahead. Her faded eyes were pale blue. Like ancient china.

'Irma Vincent Gordon,' Andrews murmured. He glanced up. 'Is that right?'

The old woman did not answer.

'She is totally deaf, sir,' the robant said.

Andrews grunted and returned to the folio. Irma Gordon was one of the original settlers of the Riga system. Origin unknown. Probably born out in space in one of the old sub-C ships. A strange feeling drifted through him. The little old creature. The centuries she had seen! The changes.

'She wants to travel?' he asked the robant.

'Yes, sir. She has come from her home to purchase a ticket.'

'Can she stand space travel?'

'She came from Riga, here to Fomalhaut IX.'

'Where does she want to go?'

'To Earth, sir,' the robant said.

'*Earth!*' Andrews' jaw dropped. He swore nervously. 'What do you mean?'

'She wishes to travel to Earth, sir.'

'You see?' Norton muttered. 'Completely crazy.'

Gripping his desk tightly, Andrews addressed the old woman. 'Madam, we can't sell you a ticket to Earth.'

'She can't hear you, sir,' the robant said.

Andrews found a piece of paper. He wrote in big letters:

CAN'T SELL YOU A TICKET TO EARTH

He held it up. The old woman's eyes moved as she studied the words. Her lips twitched. 'Why not?' she said at last. Her voice was faint and dry. Like rustling weeds.

Andrews scratched an answer.

NO SUCH PLACE

He added grimly:

MYTH – LEGEND – NEVER EXISTED

The old woman's faded eyes left the words. She gazed directly at Andrews, her face expressionless. Andrews became uneasy. Beside him, Norton sweated nervously.

'Jeez,' Norton muttered. 'Get her out of here. She'll put the hex on us.'

Andrews addressed the robant. 'Can't you make her understand? There is no such place as Earth. It's been proved a thousand times. No such primordial planet existed. All scientists agree human life arose simultaneously throughout the – '

'It is her wish to travel to Earth,' the robant said patiently. 'She is three hundred and fifty years old and they have ceased giving her sustentation treatments. She wishes to visit Earth before she dies.'

'But it's a myth!' Andrews exploded. He opened and closed his mouth, but no words came.

'How much?' the old woman said. 'How much?'

'I can't do it!' Andrews shouted. 'There isn't – '

'We have a kilo positives,' the robant said.

Andrews became suddenly quiet. 'A thousand positives.' He blanched in amazement. His jaws clamped shut, the colour draining from his face.

'How much?' the old woman repeated. 'How much?'

'Will that be sufficient?' the robant asked.

For a moment Andrews swallowed silently. Abruptly he found his voice. 'Sure,' he said. 'Why not?'

'Captain!' Norton protested. 'Have you gone nuts? You know there's no such place as Earth! How the hell can we – '

'Sure, we'll take her.' Andrews buttoned his tunic slowly, hands shaking. 'We'll take her anywhere she wants to go. Tell her that. For a thousand positives we'll be glad to take her to Earth. Okay?'

'Of course,' the robant said. 'She has saved many decades for this. She will give you the kilo positives at once. She has them with her.'

*   *   *

'Look,' Norton said. 'You can get twenty years for this. They'll take your articles and your card and they'll – '

'Shut up.' Andrews spun the dial of the intersystem vidsender. Under them the jets throbbed and roared. The lumbering transport had reached deep space. 'I want the main information library at Centaurus II,' he said into the speaker.

'Even for a thousand positives you can't do it. Nobody can do it. They tried to find Earth for generations. Directorate ships tracked down every moth-eaten planet in the whole – '

The vidsender clicked. 'Centaurus II.'

'Information library.'

Norton caught Andrews' arm. 'Please, Captain. Even for *two* kilo positives – '

'I want the following information,' Andrews said into the vidspeaker. 'All facts that are known concerning the planet Earth. Legendary birthplace of the human race.'

'No facts are known,' the detached voice of the library monitor came. 'The subject is classified as metaparticular.'

'What unverified but widely circulated reports have survived?'

'Most legends concerning Earth were lost during the Centauran–Rigan conflict of 4-B33a. What survived is fragmentary. Earth is variously described as a large ringed planet with three moons, as a small, dense planet with a single moon, as the first planet of a ten-planet system located around a dwarf white – '

'What's the most prevalent legend?'

'The Morrison Report of 5-C2 1r analysed the total ethnic and subliminal accounts of the legendary Earth. The final summation noted that Earth is generally considered to be a small third planet of a nine-planet system, with a single moon. Other than that, no agreement of legends could be constructed.'

'I see. A third planet of a nine-planet system. With a single moon.' Andrews broke the circuit and the screen faded.

'So?' Norton said.

Andrews got quickly to his feet. 'She probably knows every legend about it.' He pointed down – at the passenger quarters below. 'I want to get the accounts straight.'

'Why? What are you going to do?'

Andrews flipped open the master star chart. He ran his fingers down the index and released the scanner. In a moment it turned up a card.

He grabbed the chart and fed it into the robant pilot. 'The Emphor system,' he murmured thoughtfully.

'Emphor? We're going there?'

'According to the chart, there are ninety systems that show a third planet of nine with a single moon. Of the ninety, Emphor is the closest. We're heading there now.'

'I don't get it,' Norton protested. 'Emphor is a routine trading system. Emphor III isn't even a Class D check point.'

Captain Andrews grinned tightly. 'Emphor III has a single moon, and it's the third of nine planets. That's all we want. Does anybody know any more about Earth?' He glanced downwards. 'Does *she* know any more about Earth?'

'I see,' Norton said slowly. 'I'm beginning to get the picture.'

Emphor III turned silently below them. A dull red globe, suspended among sickly clouds, its baked and corroded surface lapped by the congealed remains of ancient seas. Cracked, eroded cliffs jutted starkly up. The flat plains had been dug and stripped bare. Great gouged pits pocketed the surface, endless gaping sores.

Norton's face twisted in revulsion. 'Look at it. Is anything alive down there?'

Captain Andrews frowned. 'I didn't realize it was so gutted.' He crossed abruptly to the robant pilot. 'There's supposed to be an auto-grapple some place down there. I'll try to pick it up.'

'A grapple? You mean that waste is inhabited?'

'A few Emphorites. Degenerate trading colony of some sort.' Andrews consulted the card. 'Commercial ships come here occasionally. Contact with this region has been vague since the Centauran–Rigan War.'

The passage rang with a sudden sound. The gleaming robant and Mrs Gordon emerged through the doorway into the control room. The old woman's face was alive with excitement. 'Captain! Is that – is that Earth down there?'

Andrews nodded. 'Yes.'

The robant led Mrs Gordon over to the big viewscreen. The old woman's face twitched, ripples of emotion stirring her withered features. 'I can hardly believe that's really Earth. It seems impossible.'

Norton glanced sharply at Captain Andrews.

'It's Earth,' Andrews stated, not meeting Norton's glance. 'The Moon should be around, soon.'

The old woman did not speak. She had turned her back.

Andrews contacted the auto-grapple and hooked the robant pilot on. The transport shuddered and then began to drop, as the beam from Emphor caught it and took over.

'We're landing,' Andrews said to the old woman, touching her on the shoulder.

'She can't hear you, sir,' the robant said.

Andrews grunted. 'Well, she can see.'

Below them the pitted, ruined surface of Emphor III was rising rapidly. The ship entered the cloud belt and emerged, coasting over a barren plain that stretched as far as the eye could see.

'What happened down there?' Norton said to Andrews. 'The war?'

'War. Mining. And it's old. The pits are probably bomb craters. Some of the long trenches may be scoop gouges. Looks like they really exhausted this place.'

A crooked row of broken mountain peaks shot past under them. They were nearing the remains of an ocean. Dark, unhealthy water lapped below, a vast sea, crusted with salt and waste, its edges disappearing into banks of piled debris.

'Why is it that way?' Mrs Gordon said suddenly. Doubt crossed her features. 'Why?'

'What do you mean?' Andrews said.

'I don't understand.' She stared uncertainly down at the surface below. 'It isn't supposed to be this way. Earth is green. Green and alive. Blue water and . . .' Her voice trailed off uneasily. '*Why?*'

Andrews grabbed some paper and wrote:

COMMERCIAL OPERATIONS EXHAUSTED SURFACE

Mrs Gordon studied his words, her lips twitching. A spasm moved through her, shaking the thin, dried-out body. 'Exhausted . . .' Her voice rose in shrill dismay. 'It's not supposed to be this way! I don't *want* it this way!'

The robant took her arm. 'She had better rest. I'll return her to her quarters. Please notify us when the landing has been made.'

'Sure.' Andrews nodded awkwardly as the robant led the old woman from the viewscreen. She clung to the guide rail, face distorted with fear and bewilderment.

'Something's wrong!' she wailed. 'Why is it this way? Why . . .'

The robant led her from the control room. The closing of the hydraulic safety doors cut off her thin cry abruptly.

Andrews relaxed, his body sagging. 'God.' He lit a cigarette shakily. 'What a racket she makes.'

'We're almost down,' Norton said frigidly.

Cold wind lashed at them as they stepped out cautiously. The air smelled bad – sour and acrid. Like rotten eggs. The wind brought salt and sand blowing up against their faces.

A few miles off the thick sea lay. They could hear it swishing faintly, gummily. A few birds passed silently overhead, great wings flapping soundlessly.

'Depressing damn place,' Andrews muttered.

'Yeah. I wonder what the old lady's thinking.'

Down the descent ramp came the glittering robant, helping the little old woman. She moved hesitantly, unsteady, gripping the robant's metal arm. The cold wind whipped around her frail body. For a moment she tottered – and then came on, leaving the ramp and gaining the uneven ground.

Norton shook his head. 'She looks bad. This air. And the wind.'

'I know.' Andrews moved back towards Mrs Gordon and the robant. 'How is she?' he asked.

'She is not well, sir,' the robant answered.

'Captain,' the old woman whispered.

'What is it?'

'You must tell me the truth. Is this – is this really Earth?' She watched his lips closely. 'You swear it is? You *swear*?' Her voice rose in shrill terror.

'It's Earth!' Andrews snapped irritably. 'I told you before. Of course it's Earth.'

'It doesn't look like Earth.' Mrs Gordon clung to his answer, panic-stricken. 'It doesn't look like Earth, Captain. Is it really Earth?'

'Yes!'

Her gaze wandered towards the ocean. A strange look

flickered across her tired face, igniting her faded eyes with sudden hunger. 'Is that water? I want to see.'

Andrews turned to Norton. 'Get the launch out. Drive her where she wants.'

Norton pulled back angrily. 'Me?'

'That's an order.'

'Okay.' Norton returned reluctantly to the ship. Andrews lit a cigarette moodily and waited. Presently the launch slid out of the ship, coasting across the ash towards them.

'You can show her anything she wants,' Andrews said to the robant. 'Norton will drive you.'

'Thank you, sir,' the robant said. 'She will be grateful. She has wanted all her life to stand on Earth. She remembers her grandfather telling her about it. She believes that he came from Earth, a long time ago. She is very old. She is the last living member of her family.'

'But Earth is just a — ' Andrews caught himself. 'I mean — '

'Yes, sir. But she is very old. And she has waited many years.' The robant turned to the old woman and led her gently towards the launch. Andrews stared after them sullenly, rubbing his jaw and frowning.

'Okay,' Norton's voice came from the launch. He slid the hatch open and the robant led the old woman carefully inside. The hatch closed after them.

A moment later the launch shot away across the salt flat, towards the ugly, lapping ocean.

Norton and Captain Andrews paced restlessly along the shore. The sky was darkening. Sheets of salt blew against them. The mud flats stank in the gathering gloom of night. Dimly, off in the distance, a line of hills faded into the silence and vapours.

'Go on,' Andrews said. 'What then?'

'That's all. She got out of the launch. She and the robant. I stayed inside. They stood looking across the ocean. After a while the old woman sent the robant back to the launch.'

'Why?'

'I don't know. She wanted to be alone, I suppose. She stood for a time by herself. On the shore. Looking over the water. The wind rising. All at once she just sort of settled down. She sank down in a heap, into the salt ash.'

'Then what?'

'While I was pulling myself together, the robant leaped out and ran to her. It picked her up. It stood for a second and then it started for the water. I leaped out of the launch, yelling. It stepped into the water and disappeared. Sank down in the mud and filth. Vanished.' Norton shuddered. 'With her body.'

Andrews tossed his cigarette savagely away. The cigarette rolled off, glowing behind them. 'Anything more?'

'Nothing. It all happened in a second. She was standing there, looking over the water. Suddenly she quivered – like a dead branch. Then she just sort of dwindled away. And the robant was out of the launch and into the water with her before I could figure out what was happening.'

The sky was almost dark. Huge clouds drifted across the faint stars. Clouds of unhealthy night vapours and particles of waste. A flock of immense birds crossed the horizon, flying silently.

Against the broken hills the Moon was rising. A diseased, barren globe, tinted faintly yellow. Like old parchment.

'Let's get back in the ship,' Andrews said. 'I don't like this place.'

'I can't figure out why it happened. The old woman.' Norton shook his head.

'The wind. Radio-active toxins. I checked with Centaurus

II. The war devastated the whole system. Left the planet a lethal wreck.'

'Then we won't – '

'No. We won't have to answer for it.' They continued for a time in silence. 'We won't have to explain. It's evident enough. Anybody coming here, especially an old person – '

'Only nobody would come here,' Norton said bitterly. 'Especially an old person.'

Andrews didn't answer. He paced along, head down, hands in pockets. Norton followed silently behind. Above them, the single moon grew brighter as it escaped the mists and entered a patch of clear sky.

'By the way,' Norton said, his voice cold and distant behind Andrews. 'This is the last trip I'll be making with you. While I was in the ship I filed a formal request for new papers.'

'Oh?'

'Thought I'd let you know. And my share of the kilo positives. You can keep it.'

Andrews flushed and increased his pace, leaving Norton behind. The old woman's death had shaken him. He lit another cigarette and then threw it away.

Damn it – the fault wasn't *his*. She had been old. Three hundred and fifty years. Senile and deaf. A faded leaf, carried off by the wind. By the poisonous wind that lashed and twisted endlessly across the ruined face of the planet.

The ruined face. Salt ash and debris. The broken line of crumbling hills. And the silence. The eternal silence. Nothing but the wind and the lapping of the thick stagnant water. And the dark birds overhead.

Something glinted. Something at his feet, in the salt ash. Reflecting the sickly pallor of the Moon.

Andrews bent down and groped in the darkness. His

fingers closed over something hard. He picked the small disc up and examined it.

'Strange,' he said.

It wasn't until they were out in deep space, roaring back towards Fomalhaut, that he remembered the disc.

He slid away from the control panel, searching his pockets for it.

The disc was worn and thin. And terribly old. Andrews rubbed it and spat on it until it was clean enough to make out. A faint impression – nothing more. He turned it over. A token? Washer? Coin?

On the back were a few meaningless letters. Some ancient, forgotten script. He held the disc to the light until he made the letters out.

E PLURIBUS UNUM*

He shrugged, tossed the ancient bit of metal into a waste disposal unit beside him, and turned his attention to the star charts, and home . . .

* Latin inscription that appears on American coins.

The Indefatigable Frog

'Zeno was the first great scientist,' Professor Hardy stated, looking sternly around his classroom. 'For example, take his paradox of the frog and the well. As Zeno showed, the frog will never reach the top of the well. Each jump is half the previous jump; a small but very real margin always remains for him to travel.'

There was silence, as the afternoon Physics 3-A Class considered Hardy's oracular utterance. Then, in the back of the room, a hand slowly went up.

Hardy stared at the hand in disbelief. 'Well?' he said. 'What is it, Pitner?'

'But in Logic we were told the frog *would* reach the top of the well. Professor Grote said – '

'The frog will not!'

'Professor Grote says he will.'

Hardy folded his arms. 'In this class the frog will never reach the top of the well. I have examined the evidence myself. I am satisfied that he will always be a small distance away. For example, if he jumps – '

The bell rang.

All the students rose to their feet and began to move towards the door. Professor Hardy stared after them, his sentence half finished. He rubbed his jaw with displeasure, frowning at the horde of young men and women with their bright, vacant faces.

When the last of them had gone, Hardy picked up his pipe and went out of the room into the hall. He looked up and down. Sure enough, not far off was Grote, standing by the drinking fountain, wiping his chin.

'Grote!' Hardy said. 'Come here!'

Professor Grote looked up, blinking. 'What?'

'Come here,' Hardy strode up to him. 'How dare you try to teach Zeno? He was a scientist, and as such he's my property to teach, not yours. Leave Zeno to me!'

'Zeno was a philosopher.' Grote stared up indignantly at Hardy. 'I know what's on your mind. It's that paradox about the frog and the well. For your information, Hardy, the frog will easily get out. You've been misleading your students. Logic is on my side.'

'Logic, bah!' Hardy snorted, his eyes blazing. 'Old dusty maxims. It's obvious that the frog is trapped for ever, in an eternal prison and can never get away!'

'He will escape.'

'He will not.'

'Are you gentlemen quite through?' a calm voice said. They turned quickly around. The Dean was standing quietly behind them, smiling gently. 'If you are through, I wonder if you'd mind coming into my office for a moment.' He nodded towards his door. 'It won't take too long.'

Grote and Hardy looked at each other. 'See what you've done?' Hardy whispered, as they filed into the Dean's office. 'You've got us into trouble again.'

'You started it – you and your frog!'

'Sit down, gentlemen.' The Dean indicated two stiff-backed chairs. 'Make yourselves comfortable. I'm sorry to trouble you when you're so busy, but I do wish to speak to you for a moment.' He studied them moodily. 'May I ask what is the nature of your discussion this time?'

'It's about Zeno,' Grote murmured.

'Zeno?'

'The paradox about the frog and the well.'

'I see.' The Dean nodded. 'I see. The frog and the well.

A two-thousand-year-old saw. An ancient puzzle. And you two grown men stand in the hall arguing like a – '

'The difficulty,' Hardy said, after a time, 'is that no one has ever performed the experiment. The paradox is a pure abstraction.'

'Then you two are going to be the first to lower the frog into his well and actually see what happens.'

'But the frog won't jump in conformity to the conditions of the paradox.'

'Then you'll have to make him, that's all. I'll give you two weeks to set up control conditions and determine the truth of this miserable puzzle. I want no more wrangling, month after month. I want this settled, once and for all.'

Hardy and Grote were silent.

'Well, Grote,' Hardy said at last, 'let's get it started.'

'We'll need a net,' Grote said.

'A net and a jar.' Hardy sighed. 'We might as well be at it as soon as possible.'

The 'Frog Chamber', as it got to be called, was quite a project. The University donated most of the basement to them, and Grote and Hardy set to work at once, carrying parts and materials downstairs. There wasn't a soul who didn't know about it before long. Most of the science majors were on Hardy's side; they formed a Failure Club and denounced the frog's efforts. In the philosophy and art departments there was some agitation for a Success Club, but nothing ever came of it.

Grote and Hardy worked feverishly on the project. They were absent from their classes more and more of the time, as the two weeks wore on. The Chamber itself grew and developed, resembling more and more a long section of sewer-pipe running the length of the basement. One end of it disappeared into a maze of wires and tubes: at the other there was a door.

One day when Grote went downstairs there was Hardy already, peering into the tube.

'See here,' Grote said, 'we agreed to keep hands off unless both of us were present.'

'I'm just looking inside. It's dark in there.' Hardy grinned. 'I hope the frog will be able to see.'

'Well, there's only one way to go.'

Hardy lit his pipe. 'What do you think of trying out a sample frog? I'm itching to see what happens.'

'It's too soon.' Grote watched nervously as Hardy searched about for his jar. 'Shouldn't we wait a bit?'

'Can't face reality, eh? Here, give me a hand.'

There was a sudden sound, a scraping at the door. They looked up. Pitner was standing there, looking curiously into the room, at the elongated Frog Chamber.

'What do you want?' Hardy said. 'We're very busy.'

'Are you going to try it out?' Pitner came into the room. 'What are all the coils and relays for?'

'It's very simple,' Grote said, beaming. 'Something I worked out myself. This end here – '

'I'll show him,' Hardy said. 'You'll only confuse him. Yes, we were about to run the first trial frog. You can stay, boy, if you want.' He opened the jar and took a damp frog from it. 'As you can see, the big tube has an entrance and an exit. The frog goes in the entrance. Look inside the tube, boy. Go on.'

Pitner peered into the open end of the tube. He saw a long black tunnel. 'What are the lines?'

'Measuring lines. Grote, turn it on.'

The machinery came on, humming softly. Hardy took the frog and dropped him into the tube. He swung the metal door shut and snapped it tight. 'That's so the frog won't get out again, at this end.'

'How big a frog were you expecting?' Pitner said. 'A full-grown man could get into that.'

'Now watch.' Hardy turned the gas cock up. 'This end of the tube is warmed. The heat drives the frog up the tube. We'll watch through the window.'

They looked into the tube. The frog was sitting quietly in a little heap, staring sadly ahead.

'Jump, you stupid frog,' Hardy said. He turned the gas up.

'Not so high, you maniac!' Grote shouted. 'Do you want to stew him?'

'Look!' Pitner cried. 'There he goes.'

The frog jumped. 'Conduction carries the heat along the tube bottom,' Hardy explained. 'He has to keep on jumping to get away from it. Watch him go.'

Suddenly Pitner gave a frightened rattle. 'My God, Hardy. The frog has shrunk. He's only half as big as he was.'

Hardy beamed. 'That is the miracle. You see, at the far end of the tube there is a force field. The frog is compelled to jump towards it by the heat. The effect of the field is to reduce animal tissue according to its proximity. The frog is made smaller the farther he goes.'

'Why?'

'It's the only way the jumping span of the frog can be reduced. As the frog leaps he diminishes in size, and hence each leap is proportionally reduced. We have arranged it so that the diminution is the same as in Zeno's paradox.'

'But where does it all end?'

'That,' Hardy said, 'is the question to which we are devoted. At the far end of the tube there is a photon beam which the frog would pass through, if he ever got that far. If he could reach it, he would cut off the field.'

'He'll reach it,' Grote muttered.

'No. He'll get smaller and smaller, and jump shorter and shorter. To him, the tube will lengthen more and more, endlessly. He will never get there.'

They glared at each other. 'Don't be so sure,' Grote said.

They peered through the window into the tube. The frog had gone quite a distance up. He was almost invisible, now, a tiny speck no larger than a fly, moving imperceptibly along the tube. He became smaller. He was a pin point. He disappeared.

'Gosh,' Pitner said.

'Pitner, go away,' Hardy said. He rubbed his hands together. 'Grote and I have things to discuss.'

He locked the door after the boy.

'All right,' Grote said. 'You designed this tube. What became of the frog?'

'Why, he's still hopping, somewhere in a sub-atomic world.'

'You're a swindler. Some place along that tube the frog met with misfortune.'

'Well,' Hardy said. 'If you think that, perhaps you should inspect the tube personally.'

'I believe I will. I may find a – trap door.'

'Suit yourself,' Hardy said, grinning. He turned off the gas and opened the big metal door.

'Give me the flashlight,' Grote said. Hardy handed him the flashlight and he crawled into the tube, grunting. His voice echoed hollowly. 'No tricks, now.'

Hardy watched him disappear. He bent down and looked into the end of the tube. Grote was half-way down, wheezing and struggling. 'What's the matter?' Hardy said.

'Too tight . . .'

'Oh?' Hardy's grin broadened. He took his pipe from his mouth and set it on the table. 'Well, maybe we can do something about that.'

He slammed the metal door shut. He hurried to the other end of the tube and snapped the switches. Tubes lit up, relays clicked into place.

Hardy folded his arms. 'Start hopping, my dear frog,' he

said. 'Hop for all you're worth.'

He went to the gas cock and turned it on.

It was very dark. Grote lay for a long time without moving. His mind was filled with drifting thoughts. What was the matter with Hardy? What was he up to? At last he pulled himself on to his elbows. His head cracked against the roof of the tube.

It began to get warm. 'Hardy!' His voice thundered around him, loud and panicky. 'Open the door. What's going on?'

He tried to turn around in the tube, to reach the door, but he couldn't budge. There was nothing to do but go forward. He began to crawl, muttering under his breath. 'Just wait, Hardy. You and your jokes. I don't see what you expect to – '

Suddenly the tube leaped. He fell, his chin banging against the metal. He blinked. The tube had grown; now there was more than enough room. And his clothing! His shirt and pants were like a tent around him.

'Oh, heavens,' Grote said in a tiny voice. He rose to his knees. Laboriously he turned around. He pulled himself back through the tube the way he had come, towards the metal door. He pushed against it, but nothing happened. It was now too large for him to force.

He sat for a long time. When the metal floor under him became too warm he crawled reluctantly along the tube to a cooler place. He curled himself up and stared dismally into the darkness. 'What am I going to do?' he asked himself.

After a time a measure of courage returned to him. 'I must think logically. I've already entered the force field once, therefore I'm reduced in size by one-half. I must be about three feet high. That makes the tube twice as long.'

He got out the flashlight and some paper from his

immense pocket and did some figuring. The flashlight was almost unmanageable.

Underneath him the floor became warm. Automatically he shifted a little up the tube to avoid the heat. 'If I stay here long enough,' he murmured, 'I might be – '

The tube leaped again, rushing off in all directions. He found himself floundering in a sea of rough fabric, choking and gasping. At last he struggled free.

'One and a half feet,' Grote said, staring around him. 'I don't dare move any more, not at all.'

But when the floor heated under him he moved some more. 'Three-quarters of a foot.' Sweat broke out on his face. 'Three-quarters of one foot.' He looked down the tube. Far, far down at the end was a spot of light, the photon beam crossing the tube. If he could reach it, if only he could reach it, if only he could reach it!

He meditated over his figures for a time. 'Well,' he said at last. 'I hope I'm correct. According to my calculations I should reach the beam of light in about nine hours and thirty minutes, if I keep walking steadily.' He took a deep breath and lifted the flashlight to his shoulder.

'However,' he murmured, 'I may be rather small by that time . . .' He started walking, his chin up.

Professor Hardy turned to Pitner. 'Tell the class what you saw this morning.'

Everyone turned to look. Pitner swallowed nervously. 'Well, I was downstairs in the basement. I was asked in to see the Frog Chamber. By Professor Grote. They were going to start the experiment.'

'What experiment do you refer to?'

'The Zeno one,' he explained nervously. 'The frog. He put the frog in the tube and closed the door. And then Professor Grote turned on the power.'

'What occurred?'

'The frog started to hop. He got smaller.'

'He got smaller, you say. And then what?'

'He disappeared.'

Professor Hardy sat back in his chair. 'The frog did not reach the end of the tube, then?'

'No.'

'That's all.' There was a murmuring from the class. 'So you see, the frog did not reach the end of the tube, as expected by my colleague, Professor Grote. He will never reach the end. Alas, we shall not see the unfortunate frog again.'

There was a general stir. Hardy tapped with his pencil. He lit his pipe and puffed calmly, leaning back in his chair. 'This experiment was quite an awakener to poor Grote, I'm afraid. He has had a blow of some unusual proportion. As you may have noticed, he hasn't appeared for his afternoon classes. Professor Grote, I understand, has decided to go on a long vacation to the mountains. Perhaps after he has had time to rest and enjoy himself, and to forget – '

Grote winced. But he kept on walking. 'Don't get frightened,' he said to himself. 'Keep on.'

The tube jumped again. He staggered. The flashlight crashed to the floor and went out. He was alone in an enormous cave, an immense void that seemed to have no end, no end at all.

He kept walking.

After a time he began to get tired again. It was not the first time. 'A rest wouldn't do any harm.' He sat down. The floor was rough under him, rough and uneven. 'According to my figures it will be more like two days, or so. Perhaps a little longer . . .'

He rested, dozing a little. Later on he began to walk again. The sudden jumping of the tube had ceased to frighten him; he had grown accustomed to it. Sooner or later he would reach the photon beam and cut through it. The force field would go off and he would resume his normal size. Grote smiled a little to himself. Wouldn't Hardy be surprised to –

He stubbed his toe and fell, headlong into the blackness around him. A deep fear ran through him and he began to tremble. He stood up, staring around him.

Which way?

'My God,' he said. He bent down and touched the floor under him. Which way? Time passed. He began to walk slowly, first one way, then another. He could make out nothing, nothing at all.

Then he was running, hurrying through the darkness, this way and that, slipping and falling. All at once he staggered. The familiar sensation: he breathed a sobbing sigh of relief. He was moving in the right direction! He began to run again, calmly, taking deep breaths, his mouth open. Then once more the staggering shudder as he shrank down another notch; but he was going the right way. He ran on and on.

And as he ran the floor became rougher and rougher. Soon he was forced to stop, falling over boulders and rocks. Hadn't they smoothed the pipe down? What had gone wrong with the sanding, the steel wool –

'Of course,' he murmured. 'Even the surface of a razor blade . . . if one is small . . .'

He walked ahead, feeling his way along. There was a dim light over everything, rising up from the great stones around him, even from his own body. What was it? He looked at his hands. They glittered in the darkness.

'Heat,' he said. 'Of course. Thanks, Hardy.' In the half-light he leaped from stone to stone. He was running across an endless plain of rocks and boulders, jumping like a goat, from crag to crag. 'Or like a frog,' he said. He jumped on, stopping once in a while for breath. How long would it be? He looked at the size of the great blocks of ore piled up around him. Suddenly a terror rushed through him.

'Maybe I shouldn't figure it out,' he said. He climbed up the side of one towering cliff and leaped across to the other side. The next gulf was even wider. He barely made it, gasping and struggling to catch hold.

He jumped endlessly, again and again. He forgot how many times.

He stood on the edge of a rock and leaped.

Then he was falling, down, down, into the cleft, into the dim light. There was no bottom. On and on he fell.

Professor Grote closed his eyes. Peace came over him, his tired body relaxed.

'No more jumping,' he said, drifting down, down. 'A certain law regarding falling bodies . . . the smaller the body the less the effect of gravity. No wonder bugs fall so lightly . . . certain characteristics . . .'

He closed his eyes and allowed the darkness to take him over, at last.

'And so,' Professor Hardy said, 'we can expect to find that this experiment will go down in science as – '

He stopped, frowning. The class was staring towards the door. Some of the students were smiling, and one began to laugh. Hardy turned to see what it was.

'Shades of Charles Fort,' he said.

A frog came hopping into the room.

Pitner stood up. 'Professor,' he said excitedly. 'This confirms a theory I've worked out. The frog became so reduced in size that he passed through the spaces – '

'What?' Hardy said. 'This is another frog.'

' – through the spaces between the molecules which form the floor of the Frog Chamber. The frog would then drift slowly to the floor, since he would be proportionally less affected by the law of acceleration. And leaving the force field, he would regain his original size.'

Pitner beamed down at the frog as the frog slowly made his way across the room.

'Really,' Professor Hardy began. He sat down at his desk weakly. At that moment the bell rang, and the students began to gather their books and papers together. Presently Hardy found himself alone staring down at the frog. He shook his head. 'It can't be,' he murmured. 'The world is full of frogs. It can't be the same frog.'

A student came up to the desk. 'Professor Hardy — '

Hardy looked up.

'Yes? What is it?'

'There's a man outside in the hall wants to see you. He's upset. He has a blanket on.'

'All right,' Hardy said. He sighed and got to his feet. At the door he paused, taking a deep breath. Then he set his jaw and went out into the hall.

Grote was standing there, wrapped in a red-wool blanket, his face flushed with excitement. Hardy glanced at him apologetically.

'We still don't know!' Grote cried.

'What?' Hardy murmured. 'Say, er, Grote — '

'We still don't know whether the frog would have reached the end of the tube. He and I fell out between the molecules. We'll have to find some other way to test the paradox. The Chamber's no good.'

'Yes, true.' Hardy said. 'Say, Grote — '

'Let's discuss it later,' Grote said. 'I have to get to my classes. I'll look you up this evening.'

And he hurried off down the hall clutching his blanket.

The Turning Wheel

Bard Chai said thoughtfully, 'Cults.' He examined a tape report grinding from the receptor. The receptor was rusty and unoiled; it whined piercingly and sent up an acrid wisp of smoke. Chai shut it off as its pitted surface began to heat ugly red. Presently he finished with the tape and tossed it with a heap of refuse jamming the mouth of the disposal slot.

'What about cults?' Bard Sung-wu asked faintly. He brought himself back with an effort, and forced a smile of interest on his plump olive-yellow face. 'You were saying?'

'Any stable society is menaced by cults; our society is no exception.' Chai rubbed his finely tapered fingers together reflectively. 'Certain lower strata are axiomatically dissatisfied. Their hearts burn with envy of those the wheel has placed above them; in secret they form fanatic, rebellious bands. They meet in the dark of the night; they insidiously express inversions of accepted norms; they delight in flaunting basic mores and customs.'

'Ugh,' Sung-wu agreed. 'I mean,' he explained quickly, 'it seems incredible people could practise such fanatic and disgusting rites.' He got nervously to his feet. 'I must go, if it's permitted.'

'Wait,' snapped Chai. 'You are familiar with the Detroit area?'

Uneasily, Sung-wu nodded. 'Very slightly.'

With characteristic vigour, Chai made his decision. 'I'm sending you; investigate and make a blue-slip report. If this group is dangerous, the Holy Arm should know. It's of the worst elements – the Techno class.' He made a wry face. 'Caucasians, hulking, hairy things. We'll give you six months in Spain, on your return; you can poke over ruins of abandoned cities.'

'Caucasians!' Sung-wu exclaimed, his face turning green. 'But I haven't been well; please, if somebody else could go – '

'You, perhaps, hold to the Broken Feather theory?' Chai raised an eyebrow. 'An amazing philologist, Broken Feather; I took partial instruction from him. He held, you know, the Caucasian to be descended of Neanderthal stock. Their extreme size, thick body-hair, their general brutish cast, reveal an innate inability to comprehend anything but a purely animalistic horizontal; proselytism is a waste of time.'

He affixed the younger man with a stern eye. 'I wouldn't send you, if I didn't have unusual faith in your devotion.'

Sung-wu fingered his beads miserably. 'Elron be praised,' he muttered; 'you are too kind.'

Sung-wu slid into a lift and was raised, amid great groans and whirrings and false stops, to the top level of the Central Chamber building. He hurried down a corridor dimly lit by occasional yellow bulbs. A moment later he approached the doors of the scanning offices and flashed his identification at the robot guard. 'Is Bard Fei-p'ang within?' he inquired.

'Verily,' the robot answered, stepping aside.

Sung-wu entered the offices, bypassed the rows of rusted, discarded machines, and entered the still function-ing wing. He located his brother-in-law, hunched over some graphs at one of the desks, laboriously copying material by hand. 'Clearness be with you,' Sung-wu murmured.

Fei-p'ang glanced up in annoyance. 'I told you not to

come again; if the Arm finds out I'm letting you use the scanner for a personal plot, they'll stretch me on the rack.'

'Gently,' Sung-wu murmured, his hand on his relation's shoulder. 'This is the last time. I'm going away; one more look, a final look.' His olive face took on a pleading, piteous cast. 'The turn comes for me very soon; this will be our last conversation.'

Sung-wu's piteous look hardened into cunning. 'You wouldn't want it on your soul; no restitution will be possible at this late date.'

Fei-p'ang snorted. 'All right; but for Elron's sake, do it quickly.'

Sung-wu hurried to the mother-scanner and seated himself in the rickety basket. He snapped on the controls, clamped his forehead to the viewpiece, inserted his identity tab, and set the space-time finger into motion. Slowly, reluctantly, the ancient mechanism coughed into life and began tracing his personal tab along the future track.

Sung-wu's hands shook; his body trembled; sweat dripped from his neck, as he saw himself scampering in miniature. *Poor Sung-wu*, he thought wretchedly. The mite of a thing hurried about its duties; this was but eight months hence. Harried and beset, it performed its tasks – and then, in a subsequent continuum, fell down and died.

Sung-wu removed his eyes from the viewpiece and waited for his pulse to slow. He could stand that part, watching the moment of death; it was what came next that was too jangling for him.

He breathed a silent prayer. Had he fasted enough? In the four-day purge and self-flagellation, he had used the whip with metal points, the heaviest possible. He had given away all his money; he had smashed a lovely vase his mother had left him, a treasured heirloom; he had rolled in the filth and mud in the centre of town. Hundreds had seen him. Now, surely, all this was enough. But time was so short!

Faint courage stirring, he sat up and again put his eyes to the viewpiece. He was shaking with terror. What if it hadn't changed? What if his mortification weren't enough? He spun the controls, sending the finger tracing his time-track past the moment of death.

Sung-wu shrieked and scrambled back in horror. His future was the same, exactly the same; there had been no change at all. His guilt had been too great to be washed away in such short a time; it would take ages – and he didn't have ages.

He left the scanner and passed by his brother-in-law. 'Thanks,' he muttered shakily.

For once, a measure of compassion touched Fei-p'ang's efficient brown features. 'Bad news? The next turn brings an unfortunate manifestation?'

'Bad scarcely describes it.'

Fei-p'ang's pity turned to righteous rebuke. 'Who do you have to blame but yourself?' he demanded sternly. 'You know your conduct in this manifestation determines the next; if you look forward to a future life as a lower animal, it should make you glance over your behaviour and repent your wrongs. The cosmic law that governs us is impartial. It is true justice: cause and effect; what you do determines what you next become – there can be no blame and no sorrow. There can be only understanding and repentance.' His curiosity overcame him. 'What is it? A snake? A squirrel?'

'It's no affair of yours,' Sung-wu said, as he moved unhappily towards the exit doors.

'I'll look myself!'

'Go ahead.' Sung-wu pushed moodily out into the hall. He was dazed with despair: it hadn't changed; it was still the same.

In eight months he would die, stricken by one of the numerous plagues that swept over the inhabited parts of the world. He would become feverish, break out with red spots, turn and twist in an anguish of delirium. His bowels would drop out; his flesh would waste away; his eyes would roll up; and after an interminable time of suffering, he would die. His body would lie in a mass heap, with hundreds of others – a whole streetful of dead, to be carted away by one of the robot sweepers, happily immune. His mortal remains would be burned in a common rubbish incinerator at the outskirts of the city.

Meanwhile, the eternal spark, Sung-wu's divine soul, would hurry from this space-time manifestation to the next in order. But it would not rise; it would sink; he had watched its descent on the scanner many times. There was always the same hideous picture – a sight beyond endurance – of his soul, as it plummeted down like a stone, into one of the lowest continua, a sinkhole of a manifestation at the very bottom of the ladder.

He had sinned. In his youth, Sung-wu had got mixed up with a black-eyed wench with long flowing hair, a glittering waterfall down her back and shoulders. Inviting red lips, plump breasts, hips that undulated and beckoned unmistakably. She was the wife of a friend, from the Warrior class, but he had taken her as his mistress; he had been *certain* time remained to rectify his venality.

But he was wrong: the wheel was soon to turn for him. The plague – not enough time to fast and pray and do good works. He was determined to go down, straight down to a wallowing, foul-aired planet in a stinking red-sun system, an ancient pit of filth and decay and unending slime – a jungle world of the lowest type.

In it, he would be a shiny-winged fly, a great blue-bottomed, buzzing carrion-eater that hummed and guzzled and crawled through the rotting carcasses of great lizards, slain in combat.

From this swamp, this pest-ridden planet in a diseased, contaminated system, he would have to rise painfully up the endless rungs of the cosmic ladder he had already climbed. It had taken aeons to climb this far, to the level of a human being on the planet Earth, in the bright yellow Sol system; now he would have to do it all over again.

Chai beamed, 'Elron be with you,' as the corroded observation ship was checked by the robot crew, and finally okayed for limited flight. Sung-wu slowly entered the ship and seated himself at what remained of the controls. He waved listlessly, then slammed the lock and bolted it by hand.

As the ship limped into the late afternoon sky, he reluctantly consulted the reports and records Chai had transferred to him.

The Tinkerists were a small cult; they claimed only a few hundred members, all drawn from the Techno class, which was the most despised of the social castes. The Bards, of course, were at the top; they were the teachers of society, the holy men who guided man to clearness. Then the Poets; they turned into saga the great legends of Elron Hu, who lived (according to legend) in the hideous days of the Time of Madness. Below the Poets were the Artists; then the Musicians; then the Workers, who supervised the robot crews. After them the Businessmen, the Warriors, the Farmers and, finally, at the bottom, the Technos.

Most of the Technos were Caucasians – immense white-skinned things, incredibly hairy, like apes; their resemblance to the great apes was striking. Perhaps Broken Feather was right; perhaps they did have Neanderthal blood and were outside the possibility of clearness. Sung-wu had always considered himself an anti-racist; he disliked those who maintained the Caucasians were a race apart. Extremists believed eternal damage would result to the species if the Caucasians were allowed to intermarry.

In any case, the problem was academic; no decent, self-respecting woman of the higher classes – of Indian or Mongolian, or Bantu stock – would allow herself to be approached by a *Cauc*.

Below his ship, the barren countryside spread out, ugly and bleak. Great red spots that hadn't yet been overgrown, and slag surfaces were still visible – but by this time most ruins were covered by soil and crab grass. He could see men and robots farming; villages, countless tiny brown circles in the green fields; occasional ruins of ancient cities – gaping sores like blind mouths, eternally open to the sky. They would never close, not now.

Ahead was the Detroit area, named, so it ran, for some now forgotten spiritual leader. There were more villages here. Off to his left, the leaden surface of a body of water, a lake of some kind. Beyond that – only Elron knew. No one went that far; there was no human life there, only wild animals and deformed things spawned from radiation infestation still lying heavy in the north.

He dropped his ship down. An open field lay to his right; a robot farmer was ploughing with a metal hook welded to its waist, a section torn off some discarded machine. It stopped dragging the hook and gazed up in amazement, as Sung-wu landed the ship awkwardly and bumped to a halt.

'Clearness be with you,' the robot rasped obediently, as Sung-wu climbed out.

Sung-wu gathered up his bundle of reports and papers and stuffed them in a brief-case. He snapped the ship's lock and hurried off towards the ruins of the city. The robot went back to dragging the rusty metal hook through the hard ground, its pitted body bent double with the strain, working slowly, silently, uncomplaining.

The little boy piped, 'Whither, Bard?' as Sung-wu pushed wearily through the tangled debris and slag. He was a little black-faced Bantu, in red rags sewed and patched together. He ran alongside Sung-wu like a puppy, leaping and bounding and grinning white-teethed.

Sung-wu became immediately crafty; his intrigue with the black-haired girl had taught him elemental dodges and evasions. 'My ship broke down,' he answered cautiously; it was certainly common enough. 'It was the last ship still in operation at our field.'

The boy skipped and laughed and broke off bits of green weeds that grew along the trail. 'I know somebody who can fix it,' he cried carelessly.

Sung-wu's pulse rate changed. 'Oh?' he murmured, as if uninterested. 'There are those around here who practise the questionable art of repairing?'

The boy nodded solemnly.

'Technos?' Sung-wu pursued. 'Are there many of them here, around these old ruins?'

More black-faced boys, and some little dark-eyed Bantu girls, came scampering through the slag and ruins. 'What's the matter with your ship?' one hollered at Sung-wu. 'Won't it run?'

They all ran and shouted around him, as he advanced slowly – an unusually wild bunch, completely undisciplined. They rolled and fought and tumbled and chased each other around madly.

'How many of you,' Sung-wu demanded, 'have taken your first instruction?'

There was a sudden uneasy silence. The children looked at each other guiltily; none of them answered.

'Good Elron!' Sung-wu exclaimed in horror. 'Are you all untaught?'

Heads hung guiltily.

'How do you expect to phase yourselves with the cosmic

will? How can you expect to know the divine plan? This is really too much!'

He pointed a plump finger at one of the boys. 'Are you constantly preparing yourself for the life to come? Are you constantly purging and purifying yourself? Do you deny yourself meat, sex, entertainment, financial gain, education, leisure?'

But it was obvious; their unrestrained laughter and play proved they were still jangled, far from clear – and clearness is the only road by which a person can gain understanding of the eternal plan, the cosmic wheel which turns endlessly, for all living things.

'Butterflies!' Sung-wu snorted with disgust. 'You are no better than the beasts and birds of the field, who take no heed of the morrow. You play and game for today, thinking tomorrow won't come. Like insects – '

But the thought of insects reminded him of the shiny-winged blue-rumped fly, creeping over a rotting lizard carcass, and Sung-wu's stomach did a flip-flip; he forced it back in place and strode on, towards the line of villages emerging ahead.

Farmers were working the barren fields on all sides. A thin layer of soil over slag; a few limp wheat stalks waved, thin and emaciated. The ground was terrible, the worst he had seen. He could feel the metal under his feet; it was almost to the surface. Bent men and women watered their sickly crops with tin cans, old metal containers picked from the ruins. An ox was pulling a crude cart.

In another field, women were weeding by hand; all moved slowly, stupidly, victims of hookworm, from the soil. They were all barefoot. The children hadn't picked it up yet, but they soon would.

Sung-wu gazed up at the sky and gave thanks to Elron; here, suffering was unusually severe; trials of exceptional vividness lay on every hand. These men and women were being tempered in a hot crucible; their souls were probably purified to an astonishing degree. A baby lay in the shade, beside a half-dozing mother. Flies crawled over its eyes; its mother breathed heavily, hoarsely, her mouth open. An unhealthy flush discoloured her brown cheeks.

'Come here,' Sung-wu called sharply to the gang of black-faced children who followed along after him. 'I'm going to talk to you.'

The children approached, eyes on the ground, and assembled in a silent circle around him. Sung-wu sat down, placed his brief-case beside him, and folded his legs expertly under him in the traditional posture outlined by Elron in his seventh book of teachings.

'I will ask and you will answer,' Sung-wu stated. 'You know the basic catechisms?' He peered sharply around. 'Who knows the basic catechisms?'

One or two hands went up. Most of the children looked away unhappily.

'First!' snapped Sung-wu. '*Who are you?* You are a minute fragment of the cosmic plan.

'Second! *What are you?* A mere speck in a system so vast as to be beyond comprehension.

'Third! *What is the way of life?* To fulfil what is required by the cosmic forces.

'Fourth! *Where are you?* On one step of the cosmic ladder.

'Fifth! *Where have you been?* Through endless steps; each turn of the wheel advances or depresses you.

'Sixth! *What determines your direction at the next turn?* Your conduct in this manifestation.

'Seventh! *What is right conduct?* Submitting yourself to the eternal forces, the cosmic elements that make up the divine plan.

'Eighth! *What is the significance of suffering?* To purify the soul.

'Ninth! *What is the significance of death?* To release the person from this manifestation, so he may rise to a new rung of the ladder.

'Tenth – '

But at that moment Sung-wu broke off. Two quasi-human shapes were approaching him. Immense white-skinned figures striding across the baked fields, between the sickly rows of wheat.

Technos – coming to meet him; his flesh crawled. Caucs. Their skins glittered pale and unhealthy, like nocturnal insects, dug from under rocks.

He rose to his feet, conquered his disgust, and prepared to greet them.

Sung-wu said, 'Clearness!' He could smell them, a musky sheep smell, as they came to a halt in front of him. Two bucks, two immense sweating males, skin damp and sticky, with beards, and long disorderly hair. They wore sailcloth trousers and boots. With horror Sung-wu perceived a thick body-hair, on their chests, like woven mats – tufts in their armpits, on their arms, wrists, even the backs of their hands. Maybe Broken Feather was right; perhaps, in these great lumbering blond-haired beasts, the archaic, Neanderthal stock – the false men – still survived. He could almost see the ape, peering from behind their blue eyes.

'Hi,' the first Cauc said. After a moment he added reflectively, 'My name's Jamison.'

'Pete Ferris,' the other grunted. Neither of them observed the customary deferences; Sung-wu winced but managed not to show it. Was it deliberate, a veiled insult, or perhaps mere ignorance? This was hard to tell; in lower classes there was, as Chai said, an ugly undercurrent of resentment and envy, and hostility.

'I'm making a routine survey,' Sung-wu explained, 'on

birth and death rates in rural areas. I'll be here a few days. Is there some place I can stay? Some public inn or hostel?'

The two Cauc bucks were silent. 'Why?' one of them demanded bluntly.

Sung-wu blinked. 'Why? Why what?'

'Why are you making a survey? If you want any information we'll supply it.'

Sung-wu was incredulous. 'Do you know to whom you're talking? I'm a Bard! Why, you're ten classes down; how dare you — ' He choked with rage. In these rural areas the Technos had utterly forgotten their place. What was ailing the local Bards? Were they letting the system break apart?

He shuddered violently at the thought of what it would mean if Technos and Farmers and Businessmen were allowed to intermingle — even intermarry, and eat, and drink, in the same places. The whole structure of society would collapse. If all were to ride the same carts, use the same outhouse; it passed belief. A sudden nightmare picture loomed up before Sung-wu of Technos living and mating with women of the Bard and Poet classes. He visioned a horizontally oriented society, all persons on the same level, with horror. It went against the very grain of the cosmos, against the divine plan; it was the Time of Madness all over again. He shuddered.

'Where is the Manager of this area?' he demanded. 'Take me to him; I'll deal directly with him.'

The two Caucs turned and headed back the way they had come, without a word. After a moment of fury, Sung-wu followed behind them.

They led him through withered fields and over barren, eroded hills on which nothing grew; the ruins increased. At the edge of the city, a line of meagre villages had been set up; he saw leaning, rickety wood huts, and mud streets.

From the villages a thick stench rose, the smell of offal and death.

Dogs lay sleeping under the huts; children poked and played in the filth and rotting debris. A few old people sat on porches, vacant faced, eyes glazed and dull. Chickens pecked around, and he saw pigs and skinny cats – and the eternal rusting piles of metal, sometimes thirty feet high. Great towers of red slag were heaped up everywhere.

Beyond the villages were the ruins proper – endless miles of abandoned wreckage; skeletons of buildings; concrete walls; bathtubs and pipe; overturned wrecks that had been cars. All these were from the Time of Madness, the decade that had finally rung the curtain down on the sorriest interval in man's history. The five centuries of madness and jangledness were now known as the Age of Heresy, when man had gone against the divine plan and taken his destiny in his own hands.

They came to a larger hut, a two-storey wood structure. The Caucs climbed a decaying flight of steps; boards creaked and gave ominously under their heavy boots. Sung-wu followed them nervously; they came out on a porch, a kind of open balcony.

On the balcony sat a man, an obese copper-skinned official in unbuttoned breeches, his shiny black hair pulled back and tied with a bone against his bulging red neck. His nose was large and prominent, his face flat and wide, with many chins. He was drinking lime juice from a tin cup and gazing down at the mud street below. As the two Caucs appeared he rose slightly, a prodigious effort.

'This man,' the Cauc named Jamison said, indicating Sung-wu, 'wants to see you.'

Sung-wu pushed angrily forward. 'I am a Bard, from the Central Chamber; do you people recognize *this*?' He tore open his robe and flashed the symbol of the Holy Arm, gold worked to form a swath of flaming red. 'I insist you accord me proper treatment! I'm not here to be pushed around by any – '

He had said too much; Sung-wu forced his anger down and gripped his brief-case. The fat Indian was studying him calmly; the two Caucs had wandered to the far end of the balcony and were squatting down in the shade. They lit crude cigarettes and turned their backs.

'Do you permit this?' Sung-wu demanded, incredulous. 'This – mingling?'

The Indian shrugged and sagged down even more on his chair. 'Clearness be with you,' he murmured; 'will you join me?' His calm expression remained unchanged; he seemed not to have noticed. 'Some lime juice? Or perhaps coffee? Lime juice is good for these.' He tapped his mouth; his soft gums were lined with caked sores.

'Nothing for me,' Sung-wu muttered grumpily, as he took a seat opposite the Indian; 'I'm here on an official survey.'

The Indian nodded faintly. 'Oh?'

'Birth and death rates.' Sung-wu hesitated, then leaned towards the Indian. 'I insist you send those two Caucs away; what I have to say to you is private.'

The Indian showed no change of expression; his broad face was utterly impassive. After a time he turned slightly. 'Please go down to the street level,' he ordered. 'As you will.'

The two Caucs got to their feet, grumbling, and pushed past the table, scowling and darting resentful glances at Sung-wu. One of them hawked and elaborately spat over the railing, an obvious insult.

'Insolence!' Sung-wu choked. 'How can you allow it? Did you see them? By Elron, it's beyond belief!'

The Indian shrugged indifferently – and belched. 'All men are brothers on the wheel. Didn't Elron Himself teach that, when He was on Earth?'

'Of course. But – '

'Are not even these men our brothers?'

'Naturally,' Sung-wu answered haughtily, 'but they must know their place; they're an insignificant class. In the rare event some object wants fixing, they are called; but in the last year I do not recall a single incident when it was deemed advisable to repair anything. The need of such a class diminishes yearly; eventually such a class and the elements composing it – '

'You perhaps advocate sterilization?' the Indian inquired, heavy-lidded and sly.

'I advocate *something*. The lower classes reproduce like rabbits; spawning all the time – much faster than we Bards. I always see some swollen-up Cauc woman, but hardly a single Bard is born, these days.'

'That's about all that's left them,' the Indian murmured mildly. He sipped a little lime juice. 'You should try to be more tolerant.'

'Tolerant? I have nothing against them, as long as they – '

'It is said,' the Indian continued softly, 'that Elron Hu, Himself, was a Cauc.'

Sung-wu spluttered indignantly and started to rejoin, but the hot words stuck fast in his mouth; down the mud street something was coming.

Sung-wu demanded, 'What is it?' He leaped up excitedly and hurried to the railing.

A slow procession was advancing with solemn step. As if at a signal, men and women poured from their rickety huts and excitedly lined the street to watch. Sung-wu was transfixed, as the procession neared; his senses reeled. More and more men and women were collecting each moment; there seemed to be hundreds of them. They were a dense, murmuring mob, packed tight, swaying back and forth, faces avid. An hysterical moan passed through them, a great wind that stirred them like leaves of a tree. They were a single collective whole, a vast primitive organism, held ecstatic and hypnotized by the approaching column.

The marchers wore a strange costume: white shirts, with the sleeves rolled up; dark grey trousers of an incredibly archaic design, and black shoes. All were dressed exactly alike. They formed a dazzling double line of white shirts, grey trousers, marching calmly and solemnly, faces up, nostrils flared, jaws stern. A glazed fanaticism stamped each man and woman, such a ruthless expression that Sung-wu shrank back in terror. On and on they came, figures of grim stone in their primordial white shirts and grey trousers, a frightening breath from the past. Their heels struck the ground in a dull, harsh beat that reverberated among the rickety huts. The dogs woke; the children began to wail. The chickens flew squawking.

'Elron!' Sung-wu cried. 'What's happening?'

The marchers carried strange symbolic implements, ritualistic images with esoteric meaning that of necessity escaped Sung-wu. There were tubes and poles, and shiny webs of what looked like metal. *Metal!* But it was not rusty; it was shiny and bright. He was stunned; they looked – new.

The procession passed directly below. After the marchers came a huge rumbling cart. On it was mounted an obvious fertility symbol, a corkscrew-bore as long as a tree; it jutted from a square cube of gleaming steel; as the cart moved forward the bore lifted and fell.

After the cart came more marchers, also grim faced, eyes glassy, loaded down with pipes and tubes and armfuls of glittering equipment. They passed on, and then the street was filled by surging throngs of awed men and women, who followed after them, utterly dazed. And then came children and barking dogs.

The last marcher carried a pennant that fluttered above

her as she strode along, a tall pole, hugged tight to her chest. At the top, the bright pennant fluttered boldly. Sung-wu made its marking out, and for a moment consciousness left him. There it was, directly below; it had passed under his very nose, out in the open for all to see – unconcealed. The pennant had a great T emblazoned on it.

'They – ' he began, but the obese Indian cut him off.

'The Tinkerists,' he rumbled, and sipped his lime juice.

Sung-wu grabbed up his brief-case and scrambled towards the stairs. At the bottom, the two hulking Caucs were already moving into motion. The Indian signalled quickly to them. 'Here!' They started grimly up, little blue eyes mean, red-rimmed and cold as stone; under their pelts their bulging muscles rippled.

Sung-wu fumbled in his cloak. His shiver-gun came out; he squeezed the release and directed it towards the two Caucs. But nothing happened; the gun had stopped functioning. He shook it wildly, flakes of rust and dried insulation fluttered from it. It was useless, worn out; he tossed it away and then, with the resolve of desperation, jumped through the railing.

He, and a torrent of rotten wood, cascaded to the street. He hit, rolled, struck his head against the corner of a hut, and shakily pulled himself to his feet.

He ran. Behind him, the two Caucs pushed after him through the throngs of men and women milling aimlessly along. Occasionally he glimpsed their white, perspiring faces. He turned a corner, raced between shabby huts, leaped over a sewage ditch, climbed heaps of sagging debris, slipping and rolling, and at last lay gasping behind a tree, his brief-case still clutched.

The Caucs were nowhere in sight. He had evaded them; for the moment he was safe.

He peered around. Which way was his ship? He shielded his eyes against the late afternoon sun until he managed to make out its bent, tubular outline. It was far off to his right, barely visible in the dying glare that hung gloomily across the sky. Sung-wu got unsteadily to his feet and began walking cautiously in that direction.

He was in a terrible spot; the whole region was pro-Tinkerist – even the Chamber-appointed Manager. And it wasn't along class lines; the cult had knifed to the top level. And it wasn't just Caucs any more; he couldn't count on Bantu or Mongolian or Indian, not in this area. An entire countryside was hostile, and lying in wait for him.

Elron, it was worse than the Arm had thought! No wonder they wanted a report. A whole area had swung over to a fanatic cult, a violent extremist group of heretics, teaching a most diabolical doctrine. He shuddered – and kept on, avoiding contact with the farmers in their fields, both human and robot. He increased his pace, as alarm and horror pushed him suddenly faster.

If the thing were to spread, if it were to hit a sizable portion of mankind, it might bring back the Time of Madness.

The ship was taken. Three or four immense Caucs stood lounging around it, cigarettes dangling from their slack mouths, white-faced and hairy. Stunned, Sung-wu moved back down the hillside, prickles of despair numbing him. The ship was lost; they had got there ahead of him. What was he supposed to do now?

It was almost evening. He'd have to walk fifty miles through the darkness, over unfamiliar, hostile ground, to reach the next inhabited area. The sun was already beginning to set, the air turning cool; and in addition, he was sopping wet with filth and slimy water. He had slipped in the gloom and fallen in a sewage ditch.

He retraced his steps, mind blank. What could he do? He was helpless; his shiver-gun had been useless. He was alone, and there was no contact with the Arm. Tinkerists swarming on all sides; they'd probably gut him and sprinkle his blood over the crops – or worse.

He skirted a farm. In the fading twilight, a dim figure was working, a young woman. He eyed her cautiously as he passed; she had her back to him. She was bending over, between rows of corn. What was she doing? Was she – good Elron!

He stumbled blindly across the field towards her, caution forgotten. 'Young woman! *Stop!* In the name of Elron, stop at once.'

The girl straightened up. 'Who are you?'

Breathless, Sung-wu arrived in front of her, gripping his battered brief-case and gasping. 'Those are our *brothers*! How can you destroy them? They may be close relatives, recently deceased.' He struck out and knocked the jar from her hand; it hit the ground and the imprisoned beetles scurried off in all directions.

The girl's cheeks flushed with anger. 'It took me an hour to collect those!'

'You were killing them! Crushing them!' He was speechless with horror. 'I saw you!'

'Of course.' The girl raised her black eyebrows. 'They gnaw the corn.'

'They're our brothers!' Sung-wu repeated wildly. 'Of course they gnaw the corn; because of certain sins committed, the cosmic forces have – ' He broke off, appalled. 'Don't you *know*? You've never been told?'

The girl was perhaps sixteen. In the fading light she was a small, slender figure, the empty jar in one hand, a rock in the other. A tide of black hair tumbled down her neck. Her eyes were large and luminous; her lips full and deep red; her skin a smooth copper-brown – Polynesian, probably. He caught a glimpse of firm brown breasts as she bent to grab a beetle that had landed on its back. The sight made his pulse race; in a flash he was back three years.

'What's your name?' he asked, more kindly.

'Frija.'

'How old are you?'

'Seventeen.'

'I am a Bard; have you ever spoken to a Bard before?'

'No,' the girl murmured. 'I don't think so.'

She was almost invisible in the darkness. Sung-wu could scarcely see her, but what he saw sent his heart into an agony of paroxysms: the same cloud of black hair, the same deep red lips. This girl was younger, of course – a mere child, and from the Farmer class, at that. But she had Liu's figure, and in time she'd ripen – probably in a matter of months.

Ageless, honeyed craft worked his vocal cords. 'I have landed in this area to make a survey. Something has gone wrong with my ship and I must remain the night. I know no one here, however. My plight is such that – '

'Oh,' Frija said, immediately sympathetic. 'Why don't you stay with us, tonight? We have an extra room, now that my brother's away.'

'Delighted,' Sung-wu answered instantly. 'Will you lead the way? I'll gladly repay you for your kindness.' The girl moved off towards a vague shape looming up in the darkness. Sung-wu hurried quickly after her. 'I find it incredible you haven't been instructed. This whole area has deteriorated beyond belief. What ways have you fallen in? We'll have to spend much time together; I can see that already. Not one of you even approaches clearness – you're jangled, every one of you.'

'What does that mean?' Frija asked, as she stepped up on the porch and opened the door.

'Jangled?' Sung-wu blinked in amazement. 'We *will* have to study much together.' In his eagerness, he tripped on the top step, and barely managed to catch himself. 'Perhaps you need complete instruction; it may be necessary to start from the very bottom. I can arrange a stay at the Holy Arm for you – under my protection, of course. Jangled means out of harmony with the cosmic elements. How can you live this way? My dear, you'll have to be brought back in line with the divine plan!'

'What plan is that?' She led him into a warm living-room; a crackling fire burned in the grate. Two or three men sat around a rough wood table, an old man with long white hair and two younger men. A frail, withered old woman sat dozing in a rocker in the corner. In the kitchen, a buxom young woman was fixing the evening meal.

'Why, *the* plan,' Sung-wu answered, astounded. His eyes darted around. Suddenly his brief-case fell to the floor. 'Caucs,' he said.

They were all Caucasians, even Frija. She was deeply tanned; her skin was almost black; but she was a Cauc, nonetheless. He recalled: Caucs, in the sun, turned dark, sometimes even darker than Mongolians. The girl had tossed her work robe over a door hook; in her household shorts her thighs were as white as milk. And the old man and woman –

'This is my grandfather,' Frija said, indicating the old man. 'Benjamin Tinker.'

Under the watchful eyes of the two younger Tinkers, Sung-wu was washed and scrubbed, given clean clothes, and then fed. He ate only a little; he didn't feel very well.

'I can't understand it,' he muttered, and he listlessly pushed his plate away. 'The scanner at the central Chamber said I had eight months left. The plague will – ' He considered. 'But it can always change. The scanner goes on prediction, not certainty; multiple possibilities; free will . . . Any overt act of sufficient significance – '

Ben Tinker laughed. 'You want to stay alive?'

'Of course!' Sung-wu muttered indignantly.

They all laughed – even Frija, and the old woman in her shawl, snow white hair and mild blue eyes. They were the first Cauc women he had ever seen. They weren't big and lumbering like the male Caucs; they didn't seem to have the same bestial characteristics. The two young Cauc bucks looked plenty tough, though; they and their father were poring over an elaborate series of papers and reports, spread out on the dinner table, among the empty plates.

'This area,' Ben Tinker murmured. 'Pipes should go here. And here. Water's the main need. Before the next crop goes in, we'll dump a few hundred pounds of artificial fertilizers and plough it in. The power ploughs should be ready then.'

'After that?' one of the tow-headed sons asked.

'Then spraying. If we don't have the nicotine sprays, we'll have to try the copper dusting again. I prefer the spray, but we're still behind on production. The bore has dug us up some good storage caverns, though. It ought to start picking up.'

'And here,' a son said, 'there's going to be need of draining. A lot of mosquito breeding going on. We can try the oil, as we did over here. But I suggest the whole thing be filled in. We can use the dredge and scoop, if they're not tied up.'

Sung-wu had taken this all in. Now he rose unsteadily to his feet, trembling with wrath. He pointed a shaking finger at the elder Tinker. 'You're – meddling!' he gasped.

They looked up. 'Meddling?'

'With the plan! With the cosmic plan! Good Elron – you're interfering with the divine process. Why – ' He was staggered by a realization so alien it convulsed the very core of his being. 'You're actually going to set back turns of the wheel.'

'That,' said old Ben Tinker, 'is right.'

Sung-wu sat down again, stunned. His mind refused to take it all in. 'I don't understand; what'll happen? If you slow the wheel, if you disrupt the divine plan – '

'He's going to be a problem,' Ben Tinker murmured thoughtfully. 'If we kill him, the Arm will merely send another; they have hundreds like him. And if we don't kill him, if we send him back, he'll raise a hue and cry that'll bring the whole Chamber down here. It's too soon for this to happen. We're gaining support fast, but we need another few months.'

Sweat stood out on Sung-wu's plump forehead. He wiped it away shakily. 'If you kill me,' he muttered, 'you will sink down many rungs of the cosmic ladder. You have risen this far; why undo the work accomplished in endless ages past?'

Ben Tinker fixed one powerful blue eye on him. 'My friend,' he said slowly, 'isn't it true one's next manifestation is determined by one's moral conduct in this?'

Sung-wu nodded. 'Such is well known.'

'And what is right conduct?'

'Fulfilling the divine plan,' Sung-wu responded immediately.

'Maybe our whole Movement is part of the plan,' Ben Tinker said thoughtfully. 'Maybe the cosmic forces *want* us to drain the swamps and kill the grasshoppers and inoculate the children; after all, the cosmic forces put us all here.'

'If you kill me,' Sung-wu wailed, 'I'll be a carrion-eating fly. I *saw* it, a shiny-winged, blue-rumped fly crawling over the carcass of a dead lizard – in a rotting, steaming jungle in a filthy cesspool of a planet.' Tears came; he dabbed at them futilely. 'In an out-of-the-way system, at the bottom of the ladder!'

Tinker was amused. 'Why this?'

'I've sinned.' Sung-wu sniffed and flushed. 'I committed adultery.'

'Can't you purge yourself?'

'There's no time!' His misery rose to wild despair. 'My mind is *still* impure!' He indicated Frija, standing in the bedroom doorway, a supple white and tan shape in her household shorts. 'I continue to think carnal thoughts; I can't rid myself. In eight months the plague will turn the wheel on me – and it'll be done! If I lived to be an old man, withered and toothless – no more appetite – ' His plump body quivered in a frenzied convulsion. 'There's no *time* to purge and atone. According to the scanner, I'm going to die a young man!'

After this torrent of words, Tinker was silent, deep in thought. 'The plague,' he said, at last. 'What exactly are the symptoms?'

Sung-wu described them, his olive face turning to a sickly green. When he had finished, the three men looked significantly at each other.

Ben Tinker got to his feet. 'Come along,' he commanded briskly, taking the Bard by the arm. 'I have something to show you. It is from the old days. Sooner or later we'll advance enough to turn out our own, but now we have only these remaining few. We have to keep them guarded and sealed.'

'This is for a good cause,' one of the sons said. 'It's worth it.' He caught his brother's eye and grinned.

Bard Chai finished reading Sung-wu's blue-slip report; he tossed it suspiciously down and eyed the younger Bard. 'You're sure? There's no further need of investigation?'

'The cult will wither away,' Sung-wu murmured indifferently. 'It lacks any real support; it's merely an escape valve.'

Chai wasn't convinced. He re-read parts of the report

again. 'I suppose you're right, but we've heard so
many – '

'Lies,' Sung-wu said. 'Rumours. Gossip. May I go?'

'Eager for your vacation?' Chai smiled understandingly.
'I know how you feel. This report must have exhausted
you. Rural areas, stagnant back-waters. We must prepare
a better programme of rural education. I'm convinced
whole regions are in a jangled state. We've got to bring
clearness to these people. It's our historic role; our class
function.'

'Verily,' Sung-wu murmured, as he bowed his way out.

As he walked he fingered his beads thankfully. He
breathed a silent prayer as his fingers moved over the
surface of the little red pellets, shiny spheres that glowed
freshly in place of the faded old – the gift of the Tinkerists.
The beads would come in handy; he kept his hand on
them tightly. Nothing must happen to them, in the next
eight months. He had to watch them carefully, as he poked
around the ruined cities of Spain – and finally came down
with the plague.

He was the first Bard to wear a rosary of penicillin
capsules.

Progeny

Ed Doyle hurried. He caught a surface car, waved fifty credits in the robot driver's face, mopped his florid face with a red pocket-handkerchief, unfastened his collar, perspired and licked his lips and swallowed piteously all the way to the hospital.

The surface car slid up to a smooth halt before the great white-domed hospital building. Ed leaped out and bounded up the steps three at a time, pushing through the visitors and convalescent patients standing on the broad terrace. He threw his weight against the door and emerged in the lobby, astonishing the attendants and persons of importance moving about their tasks.

'Where?' Ed demanded, gazing around, his feet wide apart, his fists clenched, his chest rising and falling. His breath came hoarsely, like an animal's. Silence fell over the lobby. Everyone turned towards him, pausing in their work. 'Where?' Ed demanded again. 'Where is she? *They?*'

It was fortunate Janet had been delivered of a child on this of all days. Proxima Centauri was a long way from Terra and the service was bad. Anticipating the birth of his child, Ed had left Proxima some weeks before. He had just arrived in the city. While stowing his suitcase in the luggage tread at the station the message had been handed to him by a robot courier: *Los Angeles Central Hospital. At once.*

Ed hurried, and fast. As he hurried he couldn't help feeling pleased he had hit the day exactly right, almost to the hour. It was a good feeling. He had felt it before, during years of business dealings in the 'colonies', the frontier, the fringe of Terran civilization where the streets were still lit by electric lights and doors opened by hand.

That was going to be hard to get used to. Ed turned towards the door behind him, feeling suddenly foolish. He had shoved it open, ignoring the eye. The door was just now closing, sliding slowly back in place. He calmed down a little, putting his handkerchief away in his coat pocket. The hospital attendants were resuming their work, picking up their activities where they had left off. One attendant, a strapping late-model robot, coasted over to Ed and halted.

The robot balanced his noteboard expertly, his photocell eyes appraising Ed's flushed features. 'May I inquire whom you are looking for, sir? Whom do you wish to find?'

'My wife.'

'Her name, sir?'

'Janet. Janet Doyle. She's just had a child.'

The robot consulted his board. 'This way, sir.' He coasted off down the passage.

Ed followed nervously. 'Is she okay? Did I get here in time?' His anxiety was returning.

'She is quite well, sir.' The robot raised his metal arm and a side door slid back. 'In here, sir.'

Janet, in a chic blue-mesh suit, was sitting before a mahogany desk, a cigarette between her fingers, her slim legs crossed, talking rapidly. On the other side of the desk a well-dressed doctor sat listening.

'Janet!' Ed said, entering the room.

'Hi, Ed.' She glanced up at him. 'You just now get in?'

'Sure. It's – it's all over? You – I mean, it's *happened*?'

Janet laughed, her even white teeth sparkling. 'Of course. Come in and sit. This is Doctor Bish.'

'Hello, Doc.' Ed sat down nervously across from them. 'Then it's all over?'

'The event has happened,' Doctor Bish said. His voice

was thin and metallic. Ed realized with a sudden shock that the doctor was a robot. A top-level robot, made in humanoid form, not like the ordinary metal-limbed workers. It had fooled him – he had been away so long. Doctor Bish appeared plump and well fed, with kindly features and eyeglasses. His large fleshy hands rested on the desk, a ring on one finger. Pinstripe suit and necktie. Diamond tie clasp. Nails carefully manicured. Hair black and evenly parted.

But his voice had given him away. They never seemed to be able to get a really human sound into the voice. The compressed air and whirling disc system seemed to fall short. Otherwise, it was very convincing.

'I understand you've been situated near Proxima, Mr Doyle,' Doctor Bish said pleasantly.

Ed nodded. 'Yeah.'

'Quite a long way, isn't it? I've never been out there. I have always wanted to go. Is it true they're almost ready to push on to Sirius?'

'Look, doc – '

'Ed, don't be impatient.' Janet stubbed out her cigarette, glancing reprovingly up at him. She hadn't changed in six months. Small blonde face, red mouth, cold eyes like little blue rocks. And now, her perfect figure back again. 'They're bringing him here. It takes a few minutes. They have to wash him off and put drops in his eyes and take a wave shot of his brain.'

'*He?* Then it's a boy?'

'Of course. Don't you remember? You were with me when I had the shots. We agreed at the time. You haven't changed your mind, have you?'

'Too late to change your mind now, Mr Doyle,' Doctor Bish's toneless voice came, high-pitched and calm. 'Your wife has decided to call him Peter.'

'Peter.' Ed nodded, a little dazed. 'That's right. We did

decide, didn't we? Peter.' He let the word roll around in his mind. 'Yeah. That's fine. I like it.'

The wall suddenly faded, turning from opaque to transparent. Ed spun quickly. They were looking into a brightly lit room, filled with hospital equipment and white-clad attendant robots. One of the robots was moving towards them, pushing a cart. On the cart was a container, a big metal pot.

Ed's breathing increased. He felt a wave of dizziness. He went up to the transparent wall and stood gazing at the metal pot on the cart.

Doctor Bish rose. 'Don't you want to see, too, Mrs Doyle?'

'Of course.' Janet crossed to the wall and stood beside Ed. She watched critically, her arms folded.

Doctor Bish made a signal. The attendant reached into the pot and lifted out a wire tray, gripping the handles with his magnetic clamps. On the tray, dripping through the wire, was Peter Doyle, still wet from his bath, his eyes wide with astonishment. He was pink all over, except for a fringe of hair on the top of his head, and his great blue eyes. He was little and wrinkled and toothless, like an ancient withered sage.

'Golly,' Ed said.

Doctor Bish made a second signal. The wall slid back. The attendant robot advanced into the room, holding his dripping tray out. Doctor Bish removed Peter from the tray and held him up for inspection. He turned him around and around, studying him from every angle.

'He looks fine,' he said at last.

'What was the result of the wave photo?' Janet asked.

'Result was good. Excellent tendencies indicated. Very promising. High development of the – ' The doctor broke off. 'What is it, Mr Doyle?'

Ed was holding out his hands. 'Let me have him, doc. I

want to hold him.' He grinned from ear to ear. 'Let's see how heavy he is. He sure looks big.'

Doctor Bish's mouth fell open in horror. He and Janet gaped.

'Ed!' Janet exclaimed sharply. 'What's the matter with you?'

'Good heavens, Mr Doyle,' the doctor murmured.

Ed blinked. 'What?'

'If I had thought you had any such thing in mind – ' Doctor Bish quickly returned Peter to the attendant. The attendant rushed Peter from the room, back to the metal pot. The cart and robot and pot hurriedly vanished, and the wall banged back in place.

Janet grabbed Ed's arm angrily. 'Good Lord, Ed! Have you lost your mind? Come on. Let's get out of here before you do something else.'

'But – '

'Come on.' Janet smiled nervously at Doctor Bish. 'We'll run along now, doctor. Thanks so much for everything. Don't pay any attention to him. He's been out there so long, you know.'

'I understand,' Doctor Bish said smoothly. He had regained his poise. 'I trust we'll hear from you later, Mrs Doyle.'

Janet pulled Ed out into the hall. 'Ed, what's the matter with you? I've never been so embarrassed in all my life.' Two spots of red glowed in Janet's cheeks. 'I could have kicked you.'

'But what – '

'You know we aren't allowed to touch him. What do you want to do, ruin his whole life?'

'But – '

'Come on.' They hurried outside the hospital, on to the terrace. Warm sunlight streamed down on them. 'There's no telling what harm you've done. He may already be hopelessly warped. If he grows up all warped and – and neurotic and emotional, it'll be your fault.'

Suddenly Ed remembered. He sagged, his features drooping with misery. 'That's right. I forgot. Only robots can come near the children. I'm sorry, Jan. I got carried away. I hope I didn't do anything they can't fix.'

'How *could* you forget?'

'It's so different out at Prox.' Ed waved to a surface car, crestfallen and abashed. The driver drew up in front of them. 'Jan, I'm sorry as hell. I really am. I was all excited. Let's go have a cup of coffee some place and talk. I want to know what the doctor said.'

Ed had a cup of coffee and Janet sipped at a brandy frappé. The Nymphite Room was pitch black except for a vague light oozing up from the table between them. The table diffused a pale illumination that spread over everything, a ghostly radiation seemingly without source. A robot waitress moved back and forth soundless with a tray of drinks. Recorded music played softly in the back of the room.

'Go on,' Ed said.

'Go on?' Janet slipped her jacket off and laid it over the back of her chair. In the pale light her breasts glowed faintly. 'There's not much to tell. Everything went all right. It didn't take long. I chatted with Doctor Bish most of the time.'

'I'm glad I got here.'

'How was your trip?'

'Fine.'

'Is the service getting any better? Does it still take as long as it did?'

'About the same.'

'I can't see why you want to go all the way out there. It's so – so cut off from things. What do you find out there? Are plumbing fixtures really that much in demand?'

'They need them. Frontier area. Everyone wants the refinements.' Ed gestured vaguely. 'What did he tell you about Peter? What's he going to be like? Can he tell? I guess it's too soon.'

'He was going to tell me when you started acting the way you did. I'll call him on the vidphone when we get home. His wave pattern should be good. He comes from the best eugenic stock.'

Ed grunted. 'On your side, at least.'

'How long are you going to be here?'

'I don't know. Not long. I'll have to go back. I'd sure like to see him again, before I go.' He glanced up hopefully at his wife. 'Do you think I can?'

'I suppose.'

'How long will he have to stay there?'

'At the hospital? Not long. A few days.'

Ed hesitated. 'I didn't mean at the hospital, exactly. I mean with *them*. How long before we can have him? How long before we can bring him home?'

There was silence. Janet finished her brandy. She leaned back, lighting a cigarette. Smoke drifted across to Ed, blending with the pale light. 'Ed, I don't think you understand. You've been out there so long. A lot has happened since you were a child. New methods, new techniques. They've found so many things they didn't know. They're making progress, for the first time. They know what to do. They're developing a real methodology for dealing with children. For the growth period. Attitude development. Training.' She smiled brightly at Ed. 'I've been reading all about it.'

'How long before we get him?'

'In a few days he'll be released from the hospital. He'll go to a child guidance centre. He'll be tested and studied. They'll determine his various capacities and his latent abilities. The direction his development seems to be taking.'

'And then?'

'Then he's put in the proper educational division. So he'll get the right training. Ed, you know, I think he's really going to be something! I could tell by the way Doctor Bish looked. He was studying the wave pattern charts when I came in. He had a look on his face. How can I describe it?' She searched for the word. 'Well, almost – almost a greedy look. Real excitement. They take so much interest in what they're doing. He – '

'Don't say he. Say *it*.'

'Ed, really! What's got into you?'

'Nothing.' Ed glared sullenly down. 'Go on.'

'They make sure he's trained in the right direction. All the time he's there ability tests are given. Then, when he's about nine, he'll be transferred to – '

'Nine! You mean nine *years*?'

'Of course.'

'But when do we get him?'

'Ed, I thought you knew about this. Do I have to go over the whole thing?'

'My God, Jan! We can't wait nine years!' Ed jerked himself upright. 'I never heard of such a thing. Nine years? Why, he'll be half grown by then.'

'That's the point.' Janet leaned towards him, resting her bare elbow against the table. 'As long as he's growing he has to be with them. Not with us. Afterwards, when he's finished growing, when he's no longer so plastic, then we can be with him all we want.'

'Afterwards? When he's eighteen?' Ed leaped up, pushing his chair back. 'I'm going down there and get him.'

'Sit down, Ed.' Janet gazed up calmly, one supple arm thrown lightly over the back of her chair, 'Sit down and act like an adult for a change.'

'Doesn't it matter to you? Don't you care?'

'Of course I care.' Janet shrugged. 'But it's necessary. Otherwise he won't develop correctly. It's for *his* good. Not ours. He doesn't exist for us. Do you want him to have conflicts?'

Ed moved away from the table. 'I'll see you later.'

'Where are you going?'

'Just around. I can't stand this kind of place. It bothers me. I'll see you later.' Ed pushed across the room to the door. The door opened and he found himself on the shiny noonday street. Hot sunlight beat down on him. He blinked, adjusting himself to the blinding light. People streamed around him. People and noise. He moved with them.

He was dazed. He had known, of course. It was there in the back of his mind. The new developments in child care. But it had been abstract, general. Nothing to do with him. With *his* child.

He calmed himself, as he walked along. He was getting all upset for nothing. Janet was right, of course. It was for Peter's good. Peter didn't exist for them, like a dog or cat. A pet to have around the house. He was a human being, with his own life. The training was for him, not for them. It was to develop him, his abilities, his powers. He was to be moulded, realized, brought out.

Naturally, robots could do the best job. Robots could train him scientifically, according to a rational technique. Not according to emotional whim. Robots didn't get angry. Robots didn't nag and whine. They didn't spank a child or yell at him. They didn't give conflicting orders. They didn't quarrel among themselves or use the child for their own ends. And there could be no *Oedipus Complex*, with only robots around.

No complexes at all. It had been discovered long ago that neurosis could be traced to childhood training. To the way parents brought up the child. The inhibitions he was taught, the manners, the lessons, the punishments, the rewards. Neuroses, complexes, warped development, all stemmed from the subjective relationship existing between the child and the parent. If perhaps the parent could be eliminated as a factor . . .

Parents could never become objective about their children. It was always a biased, emotional projection the parent held towards the child. Inevitably, the parent's view was distorted. No parent could be a fit instructor for his child.

Robots could study the child, analyse his needs, his wants, test his abilities and interests. Robots would not try to force the child to fit a certain mould. The child would be trained along his own lines; wherever scientific study indicated his interest and need lay.

Ed came to the corner. Traffic whirred past him. He stepped absently forward.

A clang and crash. Bars dropped in front of him, stopping him. A robot safety control.

'Sir, be more careful!' the strident voice came, close by him.

'Sorry.' Ed stepped back. The control bars lifted. He waited for the lights to change. It was for Pete's own good. Robots could train him right. Later on, when he was out of growth stage, when he was not so pliant, so responsive —

'It's better for him,' Ed murmured. He said it again, half aloud. Some people glanced at him and he coloured. Of course it was better for him. No doubt about it.

Eighteen. He couldn't be with his son until he was eighteen. Practically grown up.

The lights changed. Deep in thought, Ed crossed the street with the other pedestrians, keeping carefully inside the safety lane. It was best for Peter. But eighteen years was a long time.

'A hell of a long time,' Ed murmured, frowning. 'Too damn long a time.'

Doctor 2g-Y Bish carefully studied the man standing in front of him. His relays and memory banks clicked, narrowing down the image identification, flashing a variety of comparison possibilities past the scanner.

'I recall you, sir,' Doctor Bish said at last. 'You're the man from Proxima. From the colonies. Doyle, Edwărd Doyle. Let's see. It was some time ago. It must have been – '

'Nine years ago,' Ed Doyle said grimly. 'Exactly nine years ago, practically to the day.'

Doctor Bish folded his hands. 'Sit down, Mr Doyle. What can I do for you? How is Mrs Doyle? Very engaging wife, as I recall. We had a delightful conversation during her delivery. How – '

'Doctor Bish, do you know where my son is?'

Doctor Bish considered, tapping his fingers on the desk top, the polished mahogany surface. He closed his eyes slightly, gazing off into the distance. 'Yes. Yes, I know where your son is, Mr Doyle.'

Ed Doyle relaxed. 'Fine.' He nodded, letting his breath out in relief.

'I know exactly where your son is. I placed him in the Los Angeles Biological Research Station about a year ago. He's undergoing specialized training there. Your son, Mr Doyle, has shown exceptional ability. He is, shall I say, one of the few, the very few we have found with real possibilities.'

'Can I see him?'

'See him? How do you mean?'

Doyle controlled himself with an effort. 'I think the term is clear.'

Doctor Bish rubbed his chin. His photocell brain whirred, operating at maximum velocity. Switches routed power surges, building up loads and leaping gaps rapidly, as he contemplated the man before him. 'You wish to *view* him? That's one meaning of the term. Or do you wish to talk to him? Sometimes the term is used to cover a more direct contact. It's a loose word.'

'I want to talk to him.'

'I see.' Bish slowly drew some forms from the dispenser on his desk. 'There are a few routine papers that have to be filled out first, of course. Just how long did you want to speak to him?'

Ed Doyle gazed steadily into Doctor Bish's bland face. 'I want to talk to him several hours. *Alone.*'

'Alone?'

'No robots around.'

Doctor Bish said nothing. He stroked the papers he held, creasing the edges with his nail. 'Mr Doyle,' he said carefully, 'I wonder if you're in a proper emotional state to visit your son. You have recently come in from the colonies?'

'I left Proxima three weeks ago.'

'Then you have just arrived here in Los Angeles?'

'That's right.'

'And you've come to see your son? Or have you other business?'

'I came for my son.'

'Mr Doyle, Peter is at a very critical stage. He has just recently been transferred to the Biology Station for his higher training. Up to now his training has been general. What we call the non-differentiated stage. Recently he has entered a new period. Within the last six months Peter has begun advanced work along his specific line, that of organic chemistry. He will – '

'What does Peter think about it?'

Bish frowned. 'I don't understand, sir.'

'How does *he* feel? Is it what he wants?'

'Mr Doyle, your son has the possibility of becoming one of the world's finest bio-chemists. In all the time we have worked with human beings, in their training and development, we have never come across a more alert and integrated faculty for the assimilation of data, construction of theory, formulation of material, than that which your son possesses. All tests indicate he will rapidly rise to the top of his chosen field. He is still only a child, Mr Doyle, but it is the children who must be trained.'

Doyle stood up. 'Tell me where I can find him. I'll talk to him for two hours and then the rest is up to him.'

'The rest?'

Doyle clamped his jaw shut. He shoved his hands in his pockets. His face was flushed and set, grim with determination. In the nine years he had grown much heavier, more stocky and florid. His thinning hair had turned iron-grey. His clothes were dumpy and unpressed. He looked stubborn.

Doctor Bish sighed. 'All right, Mr Doyle. Here are the papers. The law allows you to observe your boy whenever you make proper application. Since he is out of his non-differentiated stage, you may also speak to him for a period of ninety minutes.'

'Alone?'

'You can take him away from the Station grounds for that length of time.' Doctor Bish pushed the papers over to Doyle. 'Fill these out, and I'll have Peter brought here.'

He looked up steadily at the man standing before him.

'I hope you'll remember that any emotional experience at this crucial stage may do much to inhibit his

development. He has chosen his field, Mr Doyle. He must
be permitted to grow along his selected lines, unhindered
by situational blocks. Peter has been in contact with our
technical staff throughout his entire training period. He is
not accustomed to contact with other human beings. So
please be careful.'

Doyle said nothing. He grabbed up the papers and
plucked out his fountain pen.

He hardly recognized his son when the two robot
attendants brought him out of the massive concrete Station
building and deposited him a few yards from Ed's parked
surface car.

Ed pushed the door open. 'Pete!' His heart was thump-
ing heavily, painfully. He watched his son come towards
the car, frowning in the bright sunlight. It was late
afternoon, about four. A faint breeze blew across the
parking lot, rustling a few papers and bits of debris.

Peter stood slim and straight. His eyes were large, deep
brown, like Ed's. His hair was light, almost blond. More
like Janet's. He had Ed's jaw, though, the firm line, clean
and well chiselled. Ed grinned at him. Nine years it had
been. Nine years since the robot attendant had lifted the
rack up from the conveyor pot to show him the little
wrinkled baby, red as a boiled lobster.

Peter had grown. He was not a baby any longer. He was
a young boy, straight and proud, with firm features and
wide, clear eyes.

'Pete,' Ed said. 'How the hell are you?'

The boy stopped by the door of the car. He gazed at Ed
calmly. His eyes flickered, taking in the car, the robot
driver, the heavy-set man in the rumpled tweed suit
grinning nervously at him.

'Get in. Get inside.' Ed moved over. 'Come on. We have
places to go.'

The boy was looking at him again. Suddenly Ed was

conscious of his baggy suit, his unshined shoes, his grey stubbled chin. He flushed, yanking out his red pocket-handkerchief and mopping his forehead uneasily. 'I just got off the ship, Pete. From Proxima. I haven't had time to change. I'm a little dusty. Long trip.'

Peter nodded. '4.3 light years, isn't it?'

'Takes three weeks. Get in. Don't you want to get in?'

Peter slid in beside him. Ed slammed the door.

'Let's go.' The car started up. 'Drive – ' Ed peered out the window. 'Drive up there. By the hill. Out of town.' He turned to Pete. 'I hate big cities. I can't get used to them.'

'There are no large cities in the colonies, are there?' Peter murmured. 'You're unused to urban living.'

Ed settled back. His heart had begun to slow down to its normal beat. 'No, as a matter of fact it's the other way around, Pete.'

'How do you mean?'

'I went to Prox *because* I couldn't stand cities.'

Peter said nothing. The surface car was climbing, going up a steel highway into the hills. The Station, huge and impressive, spread out like a heap of cement bricks directly below them. A few cars moved along the road, but not many. Most transportation was by air, now. Surface cars had begun to disappear.

The road levelled off. They moved along the ridge of the hills. Trees and bushes rose on both sides of them. 'It's nice up here,' Ed said.

'Yes.'

'How – how have you been? I haven't seen you for a long time. Just once. Just after you were born.'

'I know. Your visit is listed in the records.'

'You been getting along all right?'

'Yes. Quite well.'

'They treating you all right?'

'Of course.'

After a while Ed leaned forward. 'Stop here,' he said to the robot driver.

The car slowed down, pulling over to the side of the road. 'Sir, there is nothing – '

'This is fine. Let us out. We'll walk from here.'

The car stopped. The door slid reluctantly open. Ed stepped quickly out of the car, on to the pavement. Peter got out slowly after him, puzzled. 'Where are we?'

'No place.' Ed slammed the door. 'Go on back to town,' he said to the driver. 'We won't need you.'

The car drove off. Ed walked to the side of the road. Peter came after him. The hill dropped away, falling down to the beginnings of the city below. A vast panorama stretched out, the great metropolis in the late afternoon sun. Ed took a deep breath, throwing his arms out. He took off his coat and tossed it over his shoulder.

'Come on.' He started down the hillside. 'Here we go.'

'Where?'

'For a walk. Let's get off this damn road.'

They climbed down the side of the hill, walking carefully, holding on to the grass and roots jutting out from the soil. Finally they came to a level place by a big sycamore tree. Ed threw himself down on the ground, grunting and wiping sweat from his neck.

'Here. Let's sit here.'

Peter sat down carefully, a little way off. Ed's blue shirt was stained with sweat. He unfastened his tie and loosened his collar. Presently he searched through his coat pockets. He brought out his pipe and tobacco.

Peter watched him fill the pipe and light it with a big sulphur match. 'What's that?' he murmured.

'This? My pipe.' Ed grinned, sucking at the pipe. 'Haven't you ever seen a pipe?'

'No.'

'This is a good pipe. I got this when I first went out to

Proxima. That was a long time ago, Pete. It was twenty-five years ago. I was just nineteen, then. Only about twice as old as you.'

He put his tobacco away and leaned back, his heavy face serious, preoccupied.

'Just nineteen. I went out there as a plumber. Repair and sales, when I could make a sale. Terran Plumbing. One of those big ads you used to see. Unlimited opportunities. Virgin lands. Make a million. Gold in the streets.' Ed laughed.

'How did you make out?'

'Not bad. Not bad at all. I own my own line, now, you know. I service the whole Proxima system. We do repairing, maintenance, building, construction. I've got six hundred people working for me. It took a long time. It didn't come easy.'

'No.'

'Hungry?'

Peter turned. 'What?'

'Are you hungry?' Ed pulled a brown paper parcel from his coat and unwrapped it. 'I still have a couple of sandwiches from the trip. When I come in from Prox I bring some food along with me. I don't like to buy in the diner. They skin you.' He held out the parcel. 'Want one?'

'No, thank you.'

Ed took a sandwich and began to eat. He ate nervously, glancing at his son. Peter sat silently, a short distance off, staring ahead without expression. His smooth handsome face was blank.

'Everything all right?' Ed said.

'Yes.'

'You're not cold, are you?'

'No.'

'You don't want to catch cold.'

A squirrel crossed in front of them, hurrying towards

the sycamore tree. Ed threw it a piece of his sandwich. The squirrel ran off a way, then came back slowly. It scolded at them, standing up on its hind feet, its great grey tail flowing out behind it.

Ed laughed. 'Look at him. Ever see a squirrel before?'

'I don't think so.'

The squirrel ran off with the piece of sandwich. It disappeared among the brush and bushes.

'Squirrels don't exist out around Prox,' Ed said.

'No.'

'It's good to come back to Terra once in a while. See some of the old things. They're going, though.'

'Going?'

'Away. Destroyed. Terra is always changing.' Ed waved around at the hillside. 'This will be gone, some day. They'll cut down the trees. Then they'll level it. Some day they'll carve the whole range up and carry it off. Use it for fill, some place along the coast.'

'That's beyond our scope,' Peter said.

'What?'

'I don't receive that type of material. I think Doctor Bish told you. I'm working with bio-chemistry.'

'I know,' Ed murmured. 'Say, how the hell did you ever get mixed up with that stuff? Bio-chemistry?'

'The tests showed that my abilities lie along those lines.'

'You enjoy what you're doing?'

'What a strange thing to ask. Of course I enjoy what I'm doing. It's the work I'm fitted for.'

'It seems funny as hell to me, starting a nine-year-old kid off on something like that.'

'Why?'

'My God, Pete. When I was nine I was bumming around town. In school sometimes, outside mostly, wandering here and there. Playing. Reading. Sneaking into the rocket launching yards all the time.' He considered. 'Doing all sorts of things. When I was sixteen I hopped over to Mars. I stayed there a while. Worked as a hasher. I went on to Ganymede. Ganymede was all sewed up tight. Nothing doing there. From Ganymede I went out to Prox. Got a work-away all the way out. Big freighter.'

'You stayed at Proxima?'

'I sure did. I found what I wanted. Nice place, out there. Now we're starting on to Sirius, you know.' Ed's chest swelled. 'I've got an outlet in the Sirius system. Little retail and service place.'

'Sirius is 8.8 light years from Sol.'

'It's a long way. Seven weeks from here. Rough grind. Meteor swarms. Keeps things hot all the way out.'

'I can imagine.'

'You know what I thought I might do?' Ed turned towards his son, his face alive with hope and enthusiasm. 'I've been thinking it over. I thought maybe I'd go out there. To Sirius. It's a fine little place we have. I drew up the plans myself. Special design to fit with the characteristics of the system.'

Peter nodded.

'Pete – '

'Yes?'

'Do you think maybe you'd be interested? Like to hop out to Sirius and take a look? It's a good place. Four clean planets. Never touched. Lots of room. Miles and miles of room. Cliffs and mountains. Oceans. Nobody around. Just a few colonists, families, some construction. Wide, level plains.'

'How do you mean, interested?'

'In going all the way out.' Ed's face was pale. His mouth twitched nervously. 'I thought maybe you'd like to come along and see how things are. It's a lot like Prox was, twenty-five years ago. It's good and clean out there. No cities.'

Peter smiled.

'Why are you smiling?'

'No reason.' Peter stood up abruptly. 'If we have to walk back to the Station we better start. Don't you think? It's getting late.'

'Sure.' Ed struggled to his feet. 'Sure, but – '

'When are you going to be back in the Sol system again?'

'Back?' Ed followed after his son. Peter climbed up the hill towards the road. 'Slow down, will you?'

Peter slowed down. Ed caught up with him.

'I don't know when I'll be back. I don't come here very often. No ties. Not since Jan and I separated. As a matter of fact I came here this time to – '

'This way.' Peter started down the road.

Ed hurried along beside him, fastening his tie and putting his coat on, gasping for breath. 'Pete, what do you say? You want to hop out to Sirius with me? Take a look? It's a nice place out there. We could work together. The two of us. If you want.'

'But I already have my work.'

'That stuff? That damn chemistry stuff?'

Peter smiled again.

Ed scowled, his face dark red. 'Why are you smiling?' he demanded. His son did not answer. 'What's the matter? What's so damn funny?'

'Nothing,' Peter said. 'Don't become excited. We have a long walk down.' He increased his pace slightly, his supple body swinging in long, even strides. 'It's getting late. We have to hurry.'

Doctor Bish examined his wrist watch, pushing back his pinstriped coat sleeve. 'I'm glad you're back.'

'He sent the surface car away,' Peter murmured. 'We had to walk down the hill on foot.'

It was dark outside. The Station lights were coming

on automatically, along the rows of buildings and laboratories.

Doctor Bish rose from his desk. 'Sign this, Peter. Bottom of this form.'

Peter signed. 'What is it?'

'Certifies you saw him in accord with the provisions of the law. We didn't try to obstruct you in any way.'

Peter handed the paper back. Bish filed it away with the others. Peter moved towards the door of the doctor's office. 'I'll go. Down to the cafeteria for dinner.'

'You haven't eaten?'

'No.'

Doctor Bish folded his arms, studying the boy. 'Well?' he said. 'What do you think of him? This is the first time you've seen your father. It must have been strange for you. You've been around us so much, in all your training and work.'

'It was – unusual.'

'Did you gain any impressions? Was there anything you particularly noticed?'

'He was very emotional. There was a distinct bias through everything he said and did. A distortion present, virtually uniform.'

'Anything else?'

Peter hesitated, lingering at the door. He broke into a smile. 'One other thing.'

'What was it?'

'I noticed – ' Peter laughed. 'I noticed a distinct odour about him. A constant pungent smell, all the time I was with him.'

'I'm afraid that's true of all of them,' Doctor Bish said. 'Certain skin glands. Waste products thrown off from the blood. You'll get used to it, after you've been around them more.'

'Do I have to be around them?'

'They're your own race. How else can you work with them? Your whole training is designed with that in mind. When we've taught you all we can, then you will – '

'It reminded me of something. The pungent odour. I kept thinking about it, all the time I was with him. Trying to place it.'

'Can you identify it now?'

Peter reflected. He thought hard, concentrating deeply. His small face wrinkled up. Doctor Bish waited patiently by his desk, his arms folded. The automatic heating system clicked on for the night, warming the room with a soft glow that drifted gently around them.

'I know!' Peter exclaimed suddenly.

'What was it?'

'The animals in the biology labs. It was the same smell. The same smell as the experimental animals.'

They glanced at each other, the robot doctor and the promising young boy. Both of them smiled, a secret, private smile. A smile of complete understanding.

'I believe I know what you mean,' Doctor Bish said. 'In fact, I know *exactly* what you mean.'

Upon the Dull Earth

Silvia ran laughing through the night brightness, between the roses and cosmos and Shasta daisies, down the gravel paths and beyond the heaps of sweet-tasting grass swept from the lawns. Stars, caught in pools of water, glittered everywhere, as she brushed through them to the slope beyond the brick wall. Cedars supported the sky and ignored the slim shape squeezing past, her brown hair flying, her eyes flashing.

'Wait for me,' Rick complained, as he cautiously threaded his way after her, along the half familiar path. Silvia danced on without stopping. 'Slow down!' he shouted angrily.

'Can't – we're late.' Without warning, Silvia appeared in front of him, blocking the path. 'Empty your pockets,' she gasped, her grey eyes sparkling. 'Throw away all metal. You know they can't stand metal.'

Rick searched his pockets. In his overcoat were two dimes and a fifty-cent piece. 'Do these count?'

'*Yes!*' Silvia snatched the coins and threw them into the dark heaps of calla lilies. The bits of metal hissed into the moist depths and were gone. 'Anything else?' She caught hold of his arm anxiously. 'They're already on their way. Anything else, Rick?'

'Just my watch.' Rick pulled his wrist away as Silvia's wild fingers snatched for the watch. '*That's* not going in the bushes.'

'Then lay it on the sundial – or the wall. Or in a hollow tree.' Silvia raced off again. Her excited, rapturous voice danced back to him. 'Throw away your cigarette case. And your keys, your belt buckle – everything metal. You know how they hate metal. Hurry, we're late!'

Rick followed sullenly after her. 'All right, *witch*.'

Silvia snapped at him furiously from the darkness. 'Don't *say* that! It isn't true. You've been listening to my sisters and my mother and – '

Her words were drowned out by the sound. Distant flapping, a long way off, like vast leaves rustling in a winter storm. The night sky was alive with the frantic poundings; they were coming very quickly this time. They were too greedy, too desperately eager to wait. Flickers of fear touched the man and he ran to catch up with Silvia.

Silvia was a tiny column of green skirt and blouse in the centre of the thrashing mass. She was pushing them away with one arm and trying to manage the faucet with the other. The churning activity of wings and bodies twisted her like a reed. For a time she was lost from sight.

'Rick!' she called faintly. 'Come here and help!' She pushed them away and struggled up. 'They're suffocating me!'

Rick fought his way through the wall of flashing white to the edge of the trough. They were drinking greedily at the blood that spilled from the wooden faucet. He pulled Silvia close against him; she was terrified and trembling. He held her tight until some of the violence and fury around them had died down.

'They're hungry,' Silvia gasped feebly.

'You're a little cretin for coming ahead. They can sear you to ash!'

'I know. They can do anything.' She shuddered, excited and frightened. 'Look at them,' she whispered, her voice husky with awe. 'Look at the size of them – their wing-spread. And they're *white*, Rick. Spotless – perfect. There's nothing in our world as spotless as that. Great and clean and wonderful.'

'They certainly wanted the lamb's blood.'

Silvia's soft hair blew against his face as the wings fluttered on all sides. They were leaving now, roaring up into the sky. Not up, really — away. Back to their own world, whence they had scented the blood. But it was not only the blood — they had come because of Silvia. *She* had attracted them.

The girl's grey eyes were wide. She reached up towards the rising white creatures. One of them swooped close. Grass and flowers sizzled as blinding white flames roared in a brief fountain. Rick scrambled away. The flaming figure hovered momentarily over Silvia and then there was a hollow *pop*. The last of the white-winged giants was gone. The air, the ground, gradually cooled into darkness and silence.

'I'm sorry,' Silvia whispered.

'Don't do it again,' Rick managed. He was numb with shock. 'It isn't safe.'

'Sometimes I forget. I'm sorry, Rick. I didn't mean to draw them so close.' She tried to smile. 'I haven't been that careless in months. Not since that other time when I first brought you out here.' The avid, wild look slid across her face. 'Did you *see* him? Power and flames! And he didn't even touch us. He just — looked at us. That was all. And everything's burned up, all around.'

Rick grabbed hold of her. 'Listen,' he grated. 'You mustn't call them again. It's wrong. This isn't their world.'

'It's not wrong — it's beautiful.'

'It's not safe!' His fingers dug into her flesh until she gasped. 'Stop tempting them down here!'

Silvia laughed hysterically. She pulled away from him, out into the blasted circle that the horde of angels had seared behind them as they rose into the sky. 'I can't *help* it,' she cried. 'I belong with them. They're my family, my people. Generations of them, back into the past.'

'What do you mean?'

'They're my ancestors. And some day I'll join them.'

'You're a little witch!' Rick shouted furiously.

'No,' Silvia answered. 'Not a witch, Rick. Don't you see? I'm a saint.'

The kitchen was warm and bright. Silvia plugged in the Silex and got a big red can of coffee down from the cupboards over the sink. 'You mustn't listen to them,' she said, as she set out plates and cups and got cream from the refrigerator. 'You know they don't understand. Look at them in there.'

Silvia's mother and her sisters, Betty Lou and Jean, stood huddled together in the living-room, fearful and alert, watching the young couple in the kitchen. Walter Everett was standing by the fireplace, his face blank, remote.

'Listen to *me*,' Rick said. 'You have this power to attract them. You mean you're not — isn't Walter your real father?'

'Oh, yes — of course he is. I'm completely human. Don't I look human?'

'But you're the only one who has the power.'

'I'm not physically different,' Silvia said thoughtfully. 'I have the ability to see, that's all. Others have had it before me — saints, martyrs. When I was a child, my mother read to me about St Bernadette. Remember where her cave was? Near a hospital. They were hovering there and she saw one of them.'

'But the blood! It's grotesque. There never was anything like that.'

'Oh, yes. The blood draws them, lamb's blood especially. They hover over battlefields. Valkyries — carrying off the dead to Valhalla. That's why saints and martyrs cut and mutilate themselves. You know where I got the idea?'

Silvia fastened a little apron around her waist and filled the Silex with coffee. 'When I was nine years old, I read of it in Homer, in the Odyssey. Ulysses dug a trench in the ground and filled it with blood to attract the spirits. The shades from the nether world.'

'That's right,' Rick admitted reluctantly. 'I remember.'

'The ghosts of people who died. They had lived once. Everybody lives here, then dies and goes there.' Her face glowed. 'We're all going to have wings! We're all going to fly. We'll all be filled with fire and power. We won't be worms any more.'

'Worms! That's what you always call me.'

'Of course you're a worm. We're all worms – grubby worms creeping over the crust of the Earth, through dust and dirt.'

'Why should blood bring them?'

'Because it's life and they're attracted by life. Blood is *uisge beatha* – the water of life.'

'Blood means death! A trough of spilled blood . . .'

'It's *not* death. When you see a caterpillar crawl into its cocoon, do you think it's dying?'

Walter Everett was standing in the doorway. He stood listening to his daughter, his face dark. 'One day,' he said hoarsely, 'they're going to grab her and carry her off. She wants to go with them. She's waiting for that day.'

'You see?' Silvia said to Rick. 'He doesn't understand either.' She shut off the Silex and poured coffee. 'Coffee for you?' she asked her father.

'No,' Everett said.

'Silvia,' Rick said, as if speaking to a child, 'if you went away with them, you know you couldn't come back to us.'

'We all have to cross sooner or later. It's all part of our life.'

'But you're only nineteen,' Rick pleaded. 'You're young and healthy and beautiful. And our marriage – what about our marriage?' He half rose from the table. 'Silvia, you've got to stop this!'

'I *can't* stop it. I was seven when I saw them first.' Silvia stood by the sink, gripping the Silex, a faraway look in her eyes. 'Remember, Daddy? We were living back in Chicago. It was winter. I fell, walking home from school.' She held up a slim arm. 'See the scar? I fell and cut myself on the gravel and slush. I came home crying – it was sleeting and the wind was howling around me. My arm was bleeding and my mitten was soaked with blood. And then I looked up and saw them.'

There was silence.

'They want you,' Everett said wretchedly. 'They're flies – bluebottles, hovering around, waiting for you. Calling you to come along with them.'

'Why not?' Silvia's grey eyes were shining and her cheeks radiated joy and anticipation. 'You've seen them, Daddy. You know what it means. Transfiguration – from clay into gods!'

Rick left the kitchen. In the living-room the two sisters stood together, curious and uneasy. Mrs Everett stood by herself, her face granite-hard, eyes bleak behind her steel-rimmed glasses. She turned away as Rick passed them.

'What happened out there?' Betty Lou asked him in a taut whisper. She was fifteen, skinny and plain, hollow cheeked, with mousy, sand-coloured hair. 'Silvia never lets us come out with her.'

'Nothing happened,' Rick answered.

Anger stirred the girl's barren face. 'That's not true. You were both out in the garden, in the dark, and – '

'Don't talk to him!' her mother snapped. She yanked the two girls away and shot Rick a glare of hatred and misery. Then she turned quickly from him.

* * *

Rick opened the door to the basement and switched on the light. He descended slowly into the cold, damp room of concrete and dirt, with its unwinking yellow light hanging from dust-covered wires overhead.

In one corner loomed the big floor furnace with its mammoth hot air pipes. Beside it stood the water heater and discarded bundles, boxes of books, newspapers and old furniture, thick with dust, encrusted with strings of spider webs.

At the far end were the washing machine and spin dryer. And Silvia's pump and refrigeration system.

From the work bench Rick selected a hammer and two heavy pipe wrenches. He was moving towards the elaborate tanks and pipes when Silvia appeared abruptly at the top of the stairs, her coffee cup in one hand.

She hurried quickly down to him. 'What are you doing down here?' she asked, studying him intently. 'Why that hammer and those two wrenches?'

Rick dropped the tools back on to the bench. 'I thought maybe this could be solved on the spot.'

Silvia moved between him and the tanks. 'I thought you understood. They've always been a part of my life. When I brought you with me the first time, you seemed to see what – '

'I don't want to lose you,' Rick said harshly, 'to anybody or anything – in this world or any other. *I'm not going to give you up.*'

'It's not giving me up!' Her eyes narrowed. 'You came down here to destroy and break everything. The moment I'm not looking you'll smash all this, won't you?'

'That's right.'

Fear replaced anger on the girl's face. 'Do you want me to be chained here? I have to go on – I'm through with this part of the journey. I've stayed here long enough.'

'Can't you wait?' Rick demanded furiously. He couldn't

keep the ragged edge of despair out of his voice. 'Doesn't it come soon enough anyhow?'

Silvia shrugged and turned away, her arms folded, her red lips tight together. 'You want to be a worm always. A fuzzy, little creeping caterpillar.'

'I want *you*.'

'You can't *have* me!' She whirled angrily. 'I don't have any time to waste with this.'

'You have higher things in mind,' Rick said savagely.

'Of course.' She softened a little. 'I'm sorry, Rick. Remember Icarus? You want to fly, too. I know it.'

'In my time.'

'Why not now? Why wait? You're afraid.' She slid lightly away from him, cunning twisting her red lips. 'Rick, I want to show you something. Promise me first – you won't tell anybody.'

'What is it?'

'Promise?' She put her hand to his mouth. 'I have to be careful. It cost a lot of money. Nobody knows about it. It's what they do in China – everything goes towards it.'

'I'm curious,' Rick said. Uneasiness flicked at him. 'Show it to me.'

Trembling with excitement, Silvia disappeared behind the huge lumbering refrigerator, back into the darkness behind the web of frost-hard freezing coils. He could hear her tugging and pulling at something. Scraping sounds, sounds of something large being dragged out.

'See?' Silvia gasped. 'Give me a hand, Rick. It's heavy. Hardwood and brass – and metal lined. It's hand-stained and polished. And that carving – see the carving! Isn't it beautiful?'

'What is it?' Rick demanded huskily.

'It's my cocoon,' Silvia said simply. She settled down in a contented heap on the floor, and rested her head happily against the polished oak coffin.

Rick grabbed her by the arm and dragged her to her feet. 'You can't sit with that coffin, down here in the basement with – ' He broke off. 'What's the matter?'

Silvia's face was twisting with pain. She backed away from him and put her finger quickly to her mouth. 'I cut myself – when you pulled me up – on a nail or something.' A thin trickle of blood oozed down her fingers. She groped in her pocket for a handkerchief.

'Let me see it.' He moved towards her, but she avoided him. 'Is it bad?' he demanded.

'Stay away from me,' Silvia whispered.

'What's wrong? Let me see it!'

'Rick,' Silvia said in a low intense voice, 'get some water and adhesive tape. As quickly as possible.' She was trying to keep down her rising terror. 'I have to stop the bleeding.'

'Upstairs?' He moved awkwardly away. 'It doesn't look too bad. Why don't you . . .'

'Hurry.' The girl's voice was suddenly bleak with fear. 'Rick, *hurry*!'

Confused, he ran a few steps.

Silvia's terror poured after him. 'No, it's too late,' she called thinly. 'Don't come back – keep away from me. It's my own fault. I trained them to come. *Keep away!* I'm sorry, Rick. *Oh* – ' Her voice was lost to him, as the wall of the basement burst and shattered. A cloud of luminous white forced its way through and blazed out into the basement.

It was Silvia they were after. She ran a few hesitant steps towards Rick, halted uncertainly, then the white mass of bodies and wings settled around her. She shrieked once. Then a violent explosion blasted the basement into a shimmering dance of furnace heat.

He was thrown to the floor. The cement was hot and dry – the whole basement crackled with heat. Windows shattered as pulsing white shapes pushed out again. Smoke and flames licked up the walls. The ceiling sagged and rained plaster down.

Rick struggled to his feet. The furious activity was dying away. The basement was a littered chaos. All surfaces were scorched black, seared and crusted with smoking ash. Splintered wood, torn cloth and broken concrete were strewn everywhere. The furnace and washing machine were in ruins. The elaborate pumping and refrigeration system – now a glittering mass of slag. One whole wall had been twisted aside. Plaster was rubbled over everything.

Silvia was a twisted heap, arms and legs doubled grotesquely. Shrivelled, carbonized remains of fire-scorched ash, settling in a vague mound. What had been left behind were charred fragments, a brittle burned-out husk.

It was a dark night, cold and intense. A few stars glittered like ice from above his head. A faint, dank wind stirred through the dripping calla lilies and whipped gravel up in a frigid mist along the path between the black roses.

He crouched for a long time, listening and watching. Behind the cedars, the big house loomed against the sky. At the bottom of the slope a few cars slithered along the highway. Otherwise, there was no sound. Ahead of him jutted the squat outline of the porcelain trough and the pipe that had carried blood from the refrigerator in the basement. The trough was empty and dry, except for a few leaves that had fallen in it.

Rick took a deep breath of thin night air and held it. Then he got stiffly to his feet. He scanned the sky, but saw no movement. They were there, though, watching and waiting – dim shadows, echoing into the legendary past, a line of god-figures.

He picked up the heavy gallon drums, dragged them to the trough and poured blood from a New Jersey abattoir, cheap-grade steer refuse, thick and clotted. It splashed against his clothes and he backed away nervously. But nothing stirred in the air above. The garden was silent, drenched with night fog and darkness.

He stood beside the trough, waiting and wondering if they were coming. They had come for Silvia, not merely for the blood. Without her there was no attraction but the raw food. He carried the empty metal cans over to the bushes and kicked them down the slope. He searched his pockets carefully, to make sure there was no metal on him.

Over the years, Silvia had nourished their habit of coming. Now she was on the other side. Did that mean they wouldn't come? Somewhere in the damp bushes something rustled. An animal or a bird?

In the trough the blood glistened, heavy and dull, like old lead. It was their time to come, but nothing stirred the great trees above. He picked out the rows of nodding black roses, the gravel path down which he and Silvia had run – violently he shut out the recent memory of her flashing eyes and deep red lips. The highway beyond the slope – the empty, deserted garden – the silent house in which her family huddled and waited. After a time, there was a dull, swishing sound. He tensed, but it was only a diesel truck lumbering along the highway, headlights blazing.

He stood grimly, his feet apart, his heels dug into the soft black ground. He wasn't leaving. He was staying there until they came. He wanted her back – at any cost.

Overhead, foggy webs of moisture drifted across the Moon. The sky was a vast barren plain, without life or warmth. The deathly cold of deep space, away from suns and living things. He gazed up until his neck ached. Cold stars, sliding in and out of the matted layer of fog. Was there anything else? Didn't they want to come, or weren't they interested in him? It had been Silvia who had interested them – now they had her.

Behind him there was a movement without sound. He sensed it and started to turn, but suddenly, on all sides, the trees and undergrowth shifted. Like cardboard props they wavered and ran together, blending dully in the night shadows. Something moved through them, rapidly, silently, then was gone.

They had come. He could feel them. They had shut off their power and flame. Cold, indifferent statues, rising among the trees, dwarfing the cedars – remote from him and his world, attracted by curiosity and mild habit.

'Silvia,' he said clearly. 'Which are you?'

There was no response. Perhaps she wasn't among them. He felt foolish. A vague flicker of white drifted past the trough, hovered momentarily and then went on without stopping. The air above the trough vibrated, then died into immobility, as another giant inspected briefly and withdrew.

Panic breathed through him. They were leaving again, receding back into their own world. The trough had been rejected; they weren't interested.

'Wait,' he muttered thickly.

Some of the white shadows lingered. He approached them slowly, wary of their flickering immensity. If one of them touched him, he would sizzle briefly and puff into a dark heap of ash. A few feet away he halted.

'You know what I want,' he said. 'I want her back. She shouldn't have been taken yet.'

Silence.

'You were too greedy,' he said. 'You did the wrong thing. She was going to come over to you, eventually. She had it all worked out.'

The dark fog rustled. Among the trees the flickering shapes stirred and pulsed responsive to his voice. '*True*,' came a detached, impersonal sound. The sound drifted around him, from tree to tree, without location or direction. It was swept off by the night wind to die into dim echoes.

Relief settled over him. They had passed — they were aware of him — listening to what he had to say.

'You think it's right?' he demanded. 'She had a long life here. We were going to marry, have children.'

There was no answer. But he was conscious of a growing tension. He listened intently, but he couldn't make out anything. Presently he realized a struggle was taking place, a conflict among them. The tension grew — more shapes flickered — the clouds, the icy stars, were obscured by the vast presence, swelling around him.

'Rick!' A voice spoke close by. Wavering, drifting back into dim regions of the trees and dripping plants. He could hardly hear it — the words were gone as soon as they were spoken. 'Rick — help me get back.'

'Where are you?' He couldn't locate her. 'What can I do?'

'I don't know.' Her voice was wild with bewilderment and pain. 'I don't understand. Something went wrong. They must have thought I — wanted to come right away. I *didn't*!'

'I know,' Rick said. 'It was an accident.'

'They were waiting. The cocoon, the trough — but it was too soon.' Her terror came across to him, from the vague distances of another universe. 'Rick, I've changed my mind. I want to come back.'

'It's not as simple as that.'

'I know. Rick, time is different on this side. I've been gone so long — your world seems to creep along. It's been years, hasn't it?'

'One week,' Rick said.

'It was their fault. You don't blame me, do you? They know they did the wrong thing. Those who did it have been punished, but that doesn't help me.' Misery and panic distorted her voice so he could hardly understand her. 'How can I come back?'

'Don't they know?'

'They say it can't be done.' Her voice trembled. 'They say they destroyed the clay part – it was incinerated. There's nothing for me to go back to.'

Rick took a deep breath. 'Make them find some other way. It's up to them. Don't they have the power? They took you over too soon – they must send you back. It's *their* responsibility.'

The white shapes shifted uneasily. The conflict rose sharply; they couldn't agree. Rick warily moved back a few paces.

'They say it's dangerous.' Silvia's voice came from no particular spot. 'They say it was attempted once.' She tried to control her voice. 'The nexus between this world and yours is unstable. There are vast amounts of free-floating energy. The power we – on this side – have isn't really our own. It's a universal energy, tapped and controlled.'

'Why can't they . . .'

'This is a higher continuum. There's a natural process of energy from lower to higher regions. But the reverse process is risky. The blood – it's a sort of guide to follow – a bright marker.'

'Like moths around a light bulb,' Rick said bitterly.

'If they send me back and something went wrong – ' She broke off and then continued, 'If they make a mistake I might be lost between the two regions. I might be absorbed by the free energy. It seems to be partly alive. It's not understood. Remember Prometheus and the fire . . .'

'I see,' Rick said, as calmly as he could.

'Darling, if they try to send me back, I'll have to find some shape to enter. You see, I don't exactly have a shape any more. There's no real material form on this side. What you see, the wings and the whiteness, are not really there. If I succeeded to make the trip back to your side . . .'

'You'd have to mould something,' Rick said.

'I'd have to take something there — something of clay. I'd have to enter it and reshape it. As He did a long time ago, when the original form was put on your world.'

'If they did it once, they can do it again.'

'The One who did that is gone. He passed on upward.' There was unhappy irony in her voice. 'There are regions beyond this. The ladder doesn't stop here. Nobody knows where it ends, it just seems to keep on going up and up. World after world.'

'Who decides about you?' Rick demanded.

'It's up to me,' Silvia said faintly. 'They say, if I want to take the chance, they'll try it.'

'What do you think you'll do?' he asked.

'I'm afraid. What if something goes wrong? You haven't seen it, the region between. The possibilities there are incredible — they terrify me. He was the only one with enough courage. Everyone else has been afraid.'

'It was their fault. They have to take the responsibility.'

'They know that.' Silvia hesitated miserably. 'Rick, darling, please tell me what to do.'

'Come back!'

Silence. Then her voice, thin and pathetic. 'All right, Rick. If you think that's the right thing.'

'It is,' he said firmly. He forced his mind not to think, not to picture or imagine anything. *He had to have her back*. 'Tell them to get started now. Tell them — '

A deafening crack of heat burst in front of him. He was lifted and tossed into a flaming sea of pure energy. They were leaving and the scalding lake of sheer power bellowed and thundered around him. For a split second he thought he glimpsed Silvia, her hands reaching imploringly towards him.

Then the fire cooled and he lay blinded in dripping, night-moistened darkness. Alone in the silence.

Walter Everett was helping him up. 'You damn fool!' he was saying, again and again. 'You shouldn't have brought them back. They've got enough from us.'

Then he was in the big, warm living-room. Mrs Everett stood silently in front of him, her face hard and expressionless. The two daughters hovered anxiously around him, fluttering and curious, eyes wide with morbid fascination.

'I'll be all right,' Rick muttered. His clothing was charred and blackened. He rubbed black ash from his face. Bits of dried grass stuck to his hair – they had seared a circle around him as they'd ascended. He lay back against the couch and closed his eyes. When he opened them, Betty Lou Everett was forcing a glass of water into his hand.

'Thanks,' he muttered.

'You should never have gone out there,' Walter Everett repeated. 'Why? Why'd you do it? You know what happened to her. You want the same thing to happen to you?'

'I want her back,' Rick said quietly.

'Are you mad? You can't get her back. She's gone.' His lips twitched convulsively. 'You saw her.'

Betty Lou was gazing at Rick intently. 'What happened out there?' she demanded. 'They came again, didn't they?'

Rick got heavily to his feet and left the living-room. In the kitchen he emptied the water in the sink and poured himself a drink. While he was leaning wearily against the sink, Betty Lou appeared in the doorway.

'What do you want?' Rick demanded.

The girl's thin face was flushed an unhealthy red. 'I know something happened out there. You were feeding them, weren't you?' She advanced towards him. 'You're trying to get her back?'

'That's right,' Rick said.

Betty Lou giggled nervously. 'But you can't. She's dead

– her body's been cremated – I saw it.' Her face worked excitedly. 'Daddy always said that something bad would happen to her, and it did.' She leaned close to Rick. 'She was a witch! She got what she deserved!'

'She's coming back,' Rick said.

'*No!*' Panic stirred the girl's drab features. 'She *can't* come back. She's dead – like she always said – worm into butterfly – she's a butterfly!'

'Go inside,' Rick said.

'You can't order me around,' Betty Lou answered. Her voice rose hysterically. 'This is *my* house. We don't want you around here any more. Daddy's going to tell you. He doesn't want you and I don't want you and my mother and sister . . .'

The change came without warning. Like a film gone dead. Betty Lou froze, her mouth half open, one arm raised, her words dead on her tongue. She was suspended, an instantly lifeless thing raised slightly off the floor, as if caught between two slides of glass. A vacant insect, without speech or sound, inert and hollow. Not dead, but abruptly thinned back to primordial inanimacy.

Into the captured shell filtered new potency and being. It settled over her, a rainbow of life that poured into place eagerly – like hot fluid – into every part of her. The girl stumbled and moaned; her body jerked violently and pitched against the wall. A china teacup tumbled from an overhead shelf and smashed on the floor. The girl retreated numbly, one hand to her mouth, her eyes wide with pain and shock.

'Oh!' she gasped. 'I cut myself.' She shook her head and gazed up mutely at him, appealing to him. 'On a nail or something.'

'*Silvia!*' He caught hold of her and dragged her to her feet, away from the wall. It was *her* arm he gripped, warm and full and mature. Stunned grey eyes, brown hair, quivering breasts — she was now as she had been those last moments in the basement.

'Let's see it,' he said. He tore her hand from her mouth and shakily examined her finger. There was no cut, only a thin white line rapidly dimming. 'It's all right, honey. You're all right. There's nothing wrong with you!'

'Rick, I was over *there*.' Her voice was husky and faint. 'They came and dragged me across with them.' She shuddered violently. 'Rick, am I actually *back*?'

He crushed her tight. 'Completely back.'

'It was so long. I was over there a century. Endless ages. I thought — ' Suddenly she pulled away. 'Rick . . .'

'What is it?'

Silvia's face was wild with fear. 'There's something wrong.'

'There's nothing wrong. You've come back home and that's all that matters.'

Silvia retreated from him. 'But they took a living form, didn't they? Not discarded clay. They don't have the power, Rick. They altered His work instead.' Her voice rose in panic. 'A mistake — they should have known better than to alter the balance. It's unstable and none of them can control the . . .'

Rick blocked the doorway. 'Stop talking like that!' he said fiercely. 'It's worth it — *anything's* worth it. If they set things out of balance, it's their own fault.'

'We can't turn it back!' Her voice rose shrilly, thin and hard, like drawn wire. 'We've set it in motion, started the waves lapping out. The balance He set up is *altered*.'

'Come on, darling,' Rick said. 'Let's go and sit in the living-room with your family. You'll feel better. You'll have to try to recover from this.'

They approached the three seated figures, two on the couch, one in the straight chair by the fireplace. The figures sat motionless, their faces blank, their bodies limp and waxen, dulled forms that did not respond as the couple entered the room.

Rick halted, uncomprehending. Walter Everett was slumped forward, newspaper in one hand, slippers on his feet; his pipe was still smoking in the deep ashtray on the arm of his chair. Mrs Everett sat with a lapful of sewing, her face grim and stern, but strangely vague. An unformed face, as if the material were melting and running together. Jean sat huddled in a shapeless heap, a ball of clay wadded up, more formless each moment.

Abruptly Jean collapsed. Her arms fell loose beside her. Her head sagged. Her body, her arms and legs filled out. Her features altered rapidly. Her clothing changed. Colours flowed in her hair, her eyes, her skin. The waxen pallor was gone.

Pressing her finger to her lips she gazed up at Rick mutely. She blinked and her eyes focused. 'Oh,' she gasped. Her lips moved awkwardly; the voice was faint and uneven, like a poor sound track. She struggled up jerkily, with unco-ordinated movements that propelled her stiffly to her feet and towards him – one awkward step at a time – like a wire dummy.

'Rick, I cut myself,' she said. 'On a nail or something.'

What had been Mrs Everett stirred. Shapeless and vague, it made dull sounds and flopped grotesquely. Gradually it hardened and shaped itself. 'My finger,' its voice gasped feebly. Like mirror echoes dimming off into darkness, the third figure in the easy chair took up the words. Soon, they were all of them repeating the phrase, four fingers, their lips moving in unison.

'My finger. I cut myself, Rick.'

Parrot reflections, receding mimicries of words and movement. And the settling shapes were familiar in every detail. Again and again, repeated around him, twice on the couch, in the easy chair, close beside him – so close he could hear her breathe and see her trembling lips.

'What is it?' the Silvia beside him asked.

On the couch one Silvia resumed its sewing – she was sewing methodically, absorbed in her work. In the deep chair another took up its newspapers, its pipe and continued reading. One huddled, nervous and afraid. The one beside him followed as he retreated to the door. She was panting with uncertainty, her grey eyes wide, her nostrils flaring.

'Rick . . .'

He pulled the door open and made his way out on to the dark porch. Machine-like, he felt his way down the steps, through the pools of night collected everywhere, towards the driveway. In the yellow square of light behind him, Silvia was outlined, peering unhappily after him. And behind her, the other figures, identical, pure repetitions, nodding over their tasks.

He found his coupé and pulled out on to the road.

Gloomy trees and houses flashed past. He wondered how far it would go. Lapping waves spreading out – a widening circle as the imbalance spread.

He turned on to the main highway; there were soon more cars around him. He tried to see into them, but they moved too swiftly. The car ahead was a red Plymouth. A heavy-set man in a blue business suit was driving, laughing merrily with the woman beside him. He pulled his own coupé up close behind the Plymouth and followed it. The man flashed gold teeth, grinned, waved his plump hands. The girl was dark-haired, pretty. She smiled at the man, adjusted her white gloves, smoothed down her hair, then rolled up the window on her side.

He lost the Plymouth. A heavy diesel truck cut in between them. Desperately he swerved around the truck and nosed in beyond the swift-moving red sedan. Presently it passed him and, for a moment, the two occupants were clearly framed. The girl resembled Silvia. The same delicate line of her small chin – the same deep lips, parting slightly when she smiled – the same slender arms and hands. It was Silvia. The Plymouth turned off and there was no other car ahead of him.

He drove for hours through the heavy night darkness. The gas gauge dropped lower and lower. Ahead of him dismal rolling countryside spread out, blank fields between towns and unwinking stars suspended in the bleak sky. Once, a cluster of red and yellow lights gleamed. An intersection – filling stations and a big neon sign. He drove on past it.

At a single-pump stand, he pulled the car off the highway, on to the oil-soaked gravel. He climbed out, his shoes crunching the stone underfoot, as he grabbed the gas hose and unscrewed the cap of his car's tank. He had the tank almost full when the door of the drab station building opened and a slim woman in white overalls, and navy shirt, with a little cap lost in her brown curls, stepped out.

'Good evening, Rick,' she said quietly.

He put back the gas hose. Then he was driving out on to the highway. Had he screwed the cap on again? He didn't remember. He gained speed. He had gone over a hundred miles. He was nearing the state line.

At a little roadside café, warm, yellow light glowed in the chill gloom of early morning. He slowed the car down and parked at the edge of the highway in the deserted parking lot. Bleary-eyed he pushed the door open and entered.

Hot, thick smells of cooking ham and black coffee surrounded him, the comfortable sight of people eating, a juke box blared in the corner. He threw himself on to a stool and hunched over, his head in his hands. A thin farmer next to him glanced at him curiously and then returned to his newspaper. Two hard-faced women across from him gazed at him momentarily. A handsome youth in denim jacket and jeans was eating red beans and rice, washing it down with steaming coffee from a heavy mug.

'What'll it be?' the pert blonde waitress asked, a pencil behind her ear, her hair tied back in a tight bun. 'Looks like you've got some hangover, mister.'

He ordered coffee and vegetable soup. Soon he was eating, his hands working automatically. He found himself devouring a ham and cheese sandwich; had he ordered it? The juke box blared and people came and went. There was a little town sprawled beside the road, set back in some gradual hills. Grey sunlight, cold and sterile, filtered down as morning came. He ate hot apple pie and sat wiping dully at his mouth with a paper napkin.

The café was silent. Outside nothing stirred. An uneasy calm hung over everything. The juke box had ceased. None of the people at the counter stirred or spoke. An occasional truck roared past, damp and lumbering, windows rolled up tight.

When he looked up, Silvia was standing in front of him. Her arms were folded and she gazed vacantly past him. A bright yellow pencil was behind her ear. Her brown hair was tied back in a hard bun. At the counter, others were sitting, other Silvias, dishes in front of them, half dozing or eating, some of them reading. Each the same as the next, except for their clothing.

He made his way back to his parked car. In half an hour he had crossed the state line. Cold, bright sunlight sparkled off dew-moist roofs and pavements as he sped through tiny unfamiliar towns.

Along the shiny morning streets he saw them moving – early risers, on their way to work. In twos and threes they walked, their heels echoing in sharp silence. At bus stops he saw groups of them collected together. In the houses, rising from their beds, eating breakfast, bathing, dressing, were more of them – hundreds of them, legions without number. A town of them preparing for the day, resuming their regular tasks, as the circle widened and spread.

He left the town behind. The car slowed under him as his foot slid heavily from the gas pedal. Two of them walked across a level field together. They carried books – children on their way to school. Repetitions, unvarying and identical. A dog circled excitedly after them, unconcerned, his joy untainted.

He drove on. Ahead a city loomed, its stern columns of office buildings sharply outlined against the sky. The streets swarmed with noise and activity as he passed through the main business section. Somewhere, near the centre of the city, he overtook the expanding periphery of the circle and emerged beyond. Diversity took the place of the endless figures of Silvia. Grey eyes and brown hair gave way to countless varieties of men and women, children and adults, of all ages and appearances. He increased his speed and raced out on the far side, on to the wide four-lane highway.

He finally slowed down. He was exhausted. He had driven for hours; his body was shaking with fatigue.

Ahead of him a carrot-haired youth was cheerfully thumbing a ride, a thin bean-pole in brown slacks and light camel's-hair sweater. Rick pulled to a halt and opened the front door. 'Hop in,' he said.

'Thanks, buddy.' The youth hurried to the car and climbed in as Rick gathered speed. He slammed the door and settled gratefully back against the seat. 'It was getting hot, standing there.'

'How far are you going?' Rick demanded.

'All the way to Chicago.' The youth grinned shyly. 'Of course, I don't expect you to drive me that far. Anything at all is appreciated.' He eyed Rick curiously. 'Which way you going?'

'Anywhere,' Rick said. 'I'll drive you to Chicago.'

'It's two hundred miles!'

'Fine,' Rick said. He steered over into the left lane and gained speed. 'If you want to go to New York, I'll drive you there.'

'You feel all right?' The youth moved away uneasily. 'I sure appreciate a lift, but . . .' He hesitated. 'I mean, I don't want to take you out of your way.'

Rick concentrated on the road ahead, his hands gripping hard around the rim of the wheel. 'I'm going fast. I'm not slowing down or stopping.'

'You better be careful,' the youth warned in a troubled voice. 'I don't want to get in an accident.'

'I'll do the worrying.'

'But it's dangerous. What if something happens? It's too risky.'

'You're wrong,' Rick muttered grimly, eyes on the road. 'It's worth the risk.'

'But if something goes wrong – ' The voice broke off uncertainly and then continued, 'I might be lost. It would be so easy. It's all so unstable.' The voice trembled with worry and fear. 'Rick, please . . .'

Rick whirled. 'How do you know my name?'

The youth was crouched in a heap against the door. His face had a soft, molten look, as if it were losing its shape and sliding together in an unformed mass. 'I want to come back,' he was saying, from within himself, 'but I'm afraid. You haven't seen it – the region between. It's nothing but energy, Rick. He tapped it a long time ago, but nobody else knows how.'

The voice lightened, became clear and treble. The hair faded to a rich brown. Grey, frightened eyes flickered up at Rick. Hands frozen, he hunched over the wheel and forced himself not to move. Gradually he decreased speed and brought the car over into the right-hand land.

'Are we stopping?' the shape beside him asked. It was Silvia's voice now. Like a new insect, drying in the sun, the shape hardened and locked into firm reality. Silvia struggled up on the seat and peered out. 'Where are we? We're between towns.'

He jammed on the brakes, reached past her and threw open the door. 'Get out!'

Silvia gazed at him uncomprehendingly. 'What do you mean?' she faltered. 'Rick, what is it? What's wrong?'

'*Get out!*'

'Rick, I don't understand.' She slid over a little. Her toes touched the pavement. 'Is there something wrong with the car? I thought everything was all right.'

He gently shoved her out and slammed the door. The car leaped ahead, out into the stream of mid-morning traffic. Behind him the small, dazed figure was pulling itself up, bewildered and injured. He forced his eyes from the rear-view mirror and crushed down the gas pedal with all his weight.

The radio buzzed and clicked in vague static when he snapped it briefly on. He turned the dial and, after a time, a big network station came in. A faint, puzzled voice, a woman's voice. For a time he couldn't make out the words. Then he recognized it and, with a pang of panic, switched the thing off.

Her voice. Murmuring plaintively. Where was the station? Chicago. The circle had already spread that far.

He slowed down. There was no point hurrying. It had already passed him by and gone on. Kansas farms – sagging stores in little old Mississippi towns – along the bleak streets of New England manufacturing cities swarms of brown-haired grey-eyed women would be hurrying.

It would cross the ocean. Soon it would take in the

whole world. Africa would be strange – kraals of white-skinned young women, all exactly alike, going about the primitive chores of hunting and fruit-gathering, mashing grain, skinning animals. Building fires and weaving cloth and carefully shaping razor-sharp knives.

In China ... he grinned inanely. She'd look strange there, too. In the austere high-collar suit, the almost monastic robe of the young Communist cadres. Parades marching up the main streets of Peiping. Row after row of slim-legged full-breasted girls, with heavy Russian-made rifles. Carrying spades, picks, shovels. Columns of cloth-booted soldiers. Fast-moving workers with their precious tools. Reviewed by an identical figure on the elaborate stand overlooking the street, one slender arm raised, her gentle, pretty face expressionless and wooden.

He turned off the highway on to a side road. A moment later he was on his way back, driving slowly, listlessly, the way he had come.

At an intersection a traffic cop waded out through traffic to his car. He sat rigid, hands on the wheel, waiting numbly.

'Rick,' she whispered pleadingly as she reached the window. 'Isn't everything all right?'

'Sure,' he answered dully.

She reached in through the open window and touched him imploringly on the arm. Familiar fingers, red nails, the hand he knew so well. 'I want to be with you so badly. Aren't we together again? Aren't I back?'

'Sure.'

She shook her head miserably. 'I don't understand,' she repeated. 'I thought it was all right again.'

Savagely he put the car into motion and hurtled ahead. The intersection was left behind.

It was afternoon. He was exhausted, riddled with fatigue. He guided the car towards his own town automat-

ically. Along the streets she hurried everywhere, on all
sides. She was omnipresent. He came to his apartment
building and parked.

The janitor greeted him in the empty hall. Rick identified
him by the greasy rag clutched in one hand, the big push-
broom, the bucket of wood shavings. 'Please,' she
implored, 'tell me what it is, Rick. Please tell me.'

He pushed past her, but she caught at him desperately.
'Rick, *I'm back*. Don't you understand? They took me too
soon and then they sent me back again. It was a mistake. I
won't ever call them again — that's all in the past.' She
followed after him, down the hall to the stairs. 'I'm never
going to call them again.'

He climbed the stairs. Silvia hesitated, then settled down
on the bottom step in a wretched, unhappy heap, a tiny
figure in thick workman's clothing and huge cleated boots.

He unlocked his apartment door and entered.

The late afternoon sky was a deep blue beyond the
windows. The roofs of nearby apartment buildings sparkled white in the sun.

His body ached. He wandered clumsily into the bathroom — it seemed alien and unfamiliar, a difficult place to
find. He filled the bowl with hot water, rolled up his
sleeves and washed his face and hands in the swirling hot
steam. Briefly, he glanced up.

It was a terrified reflection that showed out of the mirror
above the bowl, a face, tear-stained and frantic. The face
was difficult to catch — it seemed to waver and slide. Grey
eyes, bright with terror. Trembling red mouth, pulse-
fluttering throat, soft brown hair The face gazed out
pathetically — and then the girl at the bowl bent to dry
herself.

She turned and moved wearily out of the bathroom into
the living-room.

Confused, she hesitated, then threw herself on to a chair and closed her eyes, sick with misery and fatigue.

'Rick,' she murmured pleadingly. 'Try to help me. I'm back, aren't I?' She shook her head, bewildered. 'Please, Rick, I thought everything was all right.'

The Cookie Lady

'Where you going, Bubber?' Ernie Mill shouted from across the street, fixing papers for his route.

'No place,' Bubber Surle said.

'You going to see your lady friend?' Ernie laughed and laughed. 'What do you go visit that old lady for? Let us in on it!'

Bubber went on. He turned the corner and went down Elm Street. Already, he could see the house, at the end of the street, set back a little on the lot. The front of the house was overgrown with weeds, old dry weeds that rustled and chattered in the wind. The house itself was a little grey box, shabby and unpainted, the porch steps sagging. There was an old weather-beaten rocking chair on the porch with a torn piece of cloth hanging over it.

Bubber went up the walk. As he started up the rickety steps he took a deep breath. He could smell it, the wonderful warm smell, and his mouth began to water. His heart thudding with anticipation, Bubber turned the handle of the bell. The bell grated rustily on the other side of the door. There was silence for a time, then the sounds of someone stirring.

Mrs Drew opened the door. She was old, very old, a little dried-up old lady, like the weeds that grew along the front of the house. She smiled down at Bubber, holding the door wide for him to come in.

'You're just in time,' she said. 'Come on inside, Bernard. You're just in time – they're just now ready.'

Bubber went to the kitchen door and looked in. He could see them, resting on a big blue plate on top of the stove. Cookies, a plate of warm, fresh cookies right out of the oven. Cookies with nuts and raisins in them.

'How do they look?' Mrs Drew said. She rustled past him, into the kitchen. 'And maybe some cold milk, too. You like cold milk with them.' She got the milk pitcher from the window box on the back porch. Then she poured a glass of milk for him and set some of the cookies on a small plate. 'Let's go into the living-room,' she said.

Bubber nodded. Mrs Drew carried the milk and the cookies in and set them on the arm of the couch. Then she sat down in her own chair, watching Bubber plop himself down by the plate and begin to help himself.

Bubber ate greedily, as usual, intent on the cookies, silent except for chewing sounds. Mrs Drew waited patiently, until the boy had finished, and his already ample sides bulged that much more. When Bubber was done with the plate he glanced towards the kitchen again, at the rest of the cookies on the stove.

'Wouldn't you like to wait until later for the rest?' Mrs Drew said.

'All right,' Bubber agreed.

'How were they?'

'Fine.'

'That's good.' She leaned back in her chair. 'Well, what did you do in school today? How did it go?'

'All right.'

The little old lady watched the boy look restlessly around the room. 'Bernard,' she said presently, 'won't you stay and talk to me for a while?' He had some books on his lap, some school books. 'Why don't you read to me from your books? You know, I don't see too well any more and it's a comfort to me to be read to.'

'Can I have the rest of the cookies after?'

'Of course.'

Bubber moved over towards her, to the end of the

couch. He opened his books, World Geography, Principles of Arithmetic, Hoyte's Speller. 'Which do you want?'

She hesitated. 'The geography.'

Bubber opened the big blue book at random. PERU. 'Peru is bounded on the north by Ecuador and Colombia, on the south by Chile, and on the east by Brazil and Bolivia. Peru is divided into three main sections. These are, first – '

The little old lady watched him read, his fat cheeks wobbling as he read, holding his finger next to the line. She was silent, watching him, studying the boy intently as he read, drinking in each frown of concentration, every motion of his arms and hands. She relaxed, letting herself sink back in her chair. He was very close to her, only a little way off. There was only the table and lamp between them. How nice it was to have him come; he had been coming for over a month, now, ever since the day she had been sitting on her porch and seen him go by and thought to call to him, pointing to the cookies by her rocker.

Why had she done it? She did not know. She had been alone so long that she found herself saying strange things and doing strange things. She saw so few people, only when she went down to the store or the mailman came with her pension cheque. Or the garbage men.

The boy's voice droned on. She was comfortable, peaceful and relaxed. The little old lady closed her eyes and folded her hands in her lap. And as she sat, dozing and listening, something began to happen. The little old lady was beginning to change, her grey wrinkles and lines dimming away. As she sat in the chair she was growing younger, the thin fragile body filling out with youth again. The grey hair thickened and darkened, colour coming to the wispy strands. Her arms filled, too, the mottled flesh turning a rich hue as it had been once, many years before.

Mrs Drew breathed deeply, not opening her eyes. She

could feel *something* happening, but she did not know just what. *Something* was going on; she could feel it, and it was good. But what it was she did not exactly know. It had happened before, almost every time the boy came and sat by her. Especially of late, since she had moved her chair nearer to the couch. She took a deep breath. How good it felt, the warm fullness, a breath of warmth inside her cold body for the first time in years!

In her chair the little old lady had become a dark-haired matron of perhaps thirty, a woman with full cheeks and plump arms and legs. Her lips were red again, her neck even a little too fleshy, as it had been once in the long forgotten past.

Suddenly the reading stopped. Bubber put down his book and stood up. 'I have to go,' he said. 'Can I take the rest of the cookies with me?'

She blinked, rousing herself. The boy was in the kitchen, filling his pockets with cookies. She nodded, dazed, still under the spell. The boy took the last cookies. He went across the living-room to the door. Mrs Drew stood up. All at once the warmth left her. She felt tired, tired and very dry. She caught her breath, breathing quickly. She looked down at her hands. Wrinkled, thin.

'Oh!' she murmured. Tears blurred her eyes. It was gone, gone again as soon as he moved away. She tottered to the mirror above the mantel and looked at herself. Old faded eyes stared back, eyes deep-set in a withered face. Gone, all gone, as soon as the boy had left her side.

'I'll see you later,' Bubber said.

'Please,' she whispered. 'Please come back again. Will you come back?'

'Sure,' Bubber said listlessly. He pushed the door open. 'Good-bye.' He went down the steps. In a moment she heard his shoes against the sidewalk. He was gone.

* * *

'Bubber, you come in here!' May Surle stood angrily on the porch. 'You get in here and sit down at the table.'

'All right.' Bubber came slowly up on to the porch, pushing inside the house.

'What's the matter with you?' She caught his arm. 'Where you been? Are you sick?'

'I'm tired.' Bubber rubbed his forehead.

His father came through the living-room with the newspapers, in his undershirt. 'What's the matter?' he said.

'Look at him,' May Surle said. 'All worn out. What you been doing, Bubber?'

'He's been visiting that old lady,' Ralf Surle said. 'Can't you tell? He's always washed out after he's been visiting her. What do you go there for, Bub? What goes on?'

'She gives him cookies,' May said. 'You know how he is about things to eat. He'd do anything for a plate of cookies.'

'Bub,' his father said, 'listen to me. I don't want you hanging around that crazy old lady any more. Do you hear me? I don't care how many cookies she gives you. You come home too tired! No more of that. You hear me?'

Bubber looked down at the floor, leaning against the door. His heart beat heavily, laboured. 'I told her I'd come back,' he muttered.

'You can go once more,' May said, going into the dining-room, 'but only once more. Tell her you won't be able to come back again, though. You make sure you tell her nice. Now go upstairs and get washed up.'

'After dinner better have him lie down,' Ralf said, looking up the stairs, watching Bubber climb slowly, his hand on the bannister. He shook his head. 'I don't like it,' he murmured. 'I don't want him going there any more. There's something strange about that old lady.'

'Well, it'll be the last time,' May said.

* * *

Wednesday was warm and sunny. Bubber strode along, his hands in his pockets. He stopped in front of McVane's drug store for a minute, looking speculatively at the comic books. At the soda fountain a woman was drinking a big chocolate soda. The sight of it made Bubber's mouth water. That settled it. He turned and continued on his way, even increasing his pace a little.

A few minutes later he came up on to the grey sagging porch and rang the bell. Below him the weeds blew and rustled with the wind. It was almost four o'clock; he could not stay too long. But then, it was the last time anyhow.

The door opened. Mrs Drew's wrinkled face broke into smiles. 'Come in, Bernard. It's good to see you standing there. It makes me feel so young again to have you come visit.'

He went inside, looking around.

'I'll start the cookies. I didn't know if you were coming.' She padded into the kitchen. 'I'll get them started right away. You sit down on the couch.'

Bubber went over and sat down. He noticed that the table and lamp were gone; the chair was right up next to the couch. He was looking at the chair in perplexity when Mrs Drew came rustling back into the room.

'They're in the oven. I had the batter all ready. Now.' She sat down in the chair with a sigh. 'Well, how did it go today? How was school?'

'Fine.'

She nodded. How plump he was, the little boy, sitting just a little distance from her, his cheeks red and full! She could touch him, he was so close. Her aged heart thumped. Ah, to be young again. Youth was so much. It was everything. What did the world mean to the old? *When all the world is old, lad . . .*

'Do you want to read to me, Bernard?' she asked presently.

'I didn't bring any books.'

'Oh.' She nodded. 'Well, I have some books,' she said quickly. 'I'll get them.'

She got up, crossing to the bookcase. As the opened the doors, Bubber said, 'Mrs Drew, my father says I can't come here any more. He says this is the last time. I thought I'd tell you.'

She stopped, standing rigid. Everything seemed to leap around her, the room twisting furiously. She took a harsh, frightened breath. 'Bernard, you're — you're not coming back?'

'No, my father says not to.'

There was silence. The old lady took a book at random and came slowly back to her chair. After a while she passed the book to him, her hands trembling. The boy took it without expression, looking at its cover.

'Please, read, Bernard. Please.'

'All right.' He opened the book. 'Where'll I start?'

'Anywhere. Anywhere, Bernard.'

He began to read. It was something by Trollope; she only half heard the words. She put her hand to her forehead, the dry skin, brittle and thin, like old paper. She trembled with anguish. The last time?

Bubber read on, slowly, monotonously. Against the window a fly buzzed. Outside the sun began to set, the air turning cool. A few clouds came up, and the wind in the trees rushed furiously.

The old lady sat, close by the boy, closer than ever, hearing him read, the sound of his voice, sensing him close by. Was this really the last time? Terror rose up in her and she pushed it back. The last time! She gazed at him, the boy sitting so close to her. After a time she reached out her thin, dry hand. She took a deep breath. He would never be back. There would be no more times, no more. This was the last time he would sit there.

She touched his arm.

Bubber looked up. 'What is it?' he murmured.

'You don't mind if I touch your arm, do you?'

'No, I guess not.' He went on reading. The old lady could feel the youngness of him, flowing between her fingers, through her arm. A pulsating, vibrating youngness, so close to her. It had never been that close, where she could actually touch it. The feel of life made her dizzy, unsteady.

And presently it began to happen, as before. She closed her eyes, letting it move over her, filling her up, carried into her by the sound of the voice and the feel of the arm. The change, the glow, was coming over her, the warm, rising feeling. She was blooming again, filling with life, swelling into richness, as she had been, once, long ago.

She looked down at her arms. Rounded, they were, and the nails clear. Her hair. Black again, heavy and black against her neck. She touched her cheek. The wrinkles had gone, the skin pliant and soft.

Joy filled her, a growing bursting joy. She stared around her, at the room. She smiled, feeling her firm teeth and gums, red lips, strong white teeth. Suddenly she got to her feet, her body secure and confident. She turned a little, lithe, quick circle.

Bubber stopped reading. 'Are the cookies ready?' he said.

'I'll see.' Her voice was alive, deep with a quality that had dried out many years before. Now it was there again, *her* voice, throaty and sensual. She walked quickly to the kitchen and opened the oven. She took out the cookies and put them on top of the stove.

'All ready,' she called gaily. 'Come and get them.'

Bubber came past her, his gaze fastened on the sight of the cookies. He did not even notice the woman by the door.

Mrs Drew hurried from the kitchen. She went into the bedroom, closing the door after her. Then she turned, gazing into the full-length mirror on the door. Young – she was young again, filled out with the sap of vigorous youth. She took a deep breath, her steady bosom swelling. Her eyes flashed, and she smiled. She spun, her skirts flying. Young and lovely.

And this time it had not gone away.

She opened the door. Bubber had filled his mouth and his pockets. He was standing in the centre of the living-room, his face fat and dull, a dead white.

'What's the matter?' Mrs Drew said.

'I'm going.'

'All right, Bernard. And thanks for coming to read to me.' She laid her hand on his shoulder. 'Perhaps I'll see you again some time.'

'My father – '

'I know.' She laughed gaily, opening the door for him. 'Good-bye, Bernard. Good-bye.'

She watched him go slowly down the steps, one at a time. Then she closed the door and skipped back into the bedroom. She unfastened her dress and stepped out of it, the worn grey fabric suddenly distasteful to her. For a brief second she gazed at her full, rounded body, her hands on her hips.

She laughed with excitement, turning a little, her eyes bright. What a wonderful body, bursting with life. A swelling breast – she touched herself. The flesh was firm. There was so much, so many things to do! She gazed about her, breathing quickly. So many things! She started the water running in the bathtub and then went to tie her hair up.

The wind blew around him as he trudged home. It was late, the sun had set and the sky overhead was dark and cloudy. The wind that blew and nudged against him was cold, and it penetrated through his clothing, chilling him. The boy felt tired, his head ached, and he stopped every few minutes, rubbing his forehead and resting, his heart labouring. He left Elm Street and went up Pine Street. The wind screeched around him, pushing him from side to side. He shook his head, trying to clear it. How weary he was, how tired his arms and legs were. He felt the wind hammering at him, pushing and plucking at him.

He took a breath and went on, his head down. At the corner he stopped, holding on to a lamp-post. The sky was quite dark, the street lights were beginning to come on. At last he went on, walking as best he could.

'Where is that boy?' May Surle said, going out on the porch for the tenth time. Ralf flicked on the light and they stood together. 'What an awful wind.'

The wind whistled and lashed at the porch. The two of them looked up and down the dark street, but they could see nothing but a few newspapers and trash being blown along.

'Let's go inside,' Ralf said. 'He sure is going to get a licking when he gets home.'

They sat down at the dinner table. Presently May put down her fork. 'Listen! Do you hear something?'

Ralf listened.

Outside, against the front door, there was a faint sound, a tapping sound. He stood up. The wind howled outside, blowing the shades in the room upstairs. 'I'll go see what it is,' he said.

He went to the door and opened it. Something grey, something grey and dry was blowing up against the porch, carried by the wind. He stared at it, but he could not make it out. A bundle of weeds, weeds and rags blown by the wind, perhaps.

The bundle bounced against his legs. He watched it drift past him, against the wall of the house. Then he closed the door again slowly.

'What was it?' May called.

'Just the wind,' Ralf Surle said.

Exhibit Piece

'That's a strange suit you have on,' the robot pubtrans driver observed. It slid back its door and came to rest at the kerb. 'What are the little round things?'

'Those are buttons,' George Miller explained. 'They are partly functional, partly ornamental. This is an archaic suit of the twentieth century. I wear it because of the nature of my employment.'

He paid the robot, grabbed up his brief-case, and hurried along the ramp to the History Agency. The main building was already open for the day; robed men and women wandered everywhere. Miller entered a PRIVATE lift, squeezed between two immense controllers from the pre-Christian division, and in a moment was on his way to his own level, the Middle Twentieth Century.

'Gorning,' he murmured, as Controller Fleming met him at the atomic engine exhibit.

'Gorning,' Fleming responded brusquely. 'Look here, Miller. Let's have this out once and for all. What if everyone dressed like you? The Government sets up strict rules for dress. Can't you forget your damn anachronisms once in a while? What in God's name is that thing in your hand? It looks like a squashed Jurassic lizard.'

'This is an alligator hide brief-case,' Miller explained. 'I carry my study spools in it. The brief-case was an authority symbol of the managerial class of the later twentieth century.' He unzipped the brief-case. 'Try to understand, Fleming. By accustoming myself to everyday objects of my research period I transform my relation from mere intellectual curiosity to genuine empathy. You have frequently noticed I pronounce certain words oddly. The accent is that of an American businessman of the Eisenhower administration. Dig me?'

'Eh?' Fleming muttered.

'*Dig me* was a twentieth-century expression.' Miller laid out his study spools on his desk. 'Was there anything you wanted? If not I'll begin today's work. I've uncovered fascinating evidence to indicate that although twentieth-century Americans laid their own floor tiles, they did not weave their own clothing. I wish to alter my exhibits on this matter.'

'There's no fanatic like an academician,' Fleming grated. 'You're two hundred years behind times. Immersed in your relics and artifacts. Your damn authentic replicas of discarded trivia.'

'I love my work,' Miller answered mildly.

'Nobody complains about your work. But there are other things than work. You're a political-social unit here in this society. Take warning, Miller! The Board has reports on your eccentricities. They approve devotion to work . . .' His eyes narrowed significantly. 'But you go too far.'

'My first loyalty is to my art,' Miller said.

'Your what? What does that mean?'

'A twentieth-century term.' There was undisguised superiority on Miller's face. 'You're nothing but a minor bureaucrat in a vast machine. You're a function of an impersonal cultural totality. You have no standards of your own. In the twentieth century men had personal standards of workmanship. Artistic craft. Pride of accomplishment. These words mean nothing to you. You have no soul — another concept from the golden days of the twentieth century when men were free and could speak their minds.'

'Beware, Miller!' Fleming blanched nervously and

lowered his voice. 'You damn scholars. Come up out of your tapes and face reality. You'll get us all in trouble, talking this way. Idolize the past, if you want. But remember – it's gone and buried. Times change. Society progresses.' He gestured impatiently at the exhibits that occupied the level. 'That's only an imperfect replica.'

'You impugn my research?' Miller was seething. 'This exhibit is absolutely accurate! I correct it to all new data. There isn't anything I don't know about the twentieth century.'

Fleming shook his head. 'It's no use.' He turned and stalked wearily off the level, on to the descent ramp.

Miller straightened his collar and bright hand-painted necktie. He smoothed down his blue pinstripe coat, expertly lit a pipeful of two-century-old tobacco, and returned to his spools.

Why didn't Fleming leave him alone? Fleming, the officious representative of the great hierarchy that spread like a sticky grey web over the whole planet. Into each industrial, professional, and residential unit. Ah, the freedom of the twentieth century! He slowed his tape scanner a moment, and a dreamy look slid over his features. The exciting age of virility and individuality, when men were men . . .

It was just about then, just as he was settling deep in the beauty of his research, that he heard the inexplicable sounds. They came from the centre of his exhibit, from within the intricate, carefully regulated interior.

Somebody was in his exhibit.

He could hear them back there, back in the depths. Somebody or something had gone past the safety barrier set up to keep the public out. Miller snapped off his tape scanner and got slowly to his feet. He was shaking all over as he moved cautiously towards the exhibit. He killed the barrier and climbed the railing on to a concrete pavement.

A few curious visitors blinked, as the small, oddly dressed man crept among the authentic replicas of the twentieth century that made up the exhibit and disappeared within.

Breathing hard, Miller advanced up the pavement and on to a carefully tended gravel path. Maybe it was one of the other theorists, a minion of the Board, snooping around looking for something with which to discredit him. An inaccuracy here – a trifling error of no consequence there. Sweat came out on his forehead; anger became terror. To his right was a flower bed. Paul Scarlet roses and low-growing pansies. Then the moist green lawn. The gleaming white garage, with its door half up. The sleek rear of a 1954 Buick – and then the house itself.

He'd have to be careful. If it *was* somebody from the Board he'd be up against the official hierarchy. Maybe it was somebody big. Maybe even Edwin Carnap, President of the Board, the highest ranking official in the N'York branch of the World Directorate. Shakily, Miller climbed the three cement steps. Now he was on the porch of the twentieth-century house that made up the centre of the exhibit.

It was a nice little house; if he had lived back in those days he would have wanted one of his own. Three bedrooms, a ranch style California bungalow. He pushed open the front door and entered the living-room. Fireplace at one end. Dark wine-coloured carpets. Modern couch and easy chair. Low hardwood glass-topped coffee table. Copper ashtrays. A cigarette lighter and a stack of magazines. Sleek plastic and steel floor lamps. A bookcase. Television set. Picture window overlooking the front garden. He crossed the room to the hall.

The house was amazingly complete. Below his feet the floor furnace radiated a faint aura of warmth. He peered into the first bedroom. A woman's boudoir. Silk bed cover. White starched sheets. Heavy drapes. A vanity table.

Bottles and jars. Huge round mirror. Clothes visible within the closet. A dressing gown thrown over the back of a chair. Slippers. Nylon hose carefully placed at the foot of the bed.

Miller moved down the hall and peered into the next room. Brightly painted wallpaper; clowns and elephants and tight-rope walkers. The children's room. Two little beds for the two boys. Model aeroplanes. A dresser with a radio on it, pair of combs, school books, pennants, a No Parking sign, snapshots stuck in the mirror. A postage stamp album.

Nobody there, either.

Miller peered in the modern bathroom, even into the yellow-tiled shower. He passed through the dining-room, glanced down the basement stairs where the washing machine and dryer were. Then he opened the back door and examined the back yard. A lawn, and the incinerator. A couple of small trees and then the three-dimensional projected backdrop of other houses receding off into incredibly convincing blue hills. And still no one. The yard was empty – deserted. He closed the door and started back.

From the kitchen came laughter.

A woman's laugh. The clink of spoons and dishes. And smells. It took him a moment to identify them, scholar that he was. Bacon and coffee. And hot cakes. Somebody was eating breakfast. A twentieth-century breakfast.

He made his way down the hall, past a man's bedroom, shoes and clothing strewn about, to the entrance of the kitchen.

A handsome late-thirtyish woman and two teen-age boys were sitting around the little chrome and plastic breakfast table. They had finished eating; the two boys were fidgeting impatiently. Sunlight filtered through the window over the sink. The electric clock read half-past eight. The radio was chirping merrily in the corner. A big pot of black coffee rested in the centre of the table, surrounded by empty plates and milk glasses and silverware.

The woman had on a white blouse and chequered tweed skirt. Both boys wore faded blue jeans, sweatshirts, and tennis shoes. As yet they hadn't noticed him. Miller stood frozen at the doorway, while laughter and small talk bubbled around him.

'You'll have to ask your father,' the woman was saying, with mock sternness. 'Wait until he comes back.'

'He already said we could,' one of the boys protested.

'Well, ask him again.'

'He's always grouchy in the morning.'

'Not today. He had a good night's sleep. His hay fever didn't bother him. That new anti-hist the doctor gave him.' She glanced up at the clock. 'Go see what's keeping him, Don. He'll be late to work.'

'He was looking for the newspaper.' One of the boys pushed back his chair and got up. 'It missed the porch again and fell in the flowers.' He turned towards the door, and Miller found himself confronting him face to face. Briefly, the observation flashed through his mind that the boy looked familiar. Damn familiar – like somebody he knew, only younger. He tensed himself for the impact, as the boy abruptly halted.

'Gee,' the boy said. 'You scared me.'

The woman glanced quickly up at Miller. 'What are you doing out there, George?' she demanded. 'Come on back in here and finish your coffee.'

Miller came slowly into the kitchen. The woman was finishing her coffee; both boys were on their feet and beginning to press around him.

'Didn't you tell me I could go camping over the week-end up at Russian River with the group from school?'

Don demanded. 'You said I could borrow a sleeping bag from the gym because the one I had you gave to the Salvation Army because you were allergic to the kapok in it.'

'Yeah,' Miller muttered uncertainly. Don. That was the boy's name. And his brother, Ted. But how did he know that? At the table the woman had got up and was collecting the dirty dishes to carry over to the sink. 'They said you already promised them,' she said over her shoulder. The dishes clattered into the sink and she began sprinkling soap flakes over them. 'But you remember that time they wanted to drive the car and the way they said it, you'd think they had got your okay. And they hadn't, of course.'

Miller sank weakly down at the table. Aimlessly, he fooled with his pipe. He set it down in the copper ashtray and examined the cuff of his coat. What was happening? His head spun. He got up abruptly and hurried to the window, over the sink.

Houses, streets. The distant hills beyond the town. The sights and sounds of people. The three-dimensional projected backdrop was utterly convincing; or was it the projected backdrop? How could he be sure? *What was happening?*

'George, what's the matter?' Marjorie asked, as she tied a pink plastic apron around her waist and began running hot water in the sink. 'You better get the car out and get started to work. Weren't you saying last night old man Davidson was shouting about employees being late for work and standing around the water cooler talking and having a good time on company time?'

Davidson. The word stuck in Miller's mind. He knew it, of course. A clear picture leaped up; a tall, white-haired old man, thin and stern. Vest and pocket watch. And the whole office, United Electronic Supply. The twelve-storey building in downtown San Francisco. The newspaper and cigar stand in the lobby. The honking cars. Jammed parking lots. The elevator, packed with bright-eyed secretaries, tight sweaters and perfume.

He wandered out of the kitchen, through the hall, past his own bedroom, his wife's, and into the living-room. The front door was open and he stepped out on to the porch.

The air was cool and sweet. It was a bright April morning. The lawns were still wet. Cars moved down Virginia Street, towards Shattuck Avenue. Early morning commuting traffic, businessmen on their way to work. Across the street Earl Kelly cheerfully waved his *Oakland Tribune* as he hurried down the pavement towards the bus stop.

A long way off Miller could see the Bay Bridge, Yerba Buena Island, and Treasure Island. Beyond that was San Francisco itself. In a few minutes he'd be shooting across the bridge in his Buick, on his way to the office. Along with thousands of other businessmen in blue pinstripe suits.

Ted pushed past him and out on the porch. 'Then it's okay? You don't care if we go camping?'

Miller licked his dry lips. 'Ted, listen to me. There's something strange.'

'Like what?'

'I don't know.' Miller wandered nervously around on the porch. 'This is Friday, isn't it?'

'Sure.'

'I thought it was.' But how did he know it was Friday? How did he know anything? But of course it was Friday. A long hard week – old man Davidson breathing down his neck. Wednesday, especially, when the General Electric order was slowed down because of a strike.

'Let me ask you something,' Miller said to his son. 'This morning – I left the kitchen to get the newspaper.'

Ted nodded. 'Yeah. So?'

'I got up and went out of the room. *How long was I gone?* Not long, was I?' He searched for words, but his mind was a maze of disjointed thoughts. 'I was sitting at the breakfast table with you all, and then I got up and went to look for the paper. Right? And then I came back in. Right?' His voice rose desperately. 'I got up and shaved and dressed this morning. I ate breakfast. Hot cakes and coffee. Bacon. *Right?*'

'Right,' Ted agreed. 'So?'

'Like I always do.'

'We only have hot cakes on Friday.'

Miller nodded slowly. 'That's right. Hot cakes on Friday. Because your uncle Frank eats with us Saturday and Sunday and he can't stand hot cakes, so we stopped having them on week-ends. Frank is Marjorie's brother. He was in the Marines in the First World War. He was a corporal.'

'Good-bye,' Ted said, as Don came out to join him. 'We'll see you this evening.'

School books clutched, the boys sauntered off towards the big modern high school in the centre of Berkeley.

Miller re-entered the house and automatically began searching the closet for his brief-case. Where was it? Damn it, he needed it. The whole Throckmorton account was in it; Davidson would be yelling his head off if he left it anywhere, like in the True Blue Cafeteria that time they were all celebrating the Yankees' winning the series. Where the hell was it?

He straightened up slowly, as memory came. Of course. He had left it by his work desk, where he had tossed it after taking out the research tapes. While Fleming was talking to him. Back at the History Agency.

He joined his wife in the kitchen. 'Look,' he said huskily. 'Marjorie, I think maybe I won't go down to the office this morning.'

Marjorie spun in alarm. 'George, is anything wrong?'

'I'm – completely confused.'

'Your hay fever again?'

'No. My mind. What's the name of that psychiatrist the PTA recommended when Mrs Bentley's kid had that fit?' He searched his disorganized brain. 'Grunberg, I think. In the Medical-Dental building.' He moved towards the door. 'I'll drop by and see him. Something's wrong – really wrong. And I don't know what it is.'

Adam Grunberg was a large heavy-set man in his late forties, with curly brown hair and horn-rimmed glasses. After Miller had finished, Grunberg cleared his throat, brushed at the sleeve of his Brooks Bros suit, and asked thoughtfully,

'Did anything happen while you were out looking for the newspaper? Any sort of accident? You might try going over that part in detail. You got up from the breakfast table, went out on the porch, and started looking around in the bushes. And then what?'

Miller rubbed his forehead vaguely. 'I don't know. It's all confused. I don't remember looking for any newspaper. I remember coming back in the house. Then it gets clear. But before that it's all tied up with the History Agency and my quarrel with Fleming.'

'What was that again about your brief-case? Go over that.'

'Fleming said it looked like a squashed Jurassic lizard. And I said – '

'No. I mean, about looking for it in the closet and not finding it.'

'I looked in the closet and it wasn't there, of course. It's sitting beside my desk at the History Agency. On the Twentieth Century level. By my exhibits.' A strange expression crossed Miller's face. 'Good God, Grunberg.

You realize this may be nothing but an *exhibit*? You and everybody else — maybe you're not real. Just pieces of this exhibit.'

'That wouldn't be very pleasant for us, would it?' Grunberg said, with a faint smile.

'People in dreams are always secure until the dreamer wakes up,' Miller retorted.

'So you're dreaming me,' Grunberg laughed tolerantly. 'I suppose I should thank you.'

'I'm not here because I especially like you. I'm here because I can't stand Fleming and the whole History Agency.'

Grunberg pondered. 'This Fleming. Are you aware of thinking about him before you went out looking for the newspaper?'

Miller got to his feet and paced around the luxurious office, between the leather-covered chairs and the huge mahogany desk. 'I want to face this thing. I'm an exhibit. An artificial replica of the past. Fleming said something like this would happen to me.'

'Sit down, Mr Miller,' Grunberg said, in a gentle but commanding voice. When Miller had taken his chair again, Grunberg continued, 'I understand what you say. You have a general feeling that everything around you is unreal. A sort of stage.'

'An exhibit.'

'Yes, an exhibit in a museum.'

'In the N'York History Agency. Level R, the Twentieth Century level.'

'And in addition to this general feeling of — insubstantiality, there are specific projected memories of persons and places, beyond this world. Another realm in which this one is contained. Perhaps I should say, the reality within which this is only a sort of shadow world.'

'This world doesn't look shadowy to me.' Miller struck

the leather arm of the chair savagely. 'This world is completely real. That's what's wrong. I came in to investigate the noises and now I can't get back out. Good God, do I have to wander around this replica the rest of my life?'

'You know, of course, that your feeling is common to most of mankind. Especially during periods of great tension. Where — by the way — was the newspaper? Did you find it?'

'As far as I'm concerned — '

'Is that a source of irritation with you? I see you react strongly to a mention of the newspaper.'

Miller shook his head wearily. 'Forget it.'

'Yes, a trifle. The paper boy carelessly throws the newspaper in the bushes, not on the porch. It makes you angry. It happens again and again. Early in the day, just as you're starting to work. It seems to symbolize in a small way the whole petty frustrations and defeats of your job. Your whole life.'

'Personally, I don't give a damn about the newspaper.' Miller examined his wrist watch. 'I'm going — it's almost noon. Old man Davidson will be yelling his head off if I'm not at the office by — ' He broke off. 'There it is again.'

'There what is?'

'All this!' Miller gestured impatiently out the window. 'This whole place. This damn world. This *exhibition*.'

'I have a thought,' Doctor Grunberg said slowly. 'I'll put it to you for what it's worth. Feel free to reject it if it doesn't fit.' He raised his shrewd, professional eyes. 'Ever see kids playing with rocketships?'

'Lord,' Miller said wretchedly. 'I've seen commercial rocket freighters hauling cargo between Earth and Jupiter, landing at La Guardia Spaceport.'

Grunberg smiled slightly. 'Follow me through on this. A question. Is it job tension?'

'What do you mean?'

'It would be nice,' Grunberg said blandly, 'to live in the world of tomorrow. With robots and rocketships to do all the work. You could just sit back and take it easy. No worries, no cares. No frustrations.'

'My position in the History Agency has plenty of cares and frustrations.' Miller rose abruptly. 'Look, Grunberg. Either this is an exhibit on R level of the History Agency, or I'm a middle-class businessman with an escape fantasy. Right now I can't decide which. One minute I think this is real, and the next minute – '

'We can decide easily,' Grunberg said.

'How?'

'You were looking for the newspaper. Down the path, on to the lawn. *Where did it happen?* Was it on the path? On the porch? Try to remember.'

'I don't have to try. I was still on the pavement. I had just jumped over the rail past the safety screens.'

'On the pavement. Then go back there. Find the exact place.'

'Why?'

'So you can prove to yourself there's nothing on the other side.'

Miller took a deep, slow breath. 'Suppose there is?'

'There can't be. You said yourself: only one of the worlds can be real. This world is real – ' Grunberg thumped his massive mahogany desk. 'Ergo, you won't find anything on the other side.'

'Yes,' Miller said, after a moment's silence. A peculiar expression cut across his face and stayed there. 'You've found the mistake.'

'What mistake?' Grunberg was puzzled. 'What – '

Miller moved towards the door of the office. 'I'm beginning to get it. I've been putting up a false question. Trying to decide which world is real.' He grinned humourlessly back at Doctor Grunberg. 'They're both real, of course.'

He grabbed a taxi and headed back to the house. No one was home. The boys were in school and Marjorie had gone downtown to shop. He waited indoors until he was sure nobody was watching along the street, and then started down the path to the pavement.

He found the spot without any trouble. There was a faint shimmer in the air, a weak place just at the edge of the parking strip. Through it he could see faint shapes.

He was right. There it was – complete and real. As real as the pavement under him.

A long metallic bar was cut off by the edges of the circle. He recognized it; the safety railing he had leaped over to enter the exhibit. Beyond it was the safety screen system. Turned off, of course. And beyond that, the rest of the level and the far walls of the History building.

He took a cautious step into the weak haze. It shimmered around him, misty and oblique. The shapes beyond became clearer. A moving figure in a dark blue robe. Some curious person examining the exhibits. The figure moved on and was lost. He could see his own work desk now. His tape scanner and heaps of study spools. Beside the desk was his brief-case, exactly where he had expected it.

While he was considering stepping over the railing to get the brief-case, Fleming appeared.

Some inner instinct made Miller step back through the weak spot, as Fleming approached. Maybe it was the expression on Fleming's face. In any case, Miller was back and standing firmly on the concrete pavement, when Fleming halted just beyond the juncture, face red, lips twisting with indignation.

'Miller,' he said thickly. 'Come out of there.'

Miller laughed. 'Be a good fellow, Fleming. Toss me my

brief-case. It's that strange-looking thing over by the desk.
I showed it to you — remember?'

'Stop playing games and listen to me!' Fleming snapped.
'This is serious. *Carnap knows.* I had to inform him.'

'Good for you. The loyal bureaucrat.'

Miller bent over to light his pipe. He inhaled and puffed
a great cloud of grey tobacco smoke through the weak
spot, out into the R level. Fleming coughed and retreated.

'What's that stuff?' he demanded.

'Tobacco. One of the things they have around here.
Very common substance in the twentieth century. You
wouldn't know about that — your period is the second
century, B.C. The Hellenistic world. I don't know how well
you'd like that. They didn't have very good plumbing back
there. Life expectancy was damn short.'

'What are you talking about?'

'In comparison, the life expectancy of *my* research
period is quite high. And you should see the bathroom I've
got. Yellow tile. And a shower. We don't have anything
like that at the Agency leisure-quarters.'

Fleming grunted sourly. 'In other words, you're going to
stay in there.'

'It's a pleasant place,' Miller said easily. 'Of course, my
position is better than average. Let me describe it for you.
I have an attractive wife: marriage is permitted, even
sanctioned in this era. I have two fine kids — both boys —
who are going up to Russian River this week-end. They
live with me and my wife — we have complete custody of
them. The State has no power of that, yet. I have a brand
new Buick — '

'Illusions,' Fleming spat. 'Psychotic delusions.'

'Are you sure?'

'You damn fool! I always knew you were too ego-
recessive to face reality. You and your anachronistic
retreats. Sometimes I'm ashamed I'm a theoretician. I wish

I had gone into engineering.' Fleming's lips twitched. 'You're insane, you know. You're standing in the middle of an artificial exhibit, which is owned by the History Agency, a bundle of plastic and wire and struts. A replica of a past age. An imitation. And you'd rather be there than in the real world.'

'Strange,' Miller said thoughtfully. 'Seems to me I've heard the same thing very recently. You don't know a Doctor Grunberg, do you? A psychiatrist.'

Without formality, Director Carnap arrived with his company of assistants and experts. Fleming quickly retreated. Miller found himself facing one of the most powerful figures of the twenty-second century. He grinned and held out his hand.

'You insane imbecile,' Carnap rumbled. 'Get out of there before we drag you out. If we have to do that, you're through. You know what they do with advanced psychotics. It'll be euthanasia for you. I'll give you one last chance to come out of that fake exhibit – '

'Sorry,' Miller said. 'It's not an exhibit.'

Carnap's heavy face registered sudden surprise. For a brief instant his massive poise vanished. 'You still try to maintain – '

'This is a time gate,' Miller said quietly. 'You can't get me out, Carnap. You can't reach me. I'm in the past, two hundred years back. I've crossed back to a previous existence-co-ordinate. I found a bridge and escaped from your continuum to this. And there's nothing you can do about it.'

Carnap and his experts huddled together in a quick technical conference. Miller waited patiently. He had plenty of time; he had decided not to show up at the office until Monday.

After a while Carnap approached the juncture again, being careful not to step over the safety rail. 'An interesting theory, Miller. That's the strange part about psychotics. They rationalize their delusions into a logical system. *A priori*, your concept stands up well. It's internally consistent. Only – '

'Only what?'

'Only it doesn't happen to be true.' Carnap had regained his confidence; he seemed to be enjoying the interchange. 'You think you're really back in the past. Yes, this exhibit is extremely accurate. Your work has always been good. The authenticity of detail in unequalled by any of the other exhibits.'

'I tried to do my work well,' Miller murmured.

'You wore archaic clothing and affected archaic speech mannerisms. You did everything possible to throw yourself back. You devoted yourself to your work.' Carnap tapped the safety railing with his fingernail. 'It would be a shame, Miller. A terrible shame to demolish such an authentic replica.'

'I see your point,' Miller said, after a time. 'I agree with you, certainly. I've been very proud of my work – I'd hate to see it all torn down. But that really won't do you any good. All you'll succeed in doing is closing the time gate.'

'You're sure?'

'Of course. The exhibit is only a bridge, a link with the past. I passed *through* the exhibit, but I'm not there now. I'm beyond the exhibit.' He grinned tightly. 'Your demolition can't reach me. But seal me off, if you want. I don't think I'll be wanting to come back. I wish you could see this side, Carnap. It's a nice place here. Freedom, opportunity. Limited government, responsible to the people. If you don't like a job here you can quit. There's no euthanasia, here. Come on over. I'll introduce you to my wife.'

'We'll get you,' Carnap said. 'And all your psychotic figments along with you.'

'I doubt if any of my "psychotic figments" are worried. Grunberg wasn't. I don't think Marjorie is —'

'We've already begun demolition preparations,' Carnap said calmly. 'We'll do it piece by piece, not all at once. So you may have the opportunity to appreciate the scientific and — *artistic* way we take your imaginary world apart.'

'You're wasting your time,' Miller said. He turned and walked off, down the pavement, to the gravel path and up on to the front porch of his house.

In the living-room he threw himself down in the easy chair and snapped on the television set. Then he went to the kitchen and got a can of ice cold beer. He carried it happily back into the safe, comfortable living-room.

As he was seating himself in front of the television set he noticed something rolled up on the low coffee table.

He grinned wryly. It was the morning newspaper, which he had looked so hard for. Marjorie had brought it in with the milk, as usual. And of course forgotten to tell him. He yawned contentedly and reached over to pick it up. Confidently, he unfolded it — and read the big black headlines.

RUSSIA REVEALS COBALT BOMB
TOTAL WORLD DESTRUCTION AHEAD

The world's greatest science fiction authors now available in paperback from Grafton Books

Ray Bradbury

Fahrenheit 451	£2.50	☐
The Small Assassin	£2.50	☐
The October Country	£1.50	☐
The Illustrated Man	£1.95	☐
The Martian Chronicles	£1.95	☐
Dandelion Wine	£2.50	☐
The Golden Apples of the Sun	£1.95	☐
Something Wicked This Way Comes	£2.50	☐
The Machineries of Joy	£1.50	☐
Long After Midnight	£1.95	☐
The Stories of Ray Bradbury (Volume 1)	£3.95	☐
The Stories of Ray Bradbury (Volume 2)	£3.95	☐

Philip K Dick

Flow My Tears, The Policeman Said	£2.50	☐
Blade Runner (Do Androids Dream of Electric Sheep?)	£1.95	☐
Now Wait for Last Year	£1.95	☑
The Zap Gun	£1.95	☐
A Handful of Darkness	£1.50	☐
A Maze of Death	£2.50	☐
Ubik	£1.95	☐
Our Friends from Frolix 8	£1.95	☐
Clans of the Alphane Moon	£1.95	☐
The Transmigration of Timothy Archer	£2.50	☐
A Scanner Darkly	£1.95	☐
The Three Stigmata of Palmer Eldrich	£1.95	☐
The Penultimate Truth	£1.95	☐
We Can Build You	£2.50	☐

To order direct from the publisher just tick the titles you want and fill in the order form.

All these books are available at your local bookshop or newsagent, or can be ordered direct from the publisher.

To order direct from the publishers just tick the titles you want and fill in the form below.

Name _____

Address _____

_____

Send to:
Grafton Cash Sales
PO Box 11, Falmouth, Cornwall TR10 9EN.

Please enclose remittance to the value of the cover price plus:

UK 60p for the first book, 25p for the second book plus 15p per copy for each additional book ordered to a maximum charge of £1.90.

BFPO 60p for the first book, 25p for the second book plus 15p per copy for the next 7 books, thereafter 9p per book.

Overseas including Eire £1.25 for the first book, 75p for second book and 28p for each additional book.

_____

Grafton Books reserve the right to show new retail prices on covers, which may differ from those previously advertised in the text or elsewhere.